# Trekachaw
## The Crozin War

# B.R. FLORES

Trekachaw the Crozin War
Copyright © 2023 B.R.Flores

This is a work of fiction. The characters, incidents, and dialogues are products of the author's imagination and are not construed as real. Any resemblance to actual persons, living or dead, is entirely coincidental.



For media and publishing inquiries, contact:
STRATEGIES PR
Jared Kuritz
Jkuritz@strategiespr.com
P.O. Box 178122
San Diego, CA 92177

Book design by GKS Creative, Nashville

FIRST EDITION

978-1-7331623-2-6 (paperback)
978-1-7331623-3-3 (ebook)

Library of Congress Control Number: (coming soon)

I dedicate this book to my brother, Vern.
Though it took us decades to find each other,
I've known you forever.
Love you.

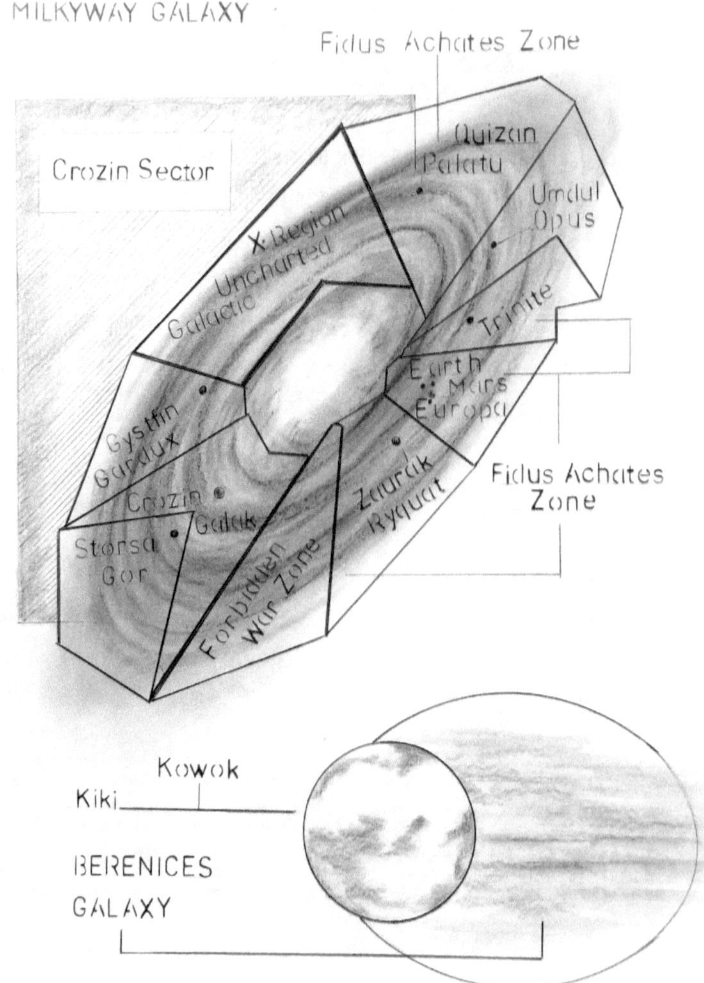

MILKYWAY GALAXY
Fidus Achates Zone
Crozin Sector
Quizan
Palatu
Umdul
Opus
X-Region
Uncharted
Galactic
Trinite
Earth
Mars
Europa
Gystfin
Gundux
Fidus Achates
Zone
Crozin
Galak
Zaurak
Ryquat
Storsa
Gor
Forbidden
War Zone
Kowok
Kiki
BERENICES
GALAXY

# Prologue

The Crozin Ukarus are dictators of a vile species obsessed with subjugating worlds. For decades they covertly sabotaged Zaurak by exploiting elected officials with the promise of elite superiority. As a diversion from the malign force to come, they created a dispute over one planet. This ruse misled the Ryquats and their adversaries within the galaxy. Meanwhile, light-years away, the invasion had already begun. The Crozins breached the Gystfins' Tocsin systems to invade their world. Those who survived the first wave fled the planet seeking refuge from previous rivals.

The Crozins' occupation of planet Gardux did not satisfy their greed and lust for power. It emboldened them. The invasion of Zaurak was coming. And upon their arrival, hordes would descend to paralyze the planet with bloodthirsty aliens. There would be no mercy or surrender.

During the first round of attacks, the chaos and shock dulled rational thinking. Because there were no warnings, it was too late to escape. That is when the mind and body become petrified by the inevitable. For those trapped in cities, divine will and hiding seemed to be the only hope left. Homes became cages or tombs for families as the world burned around them. When the Crozins crashed through their door, a young girl sacrificed herself to save her mother and two brothers. In the aftermath, the mother wrote her husband a letter of guilt and grief. Not because she believed he would ever read it, but because it was words of honor for her to live by.

*Akio,*

*If you are reading this, I'm grateful you survived. As you know by now, the Crozins and Gors attacked our planet. So that you understand my dire circumstances, I feel compelled to explain myself, not as an excuse but as a confession.*

*The invasion of Zaurak was far worse than anyone could have imagined, and there were no warnings to escape the city. What came next is difficult for me to put into words. The building shook violently from explosions all around us—one after the other, a barrage of relentless attacks. I was sure the walls would crumble, and the floors collapse beneath my feet. Thinking back, I wonder if our building was spared for a reason or if it was just pure dumb luck. But that is not important now. What's important was my lack of strength to protect our children. I froze after looking out the window as if suspended in time. There were thousands of Crozins and Gors on the ground. Even though I knew what they would do, I was unwilling to believe the inevitable. They had infiltrated the city to harvest the dead or living. As always, no exceptions except for young women taken for breeding. Wren and Benji were terrified and screaming, but I could not hear their cries, nor could I take away their fear. Kim comforted them while I did nothing. My weakness is shameful and unforgivable.*

*It had been several hours since the last explosion. Foolishly, I convinced myself we were safe. I knew the Meyer building next to ours was on fire because I could see the reflection of flames against the bedroom window. I peeked outside and heard myself gasp. Everything seemed to be burning or destroyed.*

*I found peace seeing the destruction. Since nothing was left, my fears lessened, and indeed, we would survive. That ended when the Crozins began cutting our front door with a laser. The four of us tried to hide under the bed, but there was not enough room. Kim pushed the boys as far as she could against the wall and crawled out. She ran across the room to the closet. I* stayed with Wren and Benji, afraid to move. Before Kim closed the door, she smiled and whispered that she loved me.

When the front door crashed onto the floor, Benji screamed. I covered his mouth with my hand, hoping the Crozins did not hear him. I stared into his eyes and shook my head no, but he was too young to understand that his cries would get us killed. No matter how much I tried to comfort him, he continued to cry. And Wren was making noises I'd never heard come out of a child before. I could hear our neighbors being dragged out into the hall-way screaming and begging to spare their children through the walls. The sounds of death are numbing and terrifying beyond anything I can explain.

I will never forget that I selfishly prayed their deaths would be enough for the Crozins to stop searching for us. But they were not.

What came next was an eerie silence and the sound of claws scraping against the floor as they walked toward the bedroom. I could hear that awful sniffing they make while searching for a scent.

I must inform you of Kim's sacrifice to save us from certain death with a heavy heart. When the Crozins started ripping the bed apart, our brave daughter jumped out of the closet and ran. She knew they would leave us to chase her. Like a coward, I stayed under the bed with our sons. Many hours later and long after they were gone, I crawled out. I should have traded places with her, but it was not possible at the time. Or at least that is what I tell myself.

Today I heard a stranger call out, asking if anyone was alive. I answered him because it's no longer safe to stay here. His name is Mark Keller, and he claims to know a way out of the city.

Fewer Crozins and Gors roam the streets, but their battleships remain above Zaurak as a constant reminder they could return at any moment. So, for the sake of our sons, I must go. I cannot explain it, but I feel Kim is still alive. Though I failed her, I give you my word to protect our sons with my life.

Love you always and forever,

Mya

Without the Trekachaws, the Galaxy would fall to evil.
The Crozin war had begun.

# I'VE COME TO KILL THE MONSTER WHO AWAITS MY ARROGANCE

The Umdul Language:

A KIMYO BI ЖALILI BHIEO MYINYЖBOȝ
WEHIEI EWEABЖ MYI EȝȝOGENYKO

**SOME** say nothing will stop the inevitable. Others vow this mindset is irrational or perhaps a coward's way out. So why do some succumb while others survive insurmountable odds when faced with the same adversities? No one knows why; it's just the way it is. But for Rohan, succumbing to the inevitable was not in his nature. He proved time and again that he was bulletproof to himself and Vexy. "No fear and never follow a fool" was his motto. That's all good and well, but he may have overplayed his hand this time. Suppose he continued down this same path. The outcome most likely would be grim. His failure to find a safer escape suggested their luck was running out. So, lie to her. Lying would not change the outcome. For her sake, it was best to pretend to have the answers. For all it's worth, she understood their predicament. But she refused to see the dark horse, trusting that Rohan would find a way.

Vexy fixated on the destruction below and couldn't breathe. She wished the planet were a paradox world, any world other than her own. But even at this distance, they were not safe. The shuttle was probably nothing more than false hope and more likely a death trap.

From the portal, she watched thousands of Gor and Crozin fighter jets swarm the skies of her decimated planet. They looked small, like harmless toys, but that notion was far from reality. On the surface, these sadistic aliens were capturing defenseless Ryquats. Vexy shuddered, thinking about the stacks upon stacks of marked cubicles she saw on the ground when they flew over the city. She'd seen these identical cubicles in historical documents during a previous council meeting while listening to the testimonies of past survivors from other worlds. No one wanted to believe them. The Crozins were not a threat. But they were a threat, and thousands were dying. Ryquats were being packed into cubicles, dead or alive, for later consumption. Those who lived most likely died of suffocation. If not, they froze when launched into space. There were no words to describe the wanton butchery, and no amount of torture seemed to satisfy their rage for centuries of revenge.

Vexy thought back to the moment the attack began. She screamed at Ryquats to take cover as they collapsed lifelessly to the floor. And at that very moment, Rohan appeared out of nowhere and dragged her from beneath the desk. She remembered hanging on to one of the desk legs and wondered why she did that. And then, how desperate she felt by not being able to keep up with him. Yet angry because his tight grip was hurting her hand. How long did it take to run past those familiar doors down the long hallway beyond the carnage? She heard explosions behind them, becoming distant, and the smoke had cleared. The stairs leading to the exit were within reach when a blast of hot air slammed her to the ground.

She awoke confused and in agony. Rohan was shouting her name and dragging her through a doorway onto a stairway landing. He sat her against a wall and stepped away. Trying to stop her head from spinning, she placed her hand on the floor. *Is this real?* She questioned herself. And then the burning pain when she tried to take a breath—gasping for air to fill her lungs. This was all too real. She gasped for air and felt the overwhelming panic of dying while struggling to take a second breath. The air grew darker and thicker. She muffled her coughs and gagged, fearing the monsters could hear her. They would suffocate from the black smoke and blinding dust if they stayed there any longer. The fear of dying in the stairwell was worse than the hyperbaric shock waves they'd left behind. She looked for Rohan and found him lying beside her on the landing. He had covered his nose and mouth with his bloody shirt and was motioning for her to do the same. Before she could pull up her shirt, everything went black. How long she fell unconscious was a guess. And she questioned how far Rohan had carried her through the onslaught of destruction.

For the first time in her life, she felt sheer terror when Rohan opened the utility door leading to the street. The city was on fire, and the sound was deafening. High-rise buildings were exploding and sending chunks of concrete crashing to the ground. Then a blast of hot air threw her against a wall. Her head ached, and the world was spinning. Rohan's mouth was moving, but she could not hear his screams for her to run. Run where? There was nowhere to run. Rohan grabbed her arm, and she followed.

With each step, she believed the next would be her last. Through the smoke, she realized they were on the roof of the capital, not the street below. A row of shuttles came into view from the other side. Rohan pointed at them, let go of her arm, and ran. He stopped at the first shuttle and climbed in. Rohan didn't need to tell her to run. The Crozins and Gors were close. She could hear their claws scraping the wall behind her.

She closed her eyes and saw images of young, terrified women brutally raped. The thought of being captured made her cold. But what made her shiver was so much blood when a Crozin sliced a man's throat. Those who chose to fight died sooner. If it came to that, she'd fight. What she couldn't get out of her head were the sounds Crozins made during a killing frenzy.

Their high-pitched shrills of gratification silenced the blood-curdling cries for mercy. She opened her eyes to stop the visions but could still hear the screams.

By now, most of the cities were alien occupied. Most likely, the best place to hide would be in small towns. And those trying to escape the planet's surface couldn't have made it far. From what they could tell, Rohan was the only one who navigated through the barrage of Neco lasers. And he did it remarkably unscathed.

Call it luck or skill thus far. But it was about to run out. Alien battleships and jets were swarming Zaurak's space. Vexy and Rohan knew they were as good as dead if detected. And the thought of outrunning them was that of a fool.

Rohan swept his hand across the cockpit controls, and the interior lights faded to a soft blue. The shuttle drifted into space, and the sound of silence was dire. The new war had just begun. Yet the Ryquat's defense systems and ships had already lost the fight and were being destroyed. That's when she knew nothing would ever be the same.

Looking back, she could have done more. Perhaps exposing their betrayal would have prevented the war. Still, she wasn't the only one that knew about the colluding. The Crozin sympathizers grew in numbers and gained strength by lying and silencing those who questioned their deeds. She told herself someone else would expose them. It was easier that way to ignore the problem. Eventually, they crushed anyone who resisted. In their eyes, they were exceptional, and Zaurak was expendable.

All that second-guessing was behind her. She'd try to stay alive or die with the least amount of pain. If the Crozins captured them, how they died would be up to Rohan. He needed to hear her side before it was too late.

"We need to talk. I don't want to be captured. Promise me you won't let that happen. You saw what they did. I'm nothing but a chunk of meat."

Rohan did not flinch. "If that time comes . . . I give you my word."

He waved his hand across the navigation board, and the monitor came alive with brilliant stars sprinkled across the screen.

"Vexy, come here and look at this. We're drifting toward the asteroid belt; we'll be okay. The Crozins couldn't find us inside there even if they tried. So, no more talk about being captured or dying."

Vexy let out a sigh of relief. "If you say so. Well, we may be up here for a while. What are the life support levels?"

Rohan chose not to answer. He closed three portholes with views of Zaurak while leaving the asteroid belt portholes open. Hope is what they needed. Based on previous battles, he believed staying positive increased their odds of survival. But trying to keep Vexy in a good frame of mind was like drying off in the rain.

Rohan's subtle suggestions were irritating. And she was to upset to indulge him. Then the strangest memory popped inside her head. Perhaps this was a good distraction. She recalled a therapist who gave her some free advice. At the time, she was annoyed by the unsolicited platitude. That's why she thought about it. How curious that something so absurd could be so fitting. Vexy recited the therapist's words: "The mind finds a way of protecting itself. When life is unbearable, familiarity replaces chaos."

Those words allowed her to escape the present and return to her affluent status and lavish life. At the estate, she could forget about the city. Sometimes she'd roam from room to room to enjoy its grandeur. But her favorite place was the veranda. She could see forever while hidden by the terrace of winding vines with red flowers. Oh, and that smell of fresh linen when the breeze from the north crossed over her body at night. This morning when she awoke, a subtle chill in the air meant winter was coming. So much had happened there. It was hers to share with family and cherished friends to laugh or cry. What became of them? Such a wonderful life, all gone. Rohan was the only reason she was alive. He saved her, and she took him for granted. Teasing him for attention, to make herself feel attractive. She'd do right by him and confess her admiration.

"Rohan. Do you remember when we almost? You know? Afterward, I couldn't sleep. Uh, I should have said something then."

As soon as she confessed, she regretted it. Groveling was beneath her.

Rohan's reaction was confusing, or the lack thereof. He had no response and seemed elsewhere. After an uncomfortable silence, he slurred his words when he spoke. She recalled the first time the staff introduced him. And how she felt flustered by his presence. Rohan was impressive. Big, strong, silent, and handsome to a fault. When transfers crossed her desk, she'd deny them to keep him as her Dignitary Protection Special Ops.

Three years had come and gone, yet she barely knew anything meaningful about him. He lived at her estate with his private quarters in the west wing opposite hers. Careful to be discreet, she insisted on a no-fraternizing rule with employees. Rohan knew better.

Against her own rules, those private conversations regarding her ex-husband, "the great Captain Victis," became personal. He was a good listener. But more than that, Rohan was her surrogate mate without the mess or commitment.

Rohan's face was white as a ghost. How selfish not to have noticed. The bandage she tied around his leg was blood-soaked.

"Are you okay?" Vexy asked, knowing full well he was not.

"No. What?" He sounded confused.

"No? What do you mean? Are you okay or not?"

Rohan turned his head to look at her, and she saw fear in his eyes. He slumped forward and rolled out of the pilot's seat headfirst on the deck floor.

No! He couldn't die, not now, not like this. She watched a thin stream of red blood flow across the floor before disappearing beneath a metal grate.

He was no longer the invincible man—the man of armor who protected her from danger.

Vexy felt paralyzed, staring down at him. If she did nothing, Rohan would die. *"Do something. Don't just stand there."*

Why was she talking out loud? Had she gone mad? Searching the shuttle aimlessly for something to use was a waste of time. All the while, Rohan was bleeding to death. She yanked the bottom of her tattered blouse, ripping off another strip. Working as fast as her trembling hands allowed, she struggled to tighten the old bandage around his leg before adding the new one. The blood was not coming from his leg. If not from there, where?

She rolled him to his right side and shoved her hand under his jacket. His skin was wet. Rohan had a second wound he'd hidden from her. Praying aloud, she pulled her arm out and saw blood. A lot of blood. Where was he bleeding from? This time she felt every inch of skin on his back. There it was. She should have seen it, a hole burned in the jacket.

It must have happened when they ran from the Crozins and Gors on Zaurak. Maybe when he was carrying her. Or when he laid her on the ground to fire lasers behind them? She remembered him yelling, "Vexy, get up. Can you hear me? I'm hit. Get up!"

"How could I forget that? Rohan said he'd been hit. What else did I forget?"

She remembered a flash of light through her closed eyelids startled her. That must have been what woke her. Rohan was groaning and stumbling, and then they crashed to the ground. Was he shot, then? Everything is confusing. There were too many of them, and they were chasing us!

Rohan opened his eyes. Vexy was sitting next to him on the deck and mumbling. She looked terrified and was staring at the bulkhead. Whatever was scaring her, it was inside her head. His back was on fire, and pain shot up his spine with the slightest movement. Vexy screamed, and he tried to sit up. Rohan rolled to his side, and all went black.

*Vexy was going mad, trying to untangle a living hell.*

*She heard monsters chasing her. The closer they came, the faster she ran. Screaming at Rohan, she heard Crozins' claws scraping against the shuttle hull.*

*"Where am I? Zaurak?" Rohan's voice calmed her. He held her close and whispered. The warmth of his breath against her neck gave her the courage to get up. Most men would have left her behind. But most men were not like Rohan. She crawled to her knees and felt his arms wrap around her waist. They were on the run again.*

"What happened? Where am I? I must have dozed off. It was nothing more than a bad dream." Shaking it off, she leaned over and put an ear to his chest. Rohan's heartbeat reminded her of those summer nights when she heard frogs come out to play. Both are magical. Perhaps the loud ribbits and heartbeat were meant to be heard and not seen. That's when she noticed the blood on the floor was pooling in a different direction. Were they still drifting toward the belt?

Vexy removed Rohan's jacket. The hole in his skin looked small to bleed so much. There was nothing long enough to make a bandage that could wrap around his chest. For whatever reason, she thought about plugging the hole with her finger. That's when she came up with the perfect solution. A cloth plug should do the trick. She rolled a strip on her leg, then twisted one end until it stiffened to a point. Sticking that end into the hole, she pushed down as she turned to force the cloth further into the wound. The blood slowed, but not completely. That must have hurt. Yet Rohan didn't flinch. Was he ever going to wake up?

Since she didn't know about this one, she should look at every part of his body for more injuries. The last area she checked was his no-go zone. She told herself not to stare, but she did. Rohan would never know. And she would be negligent if she didn't check there too. Vexy saw what she had been missing.

Flustered, she finished. As far as she could see, there were no more injuries. If only Rohan could tell her what to do. More importantly, what not to do. Without him, there was no hope. With that clarity, despair brings forth an acceptance of one's fate. Strangely enough, surrendering seemed to calm her. Now was the time to pray and remind herself of those moments she held dear. And that is what she did—pray.

Content, she curled up on the floor next to Rohan and only thought about good memories. Precious memories of when she was a little girl and her passion for Victis on their wedding night. But what of Rohan? She pushed him away when he tried to kiss her. How foolish of her to toy with his love. No matter the outcome, she was grateful that he waited for her.

She must have drifted off to sleep. How long was she asleep? She dreamt something but forgot the moment she woke. At least this time, it wasn't a nightmare. Nothing had changed. Same place, same problems. She'd check on Rohan and then look out a portal to see if Zaurak was still visible. To her surprise Rohan's eyes were open. Vexy grabbed his hand and kissed it several times. Nothing else mattered; Rohan was alive.

The moment was bittersweet. Blinding laser streaked past the porthole. Vexy thought for sure they'd been hit. She screamed and wrapped her arms around Rohan and hung on. The metal grates rattled hard beneath them, and they floated up. Sensors flashed, and they fell against a bulkhead and then rolled headlong onto the deck. The autopilot had engaged, and the shuttle jetted sideways. Rohan slid in one direction, and she tumbled in the other. How foolish to think they'd get out of this alive.

But all was quiet, and the lasers had stopped. The Crozins had to have seen the shuttle. Why they didn't destroy them made no sense. The sweet smell of oxygen confirmed life support had not failed. Vexy scrambled to her feet to look out the porthole. Space was ablaze with unfamiliar alien battleships in a firefight with the Crozins and Gors. It was their chance to sneak away. Vexy engaged the shuttle and headed for the asteroid belt.

THE CROZINS AND GORS CAME out of nowhere and attacked with rapid-fire lasers. The Kikis were outnumbered three to one. Captain Thude ordered his bevy to scramble and mobilize with the Umduls in deep space. He had underestimated the Crozins and ignored Pify's request.

Those able to scramble and break off did. The relentless Crozins and Gors followed in hot pursuit. As a last-ditch effort to destroy the Kikis, the Crozins fired a barrage of long-distance hyperbaric shock waves. Several Kiki jets and battleships were caught in the wave and disintegrated into vapor.

The loss was catastrophic. It took less than twenty minutes for more than half of the four hundred Kiki ships to be destroyed.

During the attack, Thude's battleship was targeted by several Crozin jets. When lasers failed, the Crozins ordered the Gor jets to sacrifice themselves and crash into the main hull near the bridge. Thude's shield held, taking the brunt of the exploding jets. Nonetheless, his battleship was damaged. Outrunning the enemy was no longer an option. Thude ordered navigation to change course for the asteroid belt. The belt was risky, but the dense terrain would conceal a battleship. It would also give the crew time to assess the damage.

The Crozins knew better than to pursue a Kiki battleship into the asteroid belt. That would be a fool's game. The Kikis' short-range sonar was superior, giving them the advantage for an ambush encounter.

It was wise that Thude chose to hide in the asteroid belt. The damage to his ship was worse than first thought. Life support was on the brink of collapsing, and the hull would vibrate apart if the telerobotic stabilizers weren't aligned and calibrated. For now, Captain Thude was unable to contact his bevy. Indeed, they would assume the worst. Be that as it may, it was imperative not to divulge their location. And he wasn't going anywhere.

With that, Thude did his best in a bad situation. But make no mistake, hiding in the shadows of the asteroid belt was a bitter pill to swallow. As well as admitting defeat. To do so was a reprehensible act for the Kiki species. Especially with such a significant loss to an inferior species. And yet, he continued to make decisions based on assumptions. Thude banked on the Gors and Crozins leaving. He assumed they would be short on patience and distracted by their insatiable, rabid thirst to be part of the genocide on Zaurak. But what if these Crozins wanted a Kiki captain more than Zaurak. Once again, Thude's opinion may or may not be correct.

In retrospect, none of this should have happened. The only reason Thude got involved was he owed Pify a favor. The Kikis preferred to remain neutral in the war. More so after hearing rumors about a lab-created genetic virus. To err on caution, the Kikis avoided the Milky Way and the Gors and Crozins. They weren't the only ones. Other species shared the same concerns. Once in a while, the Crozins were asked if there was any truth regarding the rumors. Of course, they acted insulted by the accusations and profusely denied the existence of a bio-virus. Their response was well-rehearsed and parroted by all Crozins. They claimed an overpopulated planet was the root cause of most Gor deaths. Truth being, it was all a lie.

So how and when did this begin? As far as anyone knows, it started thousands of years ago when the elite Crozin Ukarus deceived a select group of the Crozin population. Those targeted were told the Xenogenesis injection would provide a vaccine for a deadly virus spreading worldwide. Those not targeted were given a pseudo-vaccine. The elite Crozins exploited their test subjects with no remorse. And as planned, it didn't take long before the abnormalities were irreversible. For those affected, nothing would ever be the same. The mutated Crozins were reclassified as serfs and renamed Gors to degrade and divide the species.

As heartless as it may sound, Thude never cared about the Gors or the Ryquats. That is, as long as it didn't affect the Kikis. He was rethinking the coalition and his allegiance to Captain Pify. None of this was his fight.

Checking the long-range sensors validated Thude's assumption. Open space beyond the asteroid belt was free of bloodthirsty alien fighter jets. The sensors also detected the signature of a Ryquat shuttle beneath the battleship's stern. Evidently, the Kikis weren't the only ones hiding in the asteroid belt. Captain Thude ordered his crew to deal with that pesky problem after they completed repairs.

SHE WOULD NOT HAVE BELIEVED it if she hadn't seen it with her own eyes: a battleship plowing through the asteroid belt headed directly at them. Vexy ran to the pilot's seat and fastened her harness, but it was too late. Before she could engage, the massive ship scraped over the top of the shuttle, dragging them underneath. Rohan's body looked like a marionette controlled by strings as he danced to the other side of the cockpit. The shuttle rotated and pitched forward. They were about to flip when it finally came to rest. Rohan wound up sprawled out on the deck floor. Once again, chaos was her world.

Rohan concentrated on Vexy's mouth to stop his head from spinning. She was shouting something, but he could not hear her. And reading her lips didn't make sense if he got it right. All he knew for sure was his body ached, and he felt nauseous.

"Don't get up. We're in the asteroid belt stuck under a battleship." Her face was gaunt, and she looked tired. He wondered if she was giving up. But then, who could blame her?

"Did you say we're stuck? Under a ship?" he asked, trying to picture what she said. His ears were ringing, but at least he was in one piece.

"Hard to believe, right? This enormous asteroid belt and a battleship just so happened to pick the same spot. I was sure we were going to die again. But here we are. You'd think I'd be grateful to be alive. Frankly, I don't care anymore. Being tortured to death couldn't be any worse than this."

"How long was I out?" Rohan asked, making small talk as he rolled over on his side. Twice he struggled to sit up. On his third attempt, he sat up and leaned against a wall.

Vexy shrugged. "I don't know. A while, I guess. No more than a couple of hours."

"What makes you think we're stuck? A battleship, you say. Is it one of ours?" Rohan questioned, looking around for something to grab.

"Oh, we're stuck. I'm sure of that. I tried to look for something familiar, but we were too close. What I saw before we crashed doesn't look like any ship I've ever seen."

Vexy wrapped her arms around Rohan's chest in a feeble attempt to lift him. Keeping his thoughts to himself, he wished she'd let go. She was more of a hindrance than a help. Nonetheless, it seemed to make her happy. Rohan couldn't help but be amused. Vexy was grunting and groaning and getting nowhere. Rohan reached out, grabbed the control panel's edge, and pulled himself up.

His leg stopped bleeding. But now, he was bleeding from the side of his head. Still a bit foggy, he sat in the pilot's seat and ran his hand across the controls. The shuttle did not respond. He pushed on several relay tabs, but nothing. Standing on his good leg, he hopped over to the porthole to check out the massive ship above them.

"My guess is that's a Kiki ship. Let's hope it's Kiki, even though that makes no sense. They rarely enter this sector of the galaxy. I need to transmit a distress call to them, but I can't; it would give away both our locations to the Gors and Crozins," Rohan grumbled as he limped back to the pilot's seat.

"Then how will we tell them we're down here?" Vexy asked, sounding cranky.

"Hope they know we're here and allow us to board. Otherwise, not good. This shuttle's going nowhere."

THE BATTLESHIP REPAIRS AND CALIBRATIONS were completed sooner than expected. Captain Thude authorized the final countdown. Starting from the nose of the battleship, its hull rippled and hissed as if a giant serpent had awoken from a deep sleep. There was one more pesty problem to deal with before they could leave. What was the status of the wayward shuttle? The Kiki Tebna engineers advised Thude the battleship had shed it from the intake inceptor when it awoke. Now it was floating in space beneath them. This development made matters far less complicated. Thude gave orders to open the docking port above the shuttle as an invitation to enter.

This should have been easy. But par for the course, it was not. Rohan and Vexy had no clue the Kiki docking port was open. The shuttle monitor did not detect it, and they couldn't see it from the portal. Whereas to the Kikis, it appeared the Ryquats were ungrateful.

Captain Thude snapped at Watoto, "What are they waiting for?"

Watoto ruffled his feathers and shrugged his shoulders.

Thude squawked, "Fine. Let them die. Set coordinates to intercept the Umdul fleet at Proxima Centauri. Wait! Is it possible to gravitmag lock onto the shuttle?"

"Negative, Captain," chirped Watoto.

"Why not?" demanded Thude.

"The LC beam is not operable," chirped Watoto.

"Theoretically, can you center above them and descend without crashing the shuttle inside the docking bay?" questioned Thude.

"Theoretically, yes," replied Watoto.

"Theoretically? Are you mocking me? Dare insult me, pecksniffian?" snarled Thude.

"Never. I serve at your will." Watoto bowed.

"Good. Mind your caste. Evacuate the crew and secure the interior docking portholes in case of nescience error—one descent. If you fail, destroy the shuttle. Ryquats are reprehensible creatures. Still, I would be crass to leave them to die in space or at the will of Crozins or Gors," preened Captain Thude.

Vexy screamed, "No, no, no. What are they doing? They're going to crash on top of us!"

"Hang on!" yelled Rohan, bracing for the impact.

The Kiki battleship shimmered with brilliant colors as it slithered and positioned itself to devour the tiny craft. Vexy and Rohan watched from the porthole as the stars disappeared and the interior of the strange battleship appeared. Neither one said a word. But both were terrified.

A black hole opened, and an elongated tentacle-like arm uncoiled from it. At the end of the arm was a massive jaw with protruding transparent teeth. It whipped sideways in pursuit of the shuttle. The jaw opened wide and clamped onto the shuttle just in time to stop them from slamming against a bulkhead. Suspended high above the docking platform, Rohan looked down and was at a loss. *I don't know how to get out of this.*

He limped over to a locker and entered a code. A door slid open with medical supplies inside. After moving a couple of items aside, he searched with his eyes before selecting a tube with a plunger marked with lines for doses. He studied the label, then chose a few more items and placed them on a shelf next to the flight console.

Vexy was surprised to see medical supplies inside the cabinet. It would have made matters a lot easier if she'd known about it. So, what was he going to do with them now? Well, that was short-lived. He was loosening the knots.

Around and around, he unwrapped the cloth she had tied on his leg. Did he know those from her blouse? The same blouse she'd searched for inside her closet this morning.

All this in less than a day. How was it possible that Zaurak was so vulnerable? Why didn't Zaurak's defense sensors warn them? What about all those Ryquats who died his morning? They didn't wake up thinking today's the day. No one predicted that. Right? But the invasion should have been. Too late for what-ifs. What now? She should rely on her faith. Feeling sorry for herself solved nothing. Look at Rohan—cut, bleeding, bruised—and still not a complaint. He glanced in her direction and smiled. She smiled back at that handsome face she never got tired of seeing.

"Vexy, when we get out of this, we need to talk. Now would be a good time to check out my leg. Can you help me do this?" Rohan asked as he was ripping his pants. Vexy cringed at the ten-inch gash from the middle of his thigh down to his knee.

"I suppose." She wrinkled her nose and scrunched her face.

Rohan did not look pleased by her reaction. He reached out, chose a small device from the shelf, and held it up so she couldn't help but see it.

"This is a medical laser. Watch me so you can learn how to cauterize my back. How bad is it? Because it hurts like hell."

"You have a hole about an inch around. It didn't look that bad, but it bled a lot. I stuffed a piece of my blouse inside it to stop the bleeding. Sorry if it hurt." She winced.

"No apologies necessary. You did what you had to do."

Vexy was fine until she smelled his burned flesh. She felt nauseated and resisted the urge to gag by pinching her nose. By now, nothing should affect her. Yet, this bothered her more than his wounds.

Amazingly, Rohan cauterized himself and never flinched. He cut off a strip of gauze and folded it to perfection, then wrapped his leg with another roll of gauze.

He looked frustrated at her and grabbed a tube from the shelf. He snapped off the top and screwed on a thin nozzle. "Change of plans. It doesn't look like much, but this stuff works great. Kinda like what you did with your blouse. This stuff plugs holes too. Except you can leave it in. As you heal, you absorb it."

Rohan handed Vexy the tube and turned sideways in the chair. "Use the plunger to squirt the mucilage in the hole until it's full. And I'll be good as new." He grinned.

Vexy lifted his shirt. The bloody piece of cloth sticking out of the hole was disgusting. She positioned herself so Rohan couldn't see her face. Using tweezers from the ledge, she gently pulled on the end of the fabric. Being gentle was not going to work. The blood-soaked cloth had dried and was stuck inside like glue. One quick yank was a better option. That worked, but squirting blood came with it. Vexy poked the cloth back inside with her finger. She took a deep breath, pulled out the material, and jabbed the nozzle inside the wound. She squeezed until the goo filled the hole. Vexy let out a big sigh of relief. The bleeding stopped.

"Is that better?" she asked, pulling Rohan's shirt down.

"Much better." Rohan sat straight in his chair, then used a rail to help pull himself up.

"Not so fast. Sit," she ordered, holding onto his arm.

Rohan jerked away and lowered himself into the chair.

Vexy did her best to ignore him. She parted his hair with her fingers to search for the cut on his head. Rohan grumbled and picked up a packet off the shelf. He ripped it open and handed it to her. Why was he perturbed? She was trying to help, and Rohan was being difficult for no reason. This side of him she had not seen before and didn't care for it, not one bit.

There it is, she found it. The cut was smaller than she thought it would be. Vexy gently patted the dried blood from his scalp.

"Done," she announced, backing away.

The timing could not have been better. The shuttle lurched forward and began to move. They watched the tentacle slink side to side as it lowered the shuttle onto a docking platform. Its jaws opened and released the shuttle. Whatever this thing was, it coiled into a ball and disappeared inside the black hole. Vexy waited until it finished, then turned to Rohan, "Why didn't the Kikis use a cargo beam? What was that? It looked alive."

Rohan stood up and shifted his weight to his injured leg. "See, good as new. I don't know what that was," he said, walking to the hatch door while doing his best to mask his limp.

"Life support is within range. Let's find out what we've gotten ourselves into." He spoke as if all was well, but Vexy wasn't buying it.

The hatch opened to an enormous docking bay. Halfway down the ramp, he leaned over the rail. A sleek fighter jet stood out among the smaller bulky transporters at the far end of the bay.

"I was right. We're on a Kiki battleship. That's a pasha jet over there." Rohan sounded more convincing this time.

"I've never seen a Kiki ship before. They're strange, wouldn't you say? Can you tell if we're moving?"

Rohan rolled his eyes. "Not sure one way or the other. I do think the Kikis hid in the asteroid belt for the same reason we did. Since we're not going anywhere, we might as well make ourselves comfortable."

Rohan was grateful to have an excuse to sit down. He ached all over, and his leg throbbed. Not far down the ramp was a good place to sit. He hesitated once he got there. How to sit without falling would be a challenge. As much as he hated it, an unintentional groan slipped out as he sat.

"Are you okay?" asked Vexy.

Rohan put his hand up to stop her from talking. "Just a little sore, that's all."

She was getting tired of his surly attitude. "You'd tell me if you weren't . . . right?"

"You'll be the first to know." He sounded dismissive and quickly changed the subject by talking about the Kikis.

That did it. She wouldn't ask again. If he wanted to be a martyr, so be it. "Okay then. What does a Kiki look like?" she asked, gritting her teeth.

"Okay. I'll get to that. But there are a couple of things you need to know first. They don't like Ryquats. At all. When I was young, they voted to ostracize us from the Fidus Achates Coalition. From what I've experienced, Kikis are easy to provoke."

Rohan was right about the Kikis. If not downright hostile, they were notoriously rude. Daresay, being rescued by them was better than the alternative. But things could have gone better. It seemed like every move he made was another quagmire of uncertainty. Rohan was hungry, in pain, and out of ideas. Plus, Vexy needed to toughen up and not be so emotional. This was one of those times. He was describing a Kiki, and she was ignoring him. Rohan stretched his leg out, accepting the possibility of them being in the docking bay for a while.

"I hid the best anhydrate meals in the locker under the case tagged Ranine." He wondered if Vexy would get the hint he was hungry.

"You have a Ranine? What else is on the shuttle?" She perked up for the first time since all this started.

"I packed rations and supplies for weeks. The Ranine is not assembled yet."

"What kind of Ranine is it?"

Rohan frowned. "It's the 828 series . . . a heavy-duty Troodon. Anyway, back to the Kikis.

Don't forget how they feel about Ryquats. And don't tell them you're a Ryquat Viceroy. Trust me, that would only make matters worse.

"I get it, Rohan, Kikis hate Ryquats!"

"You need to take this seriously, Vexy. It's important. Before your assignment, I was a Special Ops at the edge of our galaxy near the Umduls' planet. I briefly met the Kikis twice during a disagreement with the Gystfins. They were just as rude to them. The only species the Kikis respect in this galaxy are the Umduls. But that's to be expected. The Umduls are good with most aliens except for the Crozins and Gors. I do know where the Kikis come from.

It's a distant galaxy called Coma Berenices. And their planet—Kowok—has half of the gravity of Zaurak.

"I'm guessing they know we're Ryquats because the gravity in here accommodates us. You'll feel the difference if we're allowed to leave the bay. Step lightly, or you'll bounce up and knock yourself out on the ceiling. I know; I've made that mistake more than once on space stations.

"Where was I? Oh yeah. The Kikis I've met were intelligent, courageous, and rude. More like pompous. When I first saw them, I thought they looked like a pretty chovo."

"A bird? They look like a bird?" Vexy interrupted, surprised.

"Well, not exactly," Rohan chuckled. "Kikis have colorful, shiny feathers; birdlike fingers; a face with a beak mouth; and walk upright on two skinny legs. They're beautiful. I give them that. That's what fooled me at first. You'll see what I mean. But rude or not, these Kikis saved us. So, they can't be all that bad."

"Do our linguistic chips translate, Kiki?" Vexy asked while yawning.

"Yes, at least mine did. Are you finished with all the questions?" frowned Rohan.

"Why? You said I should learn as much as possible while we wait."

"Yeah. I did, didn't I." Rohan rubbed his injured leg and flexed his foot. "Okay. Kikis have two almost-white eyes, a nose—or a beak. I'm pretty sure that's where their nose is. I couldn't tell. Their feathers cover that part of their face. They can't fly. At least I never saw one fly. What I didn't expect was they had fingers. And how graceful they move."

Vexy stretched out her legs and rolled her ankles. "Fingers? A bird with fingers. That's different. Are they shorter or taller than us?" she covered her mouth and tried not to yawn.

"They're a little shorter than the average Ryquat. Wait until you see how fast they can run. The Kiki I saw running was a blur. Must admit, I was impressed."

"Talk about seeing things. Is the Kiki ship peculiar to you?" Vexy asked, curious if she saw what she thought she saw.

"Yes. Sort of iridescent, and it slinks as if alive. Reminds me of an eel."

"Yeah. It reminded me of a mirage," waving her hand to demonstrate what she meant.

"Yeah, that too. The Kikis' feathers are iridescent like their ship." Rohan added while looking up at the black hole. Curiously, he was distracted by it.

"Do you think it will be a while before the Kikis check on us?" asked Vexy.

"Not a clue. I'm just glad to be in here instead of out there. If you don't mind, I'm going to rest my eyes while I can. Wake me up when they get here." Rohan used the rail to lie down on the ramp. "Don't worry. We're going to be okay. The Kikis may not like us, but they won't kill us. We'd already be dead if that were their intention," yawned Rohan.

He closed his eyes and saw the little boy crouched in the stairwell. He was close enough to grab him, but that would have meant leaving Vexy behind. Rohan saw the terror and desperation in his brown eyes. The boy reached out to him and screamed. Some things are not forgivable.

# two

# NEVER ENOUGH AND MUCH TO REGRET

**The Umdul Language:**
NYOVȝ ONYIUMOOGHIE ENYT
MYUMKHIE BI ȝOGȝB

**CAPTAIN** Thude's transmission with Captain Pify ended abruptly. It wasn't long before the old salt's worst trepidation came true—that nothing had gone to plan. The Crozins and Gors eradicated hundreds of Kiki battleships, and Zaurak was worse off. The numbers coming in were staggering. Now faced with a weak defense, Captain Pify requested every available Umdul battleship in the galaxy to assist in the war. To his detriment, the nearest ship would take more than a day to rendezvous. Meanwhile, he must gamble that the Crozins would not attack. Waiting in that sector to assist the Kikis could cost him his fleet.

Victis had his own conflict. Odds were, Vexy and Rohan were already dead. But there was a slim chance they made it out. Rohan sent a message just before the monitor went black: *"If we make it to the shuttle, mark coordinates 2148-0987 in the asteroid belt. We'll hide there."*

Even so, let's say they made it to the asteroid belt. Then what? How long could the shuttle sustain life? Victis wondered if he were the one stranded, would they risk flying through a swarm of Crozins to rescue him? In his heart, he knew Vexy would. Answering the question did not change his decision. Vexy and Rohan were on their own. There was too much at stake. For now, he must wait for the Umdul ships to arrive. The surviving Kiki and Ryquat battleships were transmitting exigent distress calls. And from the sounds of them, it was going to be ugly.

THE SENSORS DETECTED LESS THAN two hundred Kiki battleships, and about a hundred Ryquat ships escaped the attack on Zaurak. One after the other, war-torn ships came into view on the monitors. How they made it that far was beyond belief, yet heartbreaking. The battleships had whole sections blown off. When they disengaged, debris trailed behind them eerily in space. Ship-to-ship transmissions were coming in on all channels pleading for assistance. Most of the Ryquat battleships could transfer their injured onto other ships. Regrettably, five ships could not dock. Without that capability, the likelihood of survival radically diminished.

Meanwhile, the Kikis refused assistance. They were transferring their injured by shuttle to other Kiki ships. From what Captain Pify saw, some Kiki battleships would breach before completing the transfers. But their dire circumstances did not dictate their resolve. He wished they would accept help, but he knew they would not. Time was ticking, and hundreds of lives were hanging on to blind faith. Or perhaps they refused to accept death. No matter what, nothing could stop the inevitable once the anti-matter solar core fluctuated. Several Ryquat and Mikado captains ordered all aboard to evacuate; a breach was imminent.

As feared, the exterior of a battleship began to break apart. Frantic transmissions overlapped, requesting shuttles to rescue the fleeing Ryquats. The ship's hull expanded as pods shot out into space. A fraction of a second later, the battleship exploded into a fireball. The bright light flashed across dark space and blinded those watching on monitors. What came next was horrifying. Razor-sharp projectiles from the explosion hit a Ryquat and Kiki battleship. Sections of the ships were sliced off and spiraled away. Moments later, they both exploded, sending another wave of destruction. A third flash appeared on the monitors. It was an Umdul jet caught in the path of shrapnel.

The chain reaction ignited a fireball of destruction. It seemed forever before the cold, dark space returned. Everyone held their breath and watched the disaster unfold until the last fragment of wreckage sped past them into the abyss. Three battleships and an Umdul jet were gone. What remained was a graveyard of bodies and waste.

If one didn't know better, what appeared to be a frenzy of Ryquats and Umduls scrambling to shuttles was, in fact, a concerted operation. Lives were at stake depending on how fast help could reach them.

The Trekachaws saved precious time. They were searching for survivors before the shuttles cleared the docking bays.

What they were about to witness would shock even the most hardened. Thousands of bodies were suspended in space amid the desolate waste. What looked strange was the familiar sections of a once-mighty battleship they called home still intact.

Every person on those ships was significant. Yet now, they were meaningless. And what of those final words spoken never to be heard—life, love, and promise all gone.

But even though they had no voice, their frozen faces told the cruel stories of their demise. Some ran scared as they turned to stone, while others accepted fate holding on to one another. Many clung to precious relics, knowing death was near. How did they choose? Only they knew. In the end, it didn't matter. They all shared the same horrific grave. Their bodies were testimonies of the tragedies created by war.

Azha and Victis searched for anyone in a vita brevis suit, but there were none in the sea of dead bodies. As they were about to give up, they saw Phera, Duroc, and Boo flying toward them. Somewhere out there, they found Ryquats still alive in suits.

Phera sped past, "Hurry! There's more that way."

Azha and Victis streaked in the direction Phera came from. Along the way, they crossed paths with several more Trekachaws holding on to Ryquats headed for a ship. Nothing could have prepared Azha for the few waiting to be rescued amid the magnitude of dead floating in space. The Crozin and Gors were masters at creating a bloody trail of carnage.

They were winning, and some of it was his fault. So self-assured yet unaware. The first all-powerful Trekachaw. He had placed himself above King Myosis or anyone who questioned his conviction to save the Quizans from genocide. It was naive of him to have such thoughts of grandeur. Perhaps even believing he was a prophecy. Now, he must fight a war that spread across the galaxy. Truth being, he never had a choice. He was destined to be a quantum leap in evolution.

Why him? Azha often asked himself that question. And how could his fate be controlled? He recalled doubting himself when his Human half, Cole, saw his Trekachaw body for the first time on Earth. How confusing it all was. And then there was his weak Quizan half, more logical but lacking the warrior half necessary to survive. Together they were powerful, but his two souls were at odds in a tug-of-war for dominance. For now, he must not allow Cole to surface. That threat shook him to the core.

Coming toward him was a handful of Ryquats flying on their own. But those were the exception. Victis did not appear to be affected by any of it. But then, on Trinite, he'd endured much worse.

Azha flew behind Victis not because he was afraid but because he did not want Victis to see how troubled he was. Seeing the dead up close made him feel sick, especially his Human half. On Palatu, the Quizan deaths did not affect Cole. Not so with Ryquats. Ryquats were just as human as those on Earth. But here was not the time nor place to judge. Azha asked Cole not to look and to silence his anguish.

Azha shook Cole off and grabbed the nearest suit. He looked into her eyes; she was alive and looking back. He couldn't tell if she was more afraid of death or him. Even so, she didn't resist.

Hours passed, and they were still finding live Ryquats among the deceased. Twenty-two succumbed to injuries while en route to a battleship. There would never be an exact loss from the destroyed battleships because it was unknown how many Ryquats from Zaurak had boarded during the melee. In addition, not one Kiki was found alive. Their death toll was still unknown.

Captain Pify requested notification if any information was heard relevant to Captain Thude's ship. Several reports confirmed there was nothing to report. At this point, expecting anything to change was unrealistic. Captain Pify accepted that Captain Thude's ship was a casualty of war. He would greatly miss his Kiki friend and formidable ally. It was a costly and sad day.

However, sometimes in the darkest hour, a revelation can restore blind faith. Such was the case when a transmission confirmed Captain Thude was alive and entering Zaurak's orbit.

Thude would have much to explain, and Pify had plenty of questions. Everything that could go wrong did. Even so, adversity was far from over. Captain Pify was trying to ignore the sharp pains in his chest. He had two previous artificial heart transplants and was savvy about what it felt like when they failed.

Pify rationalized, telling himself he had several hours before the pain would become unbearable. Considering the risks, he'd speak with Thude before informing his Toogus to run a diagnostic. He heard Thude's request to dock. But this time was different. The pain became excruciating and the old salt Umdul could not wait any longer. Pify requested his personal Toogus to the bridge, fearing he could not walk to the surgical bay on his own. Toogus Oiba waddled-ran across the bridge and began sticking patches on Captain Pify's face and chest, even when Pify verbally resisted.

"Enough, Oiba. Escort from bailiwick without show. Much to tell, much to learn. Forthwith obligated sensitive burden," grumbled Pify. He was angry at himself for being old and weak when he needed to be strong.

Oiba insisted on Pify sitting in a transport dooly. When he refused, Oiba was not surprised. Nor was he flustered when Pify abruptly added not to ask again. Halfway to the infirmary, Captain Thude met them in the corridor. Following close behind, he figured Pify's heart was the problem. Still, Captain Thude felt compelled to ask and picked up his pace to walk beside the old salt. "Is it your heart?"

Pify wobbled sideways to look up at Thude. "Bad heart short-lived. New models attune mind post hoc old Pify spry, you see. Talk delay, pain great. Victis, you trust as me. *Oiba*." Captain Pify grabbed his chest and collapsed into Oiba's arms.

Not long ago, Captain Pify and Thude boasted about their upcoming grand retirement ceremony from the Fidus Achates. Neither one admitted to the other that the real reason was failing health. Of course, this was before the attack on Zaurak. Retiring became a figment of their imagination, replaced by trying to stay alive.

Several Umduls pushed Thude aside as they ran, carrying Pify down the corridor. Surrounded by Toogus, Pify disappeared behind the doors that spun shut. Captain Thude stood outside, fearing the worst. If Pify died, it would conclude their pact.

RUMORS ABOUT CAPTAIN PIFY'S RELAPSE spread quickly throughout the battleships, and the Toogus had not provided an update. Most were in denial, and the Umdul captains refused to believe the rumors until they heard directly from Oiba.

The first time Phera heard about Pify was from two Umduls quarreling about his condition. It took a moment for it to sink in. Then her stripes turned a sickly grey. She loved Pify and would be lost without him. She flashed into energy and headed for the surgical bay waiting room.

No one was there. She waited and paced, and no one came. How long would it take before someone would tell her something? She could feel her stripes turning purple with rage wanting to do things she'd regret.

*Revenge! It's wrong, but that's all I have left. How ludicrous for him to suffer needlessly. What does it take to convince a Quizan to merge? I gave sound reasons why a Quizan merge with Pify would be exceptional, and not a single Quizan volunteered. I will never forgive the Quizans for their selfish ignorance if he dies.*

Captain Victis and Azha morphed into body form next to Phera. No one said a word because they knew it would be impossible to control their emotions. Captain Thude stomped in and stood next to them. "Any word?"

Victis shook his head and cleared his throat before speaking. "Has Pify told you anything about us? That is, the Trekachaws, or how we got in this mess?"

Captain Thude stretched his neck. "Are you Victis?"

"Yes, I am." Victis was quite intrigued and distracted by the strange creature called Thude.

Thude stretched his neck even further, trying to look at Victis eye to eye. "Pify told me to talk to you if he wasn't available. Wouldn't you agree this qualifies as one of those times?"

Victis was curious how long Thude would stretch his neck to be as tall as him. He was going to get a neckache. "I'll tell you whatever I can; it's the least I can do considering your loss. May I suggest we walk to Pify's bailiwick on the bridge where we can speak in private? On the way, I need to update the Umdul crew," Victis's words were strained. He was trying to control his emotions and the color of his stripes.

Phera was distant and noticeably not well. Azha was not attached to Pify like Victis and Phera. He'd stay with her for as long as she needed him. Victis did not have the luxury of being upset or someone taking his place. The war was relentless and without Pify all the burden fell on him.

WALKING WITH THUDE TO THE bridge was a sobering experience for Victis. Several times he tried to start a conversation with the bird only to be shushed. If Thude is the normal Kiki, they're all obnoxious, disrespectful, and arrogant. No wonder the Kikis have a crass reputation.

Tired of the attitude, Victis decided to say whatever he felt like. "I'll start from the beginning. I am a Trekachaw."

Thude cackled and interrupted in a snide tone, "That much I figured out on my own. If that's your beginning, skip to the middle."

Thude's insolence caught Victis by surprise. Victis felt his stripes turning red. If that cocky little bird spoke to him that way under any other circumstances, he'd show him what a Trekachaw could do.

Victis glared down at Thude before continuing. "Pify and I knew each other long before I merged with a Quizan. He is like a father to my Ryquat half. My love and admiration for him have not lessened since becoming a Trekachaw. If you were unaware, his health has been failing for some time. Phera and I have tried to persuade a Quizan to merge with him."

Thude interrupted, "Captain Pify advised me of your new species and abilities. Although, I can sense the inferior Ryquat that burdens you. Even so, I'm somewhat impressed. However, you're distracted by foolish emotions that I find irritating. I deserve your full attention, nothing less. To clarify, I have known Pify longer than you. Stop fixating on what you cannot control. He is receiving another heart and will be fine." Thude's tone was sharp and condescending. Victis ignored the damn bird rather than saying something he may regret.

It was not a good time for Victis to meet with the Umdul crew knowing his red stripes would upset them. He was angry and grieving, and that was difficult to hide. Standing outside the bridge, he concentrated on changing to green. Captain Thude stared with curiosity. But it didn't take long before his face changed back to a puckered beak.

"The gravity on this ship is unacceptable and causing me discomfort. Decrease it, or I will leave."

Victis had to control his stripes. "The gravity can be adjusted. Stay here. I'll talk to the bridge about it."

"Do more than talk," snapped Thude.

Victis could feel his stripes turning purple. It took a moment to calm himself down. No wonder Ryquats disliked Kikis. Thude was a mean, nasty bird.

Glancing down, he saw green again and walked onto the bridge before something else was said. The crew was beside themselves with worry. Several ran up to him, spun around, then waddled away. He tried to comfort them, but they continued in the Umdul way. Weeping, moaning, and frequent face patting was shared. Victis asked several times to adjust the gravity for the Kiki, but they didn't hear a word he was saying. He resorted to yelling and then apologized. That was harsh, but at least it worked. The Umduls graciously returned the apology and began waving their stubby hands across panels and pushing icons. Watching the stocky little bodies bouncing in the light gravity across the bridge should have amused him. But seeing their sad faces, it was not. With any luck, the ill-tempered Kiki captain would be in better spirits.

Victis and Thude made their way to Pify's bailiwick and sat on the floor instead of the small, uncomfortable Umdul chairs. Victis gathered his thoughts before speaking.

"As you requested, from the middle. Ten years ago, Ryquats discovered a planet rich in raw materials. As a result, the Ryquats entered a contract with the Gystfins to extract the minerals from Palatu. In return, they received a percentage of the raw materials.

"One Ryquat captain was assigned to oversee the mining. That captain was Doug Smyth. Now we know he's a traitor who conspired with the Crozins and a corrupt faction of Gystfin addicts. Have you had any contact with Gystfins?" Victis asked to see if Thude was listening.

Thude's feathers ruffled. "Limited, no encounters. I heard they're in demand when manual labor is required, and they'll take risks no other species will. I've also heard they're not to be trusted. Does that cover it?" Thude replied as if bored.

"You heard correct. The Gystfins hunted an indigenous Palatu species called Quizans for sport. But I'm getting ahead of myself. Where was I?" asked Victis.

"Doug Smyth," Thude snapped as he stood up to stretch and fluff his tail feathers. "No further explanation is necessary." Thude ended the conversation abruptly.

Victis was losing his patience. He hoped the nasty bird was leaving. But Thude slowly sat down. Victis found it curious that Thude's legs bent backward and folded out of sight beneath his body.

"Why are you staring at my legs? How dare you stare at me as if you disapprove," Thude squawked in defense.

"No. That's not it at all. The way you sat down reminds me of, well, a bird. On Zaurak, we have a rather large bird called a chovo." Victis immediately regretted the comparison.

"Ryquats eat the bird you call chovo and their eggs? Do you see me that way?" Thude cackled with a sharp tongue, and his feathers spiked on the back of his long neck.

"No. Maybe? Well, that thought may have crossed my mind. Don't you eat fish? If you met an advanced species that looked like a fish, wouldn't that same thought cross your mind? Nothing I say now is going to matter. What do you want me to say? That I apologize for my thoughts. Okay. I apologize," Victis countered in a surly voice.

"You just compared me to a chovo. Your ignorance is appalling. Spare me any further insults, Trekachaw. Must I bear the burden of educating you? Yes, Kikis lay eggs. But we are not like other birds. We have evolved. During my cockerel prime years, I hatched three beautiful Kikis. One bink and two pulks. Unequivocally, the thought of eating an egg is revolting. Ryquats are barbaric and disgusting."

"You're a female Kiki?" Victis blurted out, surprised.

"That's your response? Why would you ask such a question? Of course, I'm a female! How insulting. You're no better than a Ryquat," screeched Thude.

"How am I supposed to tell the difference? You all look the same," growled Victis.

"Imbecile, I am a pulk. A female!" Thude squawked, outraged. She stood up, and her voice lowered. "Why are your stripes turning red?"

Victis thought to himself, *One more insult, and Pify will be extremely disappointed in me.* His yellow eyes narrowed. "Red is bad for you. My turn to be insulting. You are crass, arrogant, and boast of superiority when your defects imply the opposite. You are inferior, not the Ryquats. Pay close attention, bird, because this is the only warning you'll get. If my stripes turn purple, I suggest you run."

Thude's feathers quivered on her back. She tried to stare back but blinked and looked away.

Victis waited for Thude to stop quivering. "Now that's better. Let's be civil. What do you want to know?"

Thude's voice improved, but her need to chastise Ryquats did not. "Did you know Ryquats started this war? Their disrespect for the Crozin regions was, well, reprehensible. That foolish challenge gave the Crozins an excuse to renege on boundary decrees. I'm here because Captain Pify asked me for a favor. My Kiki bevy was supposed to be a diversion at Zaurak. I should have joined Pify first, as he requested. That mistake I shall always deeply regret. Pify was vigilant. I was not. Without a new intervention, he predicts a grim future. The Crozins and Gors will not consider a cessation with Ryquats nor their inferior Humans. One side will either dominate or destroy the inhabitants of this galaxy. Kikis are not of this galaxy. So why should we sacrifice ourselves for Ryquats? Pify's reputation and my admiration for him has limits." Thude almost sounded reasonable.

Strangely enough, Victis understood Thude's perspective. It was strategic for him to honor Pify's alliance with the Kikis. The old salt always had a good reason for everything he did.

Thude's voice sounded sad. "Pify is a visionary. He believes the Trekachaws and Kikis will become trusted allies. Our alliance should be about the future, not just the present." Victis took a step back, wondering if he had misjudged the bird. "I agree."

"Splendid. One final question. How do Quizans and Trekachaws absorb energy?" Thude reached up and touched Victis's chest.

"We absorb energy through our stripes. We prefer solar, but other sources will suffice." Victis was surprised that Thude touched him.

"Your explanation is sufficient. Pify answered my other questions. You'll learn that I am not without compassion. I rescued a stranded Ryquat shuttle in the asteroid belt," she divulged while running her finger up a stripe on his leg.

Victis took another step back. "That could be Vexy and Rohan."

"What if it's not the Vexy and Rohan Ryquats you claim? What if Ukaru Crozin or Jarb Gor purloined the Ryquat shuttle?" she squinted.

"We'll kill them," scowled Victis.

"I should hope so. First, torture for information, then kill. Agree? The shuttle I speak of is docked in the cargo bay above the stern porthole." Thude puckered her beak and stretched her neck toward Victis.

Victis turned sideways, thinking she might peck him. "I would like Azha to assist me."

"My rules apply to Azha as well. Before we depart, I must confess. I find male Trekachaws pulchritudinous," cooed Thude.

"Okay? I have no idea what that means. But thank you."

Victis transmitted ship to ship, stepping sideways away from Thude. "Akio, have Azha meet me at the airlock gate outside the Kikis' lower shuttle docking bay. Mark urgent and classified. Code *endo dens* on all frequencies until further notice." Victis flashed into energy and was gone.

Thude welcomed solitary to consider her options. If she requested assistance from allies in her galaxy, it could cause a ripple effect in the universe. Before doing anything, she'd wait until the Toogus confirmed Pify was stable enough to take command. If it were bad news, she'd offer a new world to the Umduls and Trekachaws in her galaxy. Until then, she'd wait for the incoming Umdul ships and what remained of her Kiki bevy to mobilize.

Meanwhile, she'd contact the Crozins to explain her position and request to reinstate the truce with the Kikis if all else failed. The Ryquats and Gystfins were expendable. She'd keep this to herself. Captain Pify was the only one she knew well enough to trust.

Azha morphed into body form, planting both feet firmly on the Kiki deck. He quickly realized he had overestimated the gravity. The force caused him to flip in the air until he stopped with his toes touching the ceiling. Laughing out loud, he lightly pushed off and landed upright on the deck floor.

Victis landed next to him. "Different, isn't it?"

"Different is one way of putting it. Ha, I call it a blast."

"Yeah, too bad we can't compete in a one-push ricochet bounce."

Azha thought about it for a moment. "If we get a chance, I accept the challenge."

"War now. Later, bounce on, Azha. Right now, you're here because there's a good chance Vexy and Rohan's shuttle is inside this bay. If we find Crozins or Gors, we'll wait here for Captain Thude. I gave her my word not to kill them."

"No problem. Is Thude the Kiki captain?"

"Yes. Of this ship and a fleet they call bevy. Also, captains are mikados," explained Victis.

"Seems the Kikis aren't too friendly. Or am I wrong?" asked Azha.

"Ryquats . . . well, let's say they're not too high on their list. Thude's made it clear she's here for one reason—Pify asked her."

"Her?" questioned Azha.

"Don't ask; just know she's a female." Victis grinned.

"Okay. Will we remain in energy until we know who's in the shuttle?" Azha wondered why Victis was grinning.

"Yes. Let's just focus on it being Vexy and Rohan. Wouldn't this be a lucky break for a change?" He sounded skeptical. Maybe it was because he found accepting the worst case easier than another disappointment.

The energized Trekachaws followed the corridor from the airlock to the docking bay. From above, Victis spotted Rohan first, then Vexy. She looked older but just as elegant. He felt strange, or was he ashamed to face her? Seeing her reminded him of his infidelity. He alone caused the divorce by sabotaging their marriage. A forthright Ryquat would have admitted his mistake and spared her the unnecessary grief and confusion. Instead, he lied and cheated, banking on Vexy to find out. That should have ended their marriage. But no, it did not. She forgave him. All that did was make him want the divorce more. Victis remembered the day he asked her. It took an entire bottle of Caltaboone whiskey to muster up the nerve. Her tears should have affected him, but he was too relieved and drunk to care. What mattered was she said okay.

During the divorce, she remained supportive. The next step was to get his things from her house. The plan was for her not to be there. And yet, she showed up anyway. As he picked up the last moving crate from the bedroom, she stood in the doorway, begging him not to go. He waited for her to calm down and walked around her, not saying a word. She followed him to the door, asking what went wrong. But freedom was on the other side.

What he regrets is how he used her because he was lonely. Not once did Vexy voice her anger or resentment toward his insatiable love for his deceased first wife.

Nonetheless, there were times when he told himself not to take all the blame. Vexy pushed for a relationship even though he told her he was not ready. It was as if she wanted him because she couldn't have him. Maybe he was nothing more than a challenge. No matter the reason, he still mourned for Connie, and Vexy paid the price for not listening. If Vexy was still waiting for Ryquat Victis, her wait was over; he was gone.

Victis and Azha descended in body form alongside the base of the ramp. Rohan scrambled to his feet, bouncing on one leg and pointing a Neco weapon at them. "Who are you? What are you?" Rohan shouted as he walked up the ramp with Vexy glued to his side.

"Rohan, lower your weapon. I'm Victis, or at least I was. Now I'm a Trekachaw."

"Victis?" Vexy gasped, trying to catch her breath.

"Why so surprised? You knew I merged with a Quizan," Victis responded, annoyed. Already she irritated him, and for no good reason. But he was being rude, so he'd start over. "Sorry. I thought you'd seen a Trekachaw. The first time can be overwhelming." Victis offered an excuse, sounding concerned.

"I did, on a monitor. Guess I shouldn't be surprised. You told me you merged with a Quizan. But I didn't picture you this way," confessed Vexy, feeling light-headed.

Rohan stood his ground. "Vexy, do you believe this is Victis?"

Victis's stripes turned red, and his eyes glowed yellow. "Rohan, you'd already be dead if I wanted to kill you."

Vexy placed her hand on Rohan's arm. "Please do as he says. Victis, don't hurt him. Rohan is the only reason I'm alive; he's just trying to protect me."

"I don't trust them," Rohan said in a low, deep voice.

Victis's red stripes revealed he was losing his temper. Azha spoke up to intervene. "You must have been through hell and back. I'm Azha. Allow me to answer your questions?"

"I would greatly appreciate that," replied Vexy, relieved.

"Are we on a Kiki ship?" asked Rohan.

"Yes, you're on Captain Thude's battleship. She's called a Mikado and the commander of what's left of her fleet. Captain Pify asked Thude to aid in the war. What you witnessed were Kikis trying to divert the invasion on Zaurak. There were a lot more Gors and Crozins than any of us expected. That mistake cost Thude more than two hundred of her battleships. As we speak, the Umduls and Thude are discussing options. Last I heard, they're debating the adverse shift in power, including the cost and sacrifice to protect this galaxy. It wasn't well known, but before Pify asked for Thude's support, the Kikis made a truce with the Crozins. Part of the truce was not to interfere with conflicts within this galaxy. We assume that was before the Crozin invasion. The first attack was on the Gystfins' planet, Gardux. Within a few days, Zaurak succumbed to the same bloody invasion. I won't be surprised if Thude is still aligned with the Crozins. That would be a mistake for her. Pify is confident the Crozins and Gors will eventually spread to other galaxies if not stopped. What Pify thinks doesn't matter to the Kikis. Most of them believe the Crozins will not invade their world.

"If Pify fails to convince Thude that the Crozins are liars and not to be trusted, she will leave. Without her support, the Gors and Crozins will conquer Zaurak and Gardux," explained Azha.

Rohan leaned on the ramp rail. "What can I do?"

Victis's stripes faded to green. "Well, for starters, don't take the Kikis' superior attitude personally. And don't mistake Thude for a male. Not good; I found out the hard way. What do you two know about the invasion of Zaurak?"

"No one saw it coming." Rohan didn't want to talk about it. He was trying to forget the smell of burned flesh and screams of death. Those were his private demons. Besides, telling what he saw wasn't going to help.

Vexy raised her hand. "I may have some information you can use." She hesitated, questioning if she should say anything.

An alarm sounded, and the gravity adjusted for the Kikis as they entered the bay. Vexy felt weightless and was giggling. She hung onto the rail and bounced up and down on the ramp. Rohan could put weight on his injured leg and stand like nothing was wrong. The distraction was good; even Victis was laughing with them.

True to nature, the proper Kikis were irritated by the amusement. Captain Thude stiffened. "Pify's surgery was successful. Who are these Ryquats?"

Victis pointed. "That one is Vexy, my second wife. She's a Viceroy on the Ryquat Council. With her is Rohan, a Special Op assigned to her."

"You say, the second wife?" chirped Thude.

"Affirmative. My second wife, and we're divorced." Victis sounded irritated, and he was.

"Sordid bygones are distracting. I can't see the attraction. As a Trekachaw, you must be humiliated. She is unseemly and boorish. So be it. More importantly, I am not convinced the Gors and Crozins are a threat to my galaxy, but Pify has a history of being right. To err on caution, I am considering additional Kiki pashas and reinforcements from the Latuzars. They are our most trusted allies.

"I must admit, since meeting the Trekachaws, I concur with Pify. You are a worthy new species. Also, Captain Pify asked if I was willing to transport the Quizans to a suitable world outside this galaxy. That is if need be. I accepted his request," preened Captain Thude, giving Vexy a look of disapproval.

Victis glanced sideways at Azha; he did not trust the Kikis to protect the Quizans. Azha started to say something, but Victis frowned and cut him off. "Vexy, do you have anything to add?"

"Well, maybe?" she mumbled, wondering if she should talk in front of the Kiki.

Victis scowled. "Do you have something to say or not?"

Vexy crossed her arms. "With all due respect, I do if you'd give me a chance. I have an agent on Captain Smyth's battleship. Her last transmission was disturbing and cut short. She confirmed what I suspected. Captain Smyth is a traitor. For years, he conspired with a Crozin Ukaru called Narthex. And he helped the Crozins invade Zaurak. I warned the council weeks before the attack. Not that it mattered. They dismissed me. Some were even hostile. I was labeled a conspiracy fabricator and banned from future forums. By the time I convinced two Viceroys, the invasion was days away. What I'm about to tell you may seem farfetched."

"Vexy, please get to the point," barked Victis.

"You may not look the same, but you are just as rude as ever. Stop interrupting me, and I'll get to the point," snapped Vexy.

Victis knew Vexy well enough not to challenge her when she was indignant. They'd had plenty of heated arguments during their short marriage. That trip down memory lane he didn't care to visit again.

Vexy glared at Victis. "This is what I understood from her garbled transmission. She saw Captain Smyth carrying a strange device on the bridge that supposedly contained a Trekachaw's essence or energy." Vexy thought how foolish that must have sounded.

Azha corroborated, "Your informant is correct. Inside that device is Choan's energy. Choan and a female Trekachaw infiltrated two battleships to spy on them. To avoid being captured, Phera hid inside Narthex's head. She threatened to kill him by frying his brain if he disobeyed. Of course, that got his attention. She told him to take a shuttle and fly it into space. When they were out of range, she zapped his brain just enough to knock him out and took control of the shuttle. We didn't learn about Choan until later. Thanks to Phera, we have Narthex detained."

Victis nodded yes. "Eventually, all the Trekachaws will learn how to enter a brain. Think about the advantages. We could take over Crozin battleships by controlling the Ukarus. Hold on. Communications hailed me."

Victis walked away for a few moments and then walked back.

"Ah, this is interesting. Narthex's battleship and traitor Ryquat Smyth want to speak with me. If we get the chance, Smyth needs to be captured or killed. He should not be commanding a Ryquat battleship."

"Let's talk to Phera first," suggested Azha. "We should ask her about that new device. I'm guessing it's a modification of the magnetic field the Gystfins used on Quizans. Myosis is probably behind this."

Thude ruffled her feathers. "Enough parley. You have Ryquat Captain Smyth and Narthex's battleship surrounded. Destroy them if they try to retaliate or escape. How they concede will determine their fate. One *hai* from now. Reconvene at Pify's bailiwick. Include Trekachaw Phera. I want to meet her," ordered Thude.

Rohan whispered to Vexy, "What's an *hai*?"

Vexy rolled her eyes and shrugged her shoulders.

"One hour," whispered Victis.

# three

# THE FOWL JUDAS

**The Umdul Language:**
BHIEO FAIWELI JIUMTEЖ

**THUDE'S** ship was the first to feel the impact of the blast. The Crozin and Ryquat battleships exploded in space. They destroyed themselves and the captive Trekachaw on board. Victis was shocked and outraged by the loss of his friend. Choan had been with him since Trinite. His stripes flashed bright purple, and the thunder of his voice was frightening. "The Crozins murdered my daughter, tortured Connie, and now Choan! I'm going to kill Narthex!"

Vexy buried her face in Rohan's chest. Victis scared her, and the faithful agent on Smyth's ship was dead.

Thude stretched out her skinny neck and glared at Victis because she wanted Narthex alive. The arrogant bird acted as if she could stop him if he chose to kill the demon. Victis was so furious that he didn't realize she had buried her talons in his arm until he looked down.

The deep rumble in his throat became a savage growl as he leaned toward her. "Let go of my arm, or I will rip you apart!"

Thude let go and stepped back. "What! You dare threaten me?"

Victis looked at his arm where Thude left puncture wounds. "I've killed for less. You nasty, arrogant bird."

Azha grabbed Victis's arm and yelled at him to stand down.

"I heard you. Let go," snarled Victis, trying to jerk his arm away.

"Not as long as your stripes are purple," Azha feared Victis would kill Thude.

"Don't protect this nasty bird. Narthex must die. You know, he's a part of this too."

"You're right, he should die. But not now. We have Narthex; he's not going anywhere. You'll get the satisfaction of torturing him soon enough. Why not pick his brain first? Phera wants to go back inside," Azha spoke calmly, while holding firmly to Victis's arm.

The two Trekachaws locked horns in a stalemate. The outcome was anyone's guess. But to be safe, everyone moved to the other side of the bay.

Victis' stripes began to fade. "Let go; you can see I'm gaining control." Azha loosened his grip on Victis's arm. "*Baka yarous!* Let go, Azha."

"I know what that means. Cursing isn't in control, Victis."

"Let go, or I'll turn into energy," sneered Victis.

"Are you finished?" Azha was thinking he should warn Thude to leave the bay before letting go.

"Fair enough, I won't kill Narthex or the fowl Judas. Not now, anyway."

Azha slowly let go of his arm. Victis's yellow eyes locked onto Thude. "Relax, nasty bird."

Thude flapped her wings and fluttered her tail feathers. "Ryquat lizard, you are a waste of my time. Fowl Judas, indeed. Control your tizzy imbecile. Take heed. Everyone else is likely at Pify's bailiwick. Or do you want to take more time to spew your empty threats?" Thude hissed, and Victis returned the hiss.

Azha kept the peace by walking between Victis and Thude on the way to the bailiwick. Shockingly, there were no more snide remarks exchanged along the way. Nevertheless, they displayed plenty of attitudes. Victis's stripes glowed, and Thude fluffed her feathers in protest as she paraded down the corridor.

The old salt was sitting in a chair on top of the executive table at the furthest end of the room. Pify found this was the only way to be visible and heard by aliens who towered over the squatty Umdul. And as for Victis, he was glad to meet in the bailiwick. It was as good as it was going to get for seating.

Nonetheless, the Trekachaws opted to stand against the back wall. With that problem solved, Rohan, Vexy, and a few other Ryquats quietly entered the room. Looking around, they walked over to the Trekachaws. There was a good reason the Trekachaws did not sit down. The chairs were small, even for the Ryquats. Seeing no other options, Vexy sat in an uncomfortable chair. The other Ryquats squeezed into chairs the best they could. On the other side of the room, the Kikis and Umduls sat with no problem. Not long after everyone was situated one way or the other, in walked two Gystfins.

Before the protest could start, Pify announced, "Invite are two. Enemy heretofore contrary mutual rival accepted. Phera conveys for me, weak facade strong resolve."

Phera stood behind Pify for a couple of reasons. She worried about his chair being too close to the edge. And from there, she could scan the room for anyone who objected. "Pify will correct me if I misspeak. If I can't answer your question, he will. Let's get started; there's much to cover. To begin, we're outnumbered two to one. With that said, we have a strategic plan. Rohan will be captain of Choan's old battleship with Vexy. There's a crew on board awaiting your arrival. Since Pify's recovery will take a bit longer, I will remain on this battleship for as long as he needs me. Vopar, I'm assigning you as proxy captain to my ship. Don't screw it up."

Vopar smiled. "It's an honor and a privilege."

Phera nodded her head in approval. "Next. The two Gystfins join-ing us have crucial information. Serlof, raise your hand." Phera chose to ignore the apparent disdain in the room. The Trekachaws' stripes were turning red.

Serlof raised his hand and parted his lips, revealing long yellow fangs.

Phera's yellow eyes narrowed. "Stand down, Trekachaws. Serlof, you and Tysug, come over here with me."

The two Gystfins shuffled across the room with their heads bowed in submission. They stood behind Phera, consciously not looking toward the Trekachaws.

Pify was frowning, but the Trekachaws did not notice. He raised his hand and pointed at Victis. "Precedent avert!"

"Pify's right. No more disrespect from any Trekachaw!" shouted Victis.

Searching the room for Boo, Phera continued, "The Gystfins are here as allies. Serlof is a high-ranking Dux Ducis dignitary. He honors us by agreeing with our efforts to defeat the Crozins and Gors. With him is Tysug, a Kogbor battleship captain. Where's Boo?"

Boo stepped into view. He had been standing behind several other Trekachaws.

"You are the new Gystfin liaison. Serlof will be on your ship as a guest and adviser. Tysug and roughly two hundred Gystfin battleships will coordinate with you and Serlof. Their home planet, Gardux, was invaded just before Zaurak. The Crozins and Gors occupied their major cities and, like Zaurak, harvested the Gystfins for food. Pify promised the Gystfins sanction on planet Trinite until Gardux is safe. The Umduls will protect Trinite from future Crozin invasions while they continue to help us fight this war. Serlof has been transmitting coded messages to alert wayward Gystfin passenger ships and battleships away from Gardux. No ships have responded.

"However, we have intercepted several transmissions with a Special Ops on Zaurak. From what we've heard, he is a successful ground fighter. Victis, Azha, Clyde, Zeta, Vious, and Nikki, return to Zaurak and join them. I can't be with you on this one. With that said, locating the Special Ops is imperative. Before you leave, get with Victis or Clyde for training. They will teach you how to enter a Crozin's brain. You'll be able to hear their thoughts and speak with them while in energy. More importantly, how to cause pain and kill them. Being able to control the subconscious of a Crozin is a powerful weapon. But there is a downside. A Crozin's thoughts are revolting. So be prepared. And don't forget to fry the Crozin's brain when they are no longer useful. By the way, no one has entered a Gor's brain. I do not recommend it.

"Also, be warned about a new device. The Crozins have a magnetic energy force that can trap a Trekachaw. To circumvent the trap, never expose your energy on their ship. Hide between decks, bulkheads, or something solid until a Crozin touches whatever you're hiding in. That's when you can transfer your energy directly into the Crozin. If you must or want to leave that body, do the reverse. You can also transfer from Crozin to Crozin if they're touching each other. Choan was trapped by one of these devices, and now he's dead. You should assume all their ships have the devices by now. If there are no questions for Pify, he should return to his cabin."

Phera gently scooped Pify out of his chair and carried him from the room with Thude trailing behind.

Victis asked, "Are there any questions for me?"

Serlof hobbled over to a wall and leaned on it, trying to be subtle. Whether his pain was old or new, he didn't want others to know. "The Gors destroyed my world. I am but one of a few Dux Ducis who survived the massacre. Our magnificent ancient Armada is no more. Gone forever, as our species will be without you. I've witnessed what Trekachaws can do. I believe Trekachaws are miracles created by Jaaju to bring balance to the cosmos. We were strong and proud. Now we are proud but not strong. The past must not sway our common goal to defeat the enemy. I speak for all Gystfins when I accede to your terms. Accept my allegiance to fight this war alongside you as blood warriors. I can offer no higher honor."

Phera returned to the bailiwick, appearing upset. Her stripes were dull, and she was in a hurry to speak with Victis. What she whispered was disturbing and could jeopardize their best-laid plans.

Victis walked over to Clyde and spoke so no one else could hear him.

Azha knew Victis well enough to know whatever transpired was terrible. Victis addressed the room.

"An emergency has come to my attention that I must attend. Vious notified Belton that he was required to attend this meeting. I want him here before I return. Azha, you're with me. We won't be long." Victis sounded rattled.

Victis, Azha, and Phera flashed into energy and flew out of the meeting.

Pify was propped up in his bed, waiting for them. His hair was disheveled and sticking up on one side of his head. Fizz was visible, doing his best to groom the old salt. Pify looked pale, worried, and disappointed. His heart transplant did not go well this time. He attended the meeting against Toogus Oiba's recommendation and was paying the price for his defiance.

Phera sat down on the bed next to Pify. "I would handle this without bothering you, but I'm beside myself. What could go wrong did go wrong. It's about Thude. And since you're the only one that knows Thude, I need your advice on her. Whatever you think is best, we'll do. Thude has betrayed us. She attended the meeting knowing she was leaving our galaxy with her bevy. Thude contacted the Crozins and made a pact with them. In return, the Crozins vowed not to attack the Kikis. Thude told me the same terms apply to the Umduls and Trekachaws if they abandoned the Ryquats, Gystfins, Quizans, and Humans. That includes interference on planets Zaurak, Gardux, Palatu, and Earth."

Pify shook his head no. His eyes closed and he began to snore. Fizz curled up around a tuff of Pify's hair and yawned with sleepy eyes. The three Trekachaws turned into energy and quietly disappeared.

Belton was waiting in the bailiwick when Victis, Phera, and Azha returned to the meeting. The Ryquats, Gystfins, and Trekachaws were talking and in good spirits. Now for the bad news.

Victis clapped his hands to get everyone's attention. "I will make this short. The Crozins offered Thude amnesty to withdraw, and the Kikis accepted. Thude asked the Crozins to extend their offer to the Umduls and Trekachaws. The long and short of their terms is no interference with the Crozins reigning over Gystfins, Ryquats, Quizans, and Humans. That includes home planets. Pify is still recovering from surgery, but we spoke with him briefly. He wants no part of the deal made with the Crozins. This is a mute question, but are there any Trekachaws in favor of Thude's offer?"

Victis scanned the room for even a hint of ambiguity. "Good. Here's the new contingency. The key to winning this war is to increase the Trekachaw numbers. Belton, you do whatever it takes to convince more Quizans to merge. They need to understand that if they refuse, we won't be able to protect them much longer. Without us, the Crozins will annihilate them to prevent new Trekachaws. Clyde, you and Zeta ready the cargo ship we modified. Assist Belton with the Quizan recruitment and the trek to Earth. I want to know how many before you depart. Clyde, where will you look for suitable Humans on Earth this time?"

"Same as before. No shortage of good vets," Clyde answered with confidence. Victis was counting on him. He could not fail.

"Fair enough. Go now. Time is not on our side. The rest of you resume your previous assignments until the cargo ship returns. Azha, Takeda, Nikki, Duroc, Ajax, and Cody, you're with me to Zaurak. Akio will pilot a shuttle for transport. I chose you six because I've seen you fight, and it's about to get bloody," Victis tilted his head and grinned. But all could tell it was forced.

"Before we go, who needs training in how to kill a Crozin while in energy?"

Cody answered, "Clyde taught us every trick. We're all good to go."

# four

# HAIL MARY!

The Umdul Language:

HIEALI MYEƷYI

**AS** a senior pilot in the Fidus Achates, Akio lived in space for months at a time. After years of commuting, the family moved to an upscale townhouse a stone's throw away from the Chancellor Towers in Cape Parrish. The area was safe and close to his home base. Most of all, during brief furloughs, this location allowed him more time with the family.

Akio was well aware of the attack on Cape Parrish, but hearing Vexy's disturbing detailed version of the invasion made him physically ill. According to her, it was genocide. The Crozins were mass harvesting Ryquats leaving few survivors. Thus, his family escaping was unlikely. Akio lost control, shouting she was exaggerating. He stood up and threw a tab pad at her. Rohan and another navigator ordered Akio to leave the bridge. Rohan and Vexy briefed Victis regarding the disturbance immediately after the incident. So, it wasn't a surprise when Akio demanded to speak with him. What surprised Victis was when Akio threatened to defect and search for his family on his own. Victis understood the urgency to find loved ones and sympathized with his blatant defiance. Regardless, threatening to defect is mutiny. No matter who it is. Victis hesitated before saying something he'd regret. For now, he'd let this one go. Besides, no one would be foolish enough to make such a threat if they were really going to do it.

During the briefing, Akio learned about the mission's slim odds of success. Most likely, the shuttle would be annihilated on the way down. By some chance they weren't destroyed, returning could be worse. Akio didn't care about the odds. Any chance to rescue his family was worth it. Besides, he was Victis's best pilot.

One small shuttle, one Ryquat, and seven Trekachaws departed into hostile territory. Navigating to Zaurak while avoiding the Crozin and Gor swarms on the way down would be tricky.

Choosing a small shuttle was smart on one hand because they were less likely to be detected. On the other hand, there were plenty of disadvantages. The shuttle was slow, with a limited defense system. Plus, the ten-passenger maximum was a problem. Indeed, there were plenty of reasons they could fail. But in the end, it came down to believing in Victis. Whether Ryquat or Trekachaw, his heroic missions were legendary. If anyone could pull this off, he could.

As instructed, Akio waited in the asteroid belt. But he wasn't told how long to wait. The coordinates to the small town Victis gave him didn't make sense. Why there? Minutes seemed like hours. He was wasting precious time that could have been spent searching for his family. Akio felt like acting on impulse, not logic. He couldn't stop thinking, *What if they are hurt? What if they're dying?* He had to trust Victis and follow orders. But no matter how much he told himself to stay calm, it wasn't working. He would fly to the coordinates if he didn't hear something soon.

Victis chose a small suburban town for his base camp. It had everything he needed and was within a hundred miles of Cape Parrish. Most likely, the Ryquat residents had evacuated to avoid being captured or killed. Still, he knew better than to take anything for granted. He would use caution until he knew for sure.

For the Human Trekachaws, the narrow streets with quaint markets and small-town charm were eerily like home. Azha was amazed at how much it reminded him of Cole's Earth. And though light-years away, fond memories of Cole's childhood surfaced. His Earth soul was homesick. But then came anger. Cole retaliated by causing a sickening reflex inside their body. Azha justified himself as the dominant soul because Cole knew nothing about the galaxy. Or at least that's what he told himself. Once again, Azha prevailed, silencing his Human half. But at what cost? Cole reminded Azha that he could hurt him and that his disdain for him had not diminished.


NO ONE CAME BACK FOR him. And he wasn't going to stay there any longer. Akio set a course for the town. Luck was on his side. There was not a single Gor or Crozin ship on the way down. Although, being on the planet's surface was almost as dangerous as being in space. The Crozins could be anywhere. He'd fly the shuttle just above the narrow roadway to avoid detection.

So far, so good. But he didn't want to assume the area was safe. That could be fatal. Perhaps the Crozins had already been there. He had not crossed paths with a living thing. His nerves grew increasingly on edge. Maybe the coordinates were incorrect. Akio flew in the dark, thinking aloud, "Where are the Trekachaws? This does not feel right. I need to get out of here." Talking to himself wasn't going to change a thing. Akio knew if he saw the Crozins, it was too late. Plus, his vivid imagination about what they would do was causing him to jump at shadows. Be it luck or Captain Victis's foresight, the shuttle sensors did not detect any aliens along the way. Akio searched for a place to conceal the shuttle and wait for the Trekachaws. At the edge of town, he spotted a two-story house he could hide behind and still see the roadway.

It wasn't long before he saw light orbs streaking across the night sky. Akio breathed a sigh of relief. At last, he wasn't alone. One orb paused in front of the porthole before a sparkle appeared inside the shuttle. In a flash, the sparkle morphed into a body inside the cockpit.

It was Azha with a big grin on his face. With a friendly slap to Akio's back, he sat next to him. "Well, you almost made it on your own. Navigate through those two buildings. On the other side, there's a large warehouse. Victis and Takeda will open the hangar so you can dock inside. You'll be safe in there, and the shuttle won't be visible from the air or ground."

Akio's nerves settled, and his head cleared. He flew the shuttle inside and landed without a hitch. Five light orbs morphed into Trekachaws under cover of night to begin the mission.

Victis was quick to delegate assignments. "Akio, stay with the shuttle until we know there are survivors in Cape Parrish. If we do, you'll have a small window to find your family.

"Azha, you're with me. Duroc and Ajax, try to find out approximately how many Crozin Ukaru captains are in the city. Also, the Crozin Tajat Rakta battleships in Zaurak airspace. Takeda and Nikki, get information on the Gors. Your assignment is more difficult. Their rank is by seniority on the bridge. And it's not all that unusual to find Crozin Ukarus on the Gor ships. Akio, confirm your address is Lot-983, Building Four, Cape Parrish?"

"Yes, that's my address. Thank you for doing this, Captain."

Victis tilted his head. "You may want to hold your thanks. I can't promise we'll even make it that far. This will get bloody. Crozin blood if I have my way. Listen up, everyone. I've said this before, and it won't be the last time. We are at war. There's no room for hesitation or remorse. Hesitation will get you killed, and remorse will slow you down." Victis paused, "Questions? Good. Let's get on with it; we have a world waiting to be saved."

Azha thought about telling Victis about his rebellious Human soul. Cole continued to resist, insisting they were on Earth. For the time being, Azha would keep that aggravation to himself.

They streaked to the outskirts of Cape Parrish and hovered. There were no signs of Crozins. Victis soared to the top of a skyscraper within the city and morphed into a Trekachaw. The others followed, landing next to their captain. As far as the eye could see, the beautiful city was in ruins. The view was heartbreaking. Crumbling structures littered the streets, and burned walls remained where buildings once stood. Thick smoke choked the air, and fires raged across the horizon. Seeing the destruction for themselves gave credence to the fact that few Ryquats survived. The city was crawling with Crozins. And by now, those who escaped were hunted.

Still, Victis promised he'd check on Akio's family. That promise he intended to keep. But they needed to hurry. The cover of night was growing short. Victis considered the risk and decided that most Crozins wouldn't know what a Trekachaw light orb was. And the search would be quick. That is unless Akio's family was still alive.

Indeed, the warehouse seemed safe enough. Moonlight filtered through the windows, just enough to make it possible to see. The building was old, and Akio questioned if anyone had been inside for years. A cracked concrete pad covered the entry. From there, the warehouse had dirt floors and a wooden staircase along the back wall to a second story. The Trekachaws should have completed their task by now. Being alone again was aggravating. Akio walked up the stairs to an office that overlooked the warehouse and a bird's-eye view of the streets below. What he saw took his breath away. Sweat dripped down his face, and he froze, terrified.

Gathering on the streets below were dozens of Crozins. If they opened the hangar, he was as good as dead. The Crozins' keen noses would smell his sweat for sure. Searching for a place to hide was pointless. And the slightest sound could alert them. They would tear the warehouse apart if they suspected Ryquats were hiding inside. He needed to stay where he was and try not to breathe hard. Akio slowly squatted on the floor beneath the window and waited. He heard them talking but couldn't tell if they were getting closer. He could hear his heart beating inside his chest—*thump, thump, thump*. If the Crozins came any closer, they would hear it too. They'd come for him, searching with their long, nasty noses. Akio thought about making a break for the shuttle. That would be suicide. He'd stay there.

VICTIS EXPECTED A QUICK TURNAROUND since he was familiar with the area in Cape Parrish. That was about to change. Finding Akio's building in a city ravaged by fires and laser attacks would not be easy. Victis and the other Trekachaws regrouped to talk strategy. They would fly to the city's west side at the capital and start from there. If he remembered correctly, Akio's apartment was only a few blocks away. The only distinctive thing Victis could remember about the complex was the blue cornerstones. After telling the Trekachaws what to look for, they circled the area. Nikki was the first one to spot the blue stones. From above, it looked like the buildings in the complex had substantial damage. A few at the east end had been reduced to rubble. Victis motioned for the Trekachaws to follow him.

He chose the building with the least amount of damage. Nonetheless, the front doors had to be forced open. The moment they stepped inside the lobby, signs of a struggle were evident. Broken furniture and smeared blood told stories of how they died. That is where the tenants took their last stand. The door leading to the elevator lifts was barricaded to keep the Crozins out for as long as possible. Victis knew they would find more cursed halls and rooms with remnants of heroes and innocent lives cut short. There it was. He found what he was looking for. A sign above an archway with the number "One."

Victis and the Trekachaws flew past a charred fire escape and listened for any signs of life. They felt a breeze from an open window and stopped to watch the edge of a singed curtain catch the wind and flutter. The ashes on the floor left footprints as they walked. No one else had been there. Time was running out, and Victis was getting antsy.

Across the courtyard, Victis saw the number "Four" above the main entrance of the building. That was the number where Akio said his family lived. From the looks of it, no one survived. Be that as it may, he promised Akio to check the apartment. One after the other, six light orbs morphed into Trekachaws inside the lobby. There were no signs of a struggle, but they could smell the remnants of a fire. Sometime during the attack, an interior side door had been shut that gave access to the upper floors. The door was grey, and black residue from a fire that had burned on the other side lined the frame. It had stopped the fire from spreading. But whoever was trapped on the other side had no way out.

Victis turned the charred doorknob and pushed. The door crumbled into cinders and ash on the floor. It took a moment for him to realize what had just happened. He looked dismayed at Azha and dropped the doorknob. They were about to enter another world of grizzly remains and dreadful results. Every step down the long hallway exposed the chaos that took place. Doors torn off their hinges lay broken on the floor. Walls were scorched with laser burns when the Crozins shot at Ryquats, running for their lives. Victis could not ignore the obvious. Akio's family was gone. They were phantoms of this aftermath.

The numbers were going up in the hallway. Akio's apartment should be in front of them. Rechecking the numbers, the apartment without a door should be it. Azha flipped over a splintered door in the hallway and saw #983 attached to the top. They had found the apartment. The living room was ransacked, but there were no laser marks. What concerned Victis were the rips in the couch. Crozins' claws made them. He didn't see any signs of Crozins in the large bedroom. However, something happened because a mattress was leaning against the wall. Azha walked in behind Victis and noticed a sealed envelope on a nightstand addressed to Akio.

The letter seemed out of place. Whoever left it used a pen and paper like that of Earth. Ryquats rarely used paper. He picked it up and thought about reading it. Instead, he handed it to Victis. "You should give this to Akio." It confirmed they had found the apartment. Victis wished he had better news. Akio will be devastated and blame himself for not coming sooner. Perhaps he'd find solace and answers to his questions inside the letter. Anyone who knew him appreciated his devotion to the family. A Quizan had offered to merge with Akio. As much as he wanted to become a Trekachaw, he declined. The love for his wife and children was greater. Victis looked for anything else that might help Akio. Nothing he saw was going to make it easier. He thought about reading the letter, but that felt wrong. Those last words were for Akio's eyes only.

As they were about to leave, Takeda thought he heard a noise coming from a closet. He snapped his fingers to get the other Trekachaws' attention. Something moved inside. Victis motioned for the Trekachaws to stand back. If a Crozin were inside, he'd enter its brain to learn what the demon knew before killing it.

Victis flung the door open. Inside was a young woman on the floor curled up in a ball. Her clothes were filthy, and dirt covered the side of her face. From what he could see, she couldn't have been more than sixteen. She moaned in pain and moved ever so slightly. At some point, it looked like she tried to pull a blanket up to hide under. Now she was clinging to it for dear life. He slowly pulled it from her fingers and off to one side to get a better look. Her hair was bloody and matted to her head from the cuts on her scalp. And no telling how long it had been since she had much to eat. Her arms were nothing more than skin and bones. Looking closer, he saw her blouse was shredded on her back, and beneath were days-old slashes left by Crozin claws. These injuries told Victis this young woman was lucky to have survived the attack. But he questioned if she was at death's door. He leaned over and touched the young woman's neck to check for a pulse. She peered out from her swollen eyes and began to sob. Victis was beside himself. "Azha, go down the hallway. I saw an aqua tank inside an apartment. Hurry!" Victis glanced up and pointed the way.

Azha ran searching door to door until he saw the tank. He grabbed a couple of glasses off a counter and filled them. Running back, he cringed, thinking about what the Crozins must have done to her.

Azha kneeled next to Victis. "How can I help?"

"Help me sit her up."

Victis rolled her over and clenched his jaw when he saw her jeans were bloody and shredded. And like her back, he could see dark bruises and dried blood masking the deep open wounds. Victis wrapped his arm around her frail shoulders and gently sat her up. She tried to reach for the glass but was too weak. He held it next to her lips and tilted the glass. She gulped the water so fast she choked and spit it out. Victis lowered the glass and waited. She leaned against his chest for support and reached up to her face. He could feel her tremble, and her hand shook as she pulled matted hair from her mouth. Victis held the glass up and asked if she wanted to try again. She nodded her head and parted her chapped lips. This time, he tilted the glass slowly. She took small sips until most of the water was gone.

Whoever this young woman was, she had been through hell and survived. Victis spoke softly, not to frighten her. "I'm going to pick you up and carry you over to the bed. Is that okay?"

She looked up at him and nodded her head.

Azha threw the mattress onto the bed frame and brushed it off while the other Trekachaws kept watch for Crozins.

"Do you need help getting her out of the closet?" Azha asked, wishing he could do more.

"No. But I need one of you to go get Akio. The rest of you wait here. Whoever's going, do it now. Daylight is a few hours away. We need to be out of here before then. Tell Akio I said to fly in fast. Hover outside the bedroom window and open the main hatch. I'll carry her out the window straight into the shuttle. The rest of you, do what you can to keep the Crozins busy if they find us." Victis sounded worried, and that was rare.

Everyone wondered how this crazy plan would work. But Azha was the one who asked. "How will you get her from the window into the shuttle nine stories up?"

"Simple. I'll fly. How else?" Victis spoke in a surly voice.

"Oh yeah? Have you ever done that before?"

"No, Azha. How much could she weigh, a hundred pounds?"

Victis wiped dirt from her face. "I promise to do my best and get you out of here. But I need you to trust me."

"Are you real?" she asked with a raspy voice.

"Yes. I'm what's called a Trekachaw." He smiled.

"I'm not hallucinating?" She squinted her eyes to see him better.

"I'm quite real. Are you ready?"

"Yes," she grinned, and her body relaxed.

"So, young lady, what shall I call you?"

"Kim."

"Nice to meet you, Kim. My name is Victis," he said with a wink.

Victis cradled Kim in his arms and lifted her off the closet floor. Steadily, he rose above, testing his ability to carry her weight. Why no one had bothered to try before didn't make sense. That said, it was possible.

At last, she felt safe in his arms, whether it be a dream or reality. Victis floated to the bed and gently laid her on the mattress. The green-striped Trekachaw pulled up the sheets and tucked her in. Kim fought to keep her eyes open, fearing he wouldn't be there when she awoke. But her eyes were too heavy.

Watching his captain's compassion gave Cody strength. He didn't understand this new life yet. But he was honored to have been chosen. If not for Victis, he would still be on Earth staring at the ceiling, paralyzed from the neck down. It had been less than a year since an IED took his body. Being alive had a whole new meaning. He thought for sure he'd lost his mind when he saw the aliens from the corner of his eye. Real or not, he cried out. Victis heard him over everyone else. How remarkable. Cody turned to look out the open window, thinking this was one of those moments he should never forget. The sky seemed less smoky at night. Or perhaps the subtle breeze he felt had cleared the thick haze that choked the city. He missed Earth, his family, and the small town he came from. Zaurak made him homesick. But that was before the war on Earth when family and friends didn't pity him. Becoming a Trekachaw made him whole again. And this magnificent body gave him strength Humans could not fathom. His life was spared by this ruthless warrior with a heart of gold. He would follow Victis into hell without question. He turned away from the window and looked at his captain to volunteer. He knew he was the best Trekachaw for the task. Besides being faster, he could pilot the shuttle if Akio became disabled. Victis cocked his head to one side and agreed. To anyone who knew Victis, the head tilt was a sure giveaway that he was either very angry or very pleased; this was a good head tilt.

Cody turned into energy and streaked out the bedroom window over the moonlit city. Soaring solo in the night sky set him free. That ended with distant thunder in the direction he was headed. The thunder was not of nature but that of war. The Crozins' wrath was coming for anyone who survived. He flew faster, fearing Akio might be in their path.

During the short time Akio was left alone, the Crozins infiltrated the small town adjacent to the warehouse. Hundreds were swarming the streets and scavenging the buildings for someone to eat.

Not far from the warehouse, Cody got a bad gut feeling. Since becoming a Trekachaw, his instincts were acute, and he'd learned to pay attention to them. His gut feeling was right. He caught a whiff of Crozin stench at the edge of town. In his mind, he contemplated the worst-case scenarios if the Crozins had found the shuttle. Cody knew the answers, and none of them were good.

He dimmed his light orb and flew inside the warehouse to have a peek. There were no Crozins, and the shuttle was where they had left it. He sparkled green and circled above. Akio saw the Trekachaw and thought about running. But he slowly and very quietly got off the floor. As he tiptoed down the stairs to the shuttle, he waved and put his finger to his lips, warning the sparkling light to be quiet. Cody spiraled and morphed into body form next to him, whispering, "I take it you know about the Crozins out there?"

"Yeah! I've been scared stiff. I thought for sure those monsters would find me. They walked close enough for me to hear them more than a couple of times. How will I fly the shuttle out of here without them seeing me?" whispered Akio with his hands cupped around his mouth.

"I didn't see any Crozins in the front of the warehouse. Fly out fast and stay between the buildings," whispered Cody, thinking he should keep his fat chance to himself.

"Let's go. Anything is better than being here. Ahh, where are we going?" whispered Akio, wiping the sweat from his face.

"To your address in Cape Parrish."

"Did you find my family?" whispered Akio.

"I don't know. We found a girl hiding inside a bedroom closet."

Akio looked as if he'd seen a ghost. "What's her name?"

"She said, Kim."

Akio felt light-headed. "Kim is my daughter." His face flushed, and he shed a tear. "What about the rest of my family?"

"I don't know. I didn't know Kim was your daughter," whispered Cody.

"Did she say anything about Mya or her two brothers?"

"Sorry. That's all I know. Azha found a letter addressed to you. But he didn't open it. Maybe it will explain more." Cody helped Akio walk up the shuttle ramp to the pilot's seat.

"Is Kim okay?"

"She'll be happy to see you. Are you okay to fly?" Cody did not want to tell Akio his daughter had met the devil and lived.

Cody turned into a dull glow and circled outside the warehouse. A swarm of Crozins was in a frenzy. Upon a closer look, he saw them devouring an animal still alive. If he could kill them, he would. Someday he would, but not now and not here. He recalled a saying on Earth: Fortune favors the brave. Maybe so, but a little dumb luck couldn't hurt.

Akio switched off the interior and exterior lights before engaging the shuttle. A gentle hum grew louder as the small craft rose above the ground. Cody had returned and was in front of the shuttle giving him the signal to get ready. All he could think about was Kim. She needed him, so he'd better make it out of there alive.

He watched the hangar slide open, and Cody flashed into energy. *Fast, fly fast,* he told himself. The street in front of the warehouse was clear. Beyond that, it disappeared between two buildings. *Don't think. Just go.* That way was his best chance.

Akio flew in sideways, fearing the shuttle would scrape the sides of the buildings.

Just when he was about to celebrate, he saw a Ryquat standing in the middle of the road, frantically waving at him. If he ignored the Ryquat, the Crozins would kill him.

Cody saw him too. He watched for the Crozins as Akio landed the shuttle at an intersection nearest the Ryquat. Cody understood why Akio couldn't leave the Ryquat behind. Still, this was insane, considering the risk.

On Earth, Cody recalled the risk he took that changed his life. He saw an IED take out a Humvee in a caravan. Instead of checking the road on the way to the Humvee, he tripped another smaller explosive. That mistake is what changed his life. Should he have done things differently? Yes. He should have slowed down and checked the road like he was trained to do. Akio was making the same mistake. But it was too late now. He'd warn Akio if the Crozins swarmed the ground. Of course, Crozins were nothing if Jager-Ki jets were in the area.

Akio lowered the ramp and looked back. Instead of running toward him, the Ryquat was waving at a building. A male and a female carrying a small child ran out of the building and toward the shuttle. As they hurried up the ramp, dozens of Ryquats ran out of the building. There were far too many to transport. Akio raised the ramp and flew away into the dark. Cody watched from above as the Ryquats scattered and disappeared. Their fate was sealed; the Crozins caught their scent and swarmed the streets. Whoever those poor souls were, they were as good as dead. If Akio had hesitated, he would be too.

The Ryquat shouted, "Go back. Damn it! I said go back!"

Akio screamed, "Shut up and sit down. We'd be dead if I'd stayed."

The Ryquat cursed as he sat next to Akio. "I promised I'd get them out."

Akio concentrated on flying, "Don't make promises you can't keep. The Crozins and Gors are everywhere."

The Ryquat was a big man that looked like an Op hardened by war. Akio wondered if he knew how to fly the shuttle and if he'd yank him out of his seat.

The Ryquat shouted, "Don't lecture me. I've been living it. Most of those Ryquats you left behind to die are from the capital. Every town for miles has been invaded and harvested. Look, I get why you left, but there's a chance some survived. We fortified the attic in the town hall. The Crozins won't think anyone is up there because we camouflaged the door. Is there any way we can wait a while and then circle back?" He sounded desperate.

"No. I'm sorry. My captain is waiting for me. Maybe he can help you out."

The Ryquat sat back and crossed his arms. "How did this happen? Why weren't we ready?"

"We know a group on the council sold us out to the Crozins. But when it started, who knows? Captain Victis told us he suspects a while. One of the surviving Viceroys tried to warn those not in the group, but no one listened. The only good thing that came of this was the Crozins killed most of the traitors when they destroyed the towers. I take it you already know Gardux is under Crozin control. They invaded the Gystfins' planet just before ours. Okay, we're getting close to Cape Parrish," Akio sounded somber, looking down at the devastation.

"Any word on how long the Crozins plan on occupying Zaurak? If the Crozins have split forces to occupy both planets, they can't keep fighting both fronts."

Akio shook his head. "You're wrong. Gardux is defeated. The Crozins crushed our fleet. The Umduls joined the war. I'm not sure about the Kikis. Listen, and don't ask questions. Just believe what I have to say. You're going to meet a new species. Somehow Ryquats, or Humans from Earth, were able to fuse their bodies together with species called Quizans. They call them-selves Trekachaws. I can't explain more than that. There's no time. When we get there, don't ask them questions. And don't get in their way. By the way, I'm Akio. I take it you're an Op. Who did I pick up in the back?" Akio was no longer angry. He sounded nervous.

"Fair enough. I'm Steve. That's Roger, his wife Tina, and his daughter Talia. Other than that, I don't know much about them. They were part of a group that joined us on the road. Look, I get it. What's at stake, that is. I've been retired for a couple of years but served as a Special Ops for twenty-two years. I have plenty of experience under my belt. Damn, it looks worse than when I left," Steve uttered, looking down at the city.

"We can use all the help we can get. Do you know where there's more Ops?" Akio asked while keeping track of the Trekachaw's light.

"Last I heard, Largo. It's about a hundred miles west of where you picked me up. I'd be with the Ops, but Crozins cornered me, and I had to lay low. Before something else happens, thanks for picking me up. If we make it out alive, I'll buy you a drink," Steve offered with a crooked grin.

"I'll hold you to that drink. Get ready; we're almost there. A Trekachaw will fly out the ninth-floor window carrying a girl and enter through the hatch on the left side. There's a couple of Necos under flight control; grab one for yourself and hand me one. Cover the Trekachaw. That girl is my daughter. Can Roger or Tina shoot a laser?" asked Akio, descending at a high rate of speed.

"No. I'll tell the family to strap in and hang on."

"Here we go," warned Akio.

Akio banked hard and stopped dead in the air next to his open bedroom window. Victis was waiting with Kim cradled in his arms. His heart broke; she was near death and didn't look real. She reminded him of a doll lost in the dirt to rot. Cody did not tell Akio what to expect on purpose. Besides, how would he have described her? Kim survived the savage attacks. But she would never be the same. No one could.

Akio yelled at Steve and pointed, "Over there. Those balls of light you see flying around are other Trekachaws in energy. Don't shoot them."

A flash blinded them. Then an ear-piercing blast hit above the window. An explosion of bricks and projectiles shot inside the open hatch. Steve watched it slice through the cockpit and embed inside a bulkhead. A shower of fragments followed, and smoke filled the cabin. He watched sections of the building break apart through a thick mushroom of dust. Another blast hit the side of the building, sending hot air and fragments in every direc-tion. The entire structure was collapsing. The shuttle flipped sideways and was being pulled down by the implosion. Beneath them, another laser hit. The shock wave catapulted the shuttle upward and spinning out of control.

The autopilot stabilized the shuttle before Steve could release his harness strap clip. When he tried to stand up, he fell. His head throbbed, and he was too dizzy to get off the floor. Steve crawled across the deck and looked out of the open hatch. All that remained was a pile of rubble on the ground. He hung his head out the hatch and breathed, filling his lungs. The thick smoke inside the cabin made him cough. And the debris he crawled through had cut his knees and hands.

Glancing back, he saw Akio slumped over in the pilot's chair, bloody and unconscious. To his right, he saw the strange alien. Somehow, the Trekachaw had managed to jump from the window to the shuttle with the girl. He looked dazed and was hanging on to a rail to keep himself and the girl from falling out. Steve could not tell who was bleeding, the Trekachaw or the girl. But whoever it was, may not matter for much longer.

Steve crawled as fast as he could across the deck to the cockpit. He was almost there when the shuttle began to pitch and slowly descend. The autopilot was no longer functioning. Steve grabbed the arm of the copilot seat until he gained enough strength to pull himself forward. He sat next to Akio and took control. He adjusted the navigation screen and the latitude spectrum sensor.

The shuttle did not respond. Navigation had to be switched to manual. And that was not all. Warnings flashed across the cockpit panels of failing vector components. The hatch had to be closed if he were to fly the shuttle out of this mess. Steve rotated in the copilot's chair to get a better look. That problem would have to wait. The shuttle pitched hard and began to roll. Instead of correcting the pitch, he banked into a turn.

He heard chunks of debris tumbling across the deck and out the door. Trying again, he pushed on the relay until he heard it shut. Steve glanced up and saw the starboard was spitting distance from another structure. He pitched hard portside into a downward spin to avoid crashing. But the shuttle was out of control, and his final thoughts were disturbing. He didn't want to die and be lost in an unmarked grave. The ground was spinning and coming closer and closer. Steve wrapped his arms around the navigation lever and pulled with all his might. The shuttle flexed and torqued, leaving a vortex of air spinning on the ground as the shuttle ascended. He braced for impact but missed crashing into a Crozin transport ship docked on the street. Laser bursts erupted from below. Steve looked over at Akio. He was still unconscious and had pissed himself. For the moment, they were still alive. But the plan to sneak out under cover of darkness had ended. And it wouldn't be long before Crozin Jager-Kis would find them.

Finding a safe way out of the city was hit or miss. A split-second decision to navigate between two high-rise buildings paid off. A stream of Crozin air strikes missed their mark. To his left, lasers sliced into structures, causing them to explode in his path. The onslaught caused a firestorm that lit the coming of a new dawn. Steve considered his limited options. The answer was his Ryquat grit. He was the best pilot in the fleet before retiring. He'd get through this and brag about it on the other side.

Ahead was a clear blue sky and nowhere to hide. Circling back was the only choice. Perhaps he spoke too soon about bragging rights. Flying into the Crozins was dicey, but flying in the open was suicide. A red light coming straight at him veered and streaked past the shuttle's starboard toward a jet hot on his tail. It was not a laser. It was a Trekachaw. HUA! The light disappeared into the Crozin Jager-Ki. He counted five, maybe more jets in pursuit. Laser flashes streaked past, narrowly missing the shuttle. It had been a while since he'd flown a shuttle, but he knew better than to think he could out-navigate that many jets. Headed straight for him, two Gor V-Jaks were lining up to strike. If the Crozins didn't get him, the Gors would.

"Hail Mary, albeit the nefarious awaits," Steve repeated this in his head over and over. He was searching for a way to beat the inevitable. The Trekachaw was standing behind him, "Pull up! We're in control of the Jager-Kis!"

The mighty alien had braced himself for the steep ascent while holding Kim tight against his chest with one arm.

Steve banked hard, clearing the structures, and soared skyward. The Trekachaw roared, sending chills up Steve's spine. What was this creature? To focus on what he could not control, Steve chanted to distract himself from panicking, *"Into the light, we shall receive mercy when touched by the heavens."*

Beneath the shuttle, two Gor V-Jaks exploded, creating a shock wave that rattled his thoughts.

Steve aimed for the stars and unto the son of God. He was convinced space was a fitting place for this life to end and his heavenly one to begin. To his right, four Crozin Jager-Kis mirrored his flight. Howbeit, today was not his day to die. Divine intervention had spared him for a higher purpose. Fighting evil was his calling.

Sometime during this crazy ride, the Trekachaw had harnessed Kim into a chair. He was limping and bleeding from cuts on both legs. The giant creature was not immortal after all. Those piercing yellow eyes must have caught him staring at his injured legs.

"I heal fast. Got to admit that was ace flying you did back there. You're in the clear now. The other Trekachaws killed the Crozin pilots and took control of the jets you saw fly past us. Today was a good day," smiled the green-striped Trekachaw.

Akio moaned and leaned back in the pilot's chair. His hands trembled as he reached up to feel the cuts on his head. He looked at the blood on his hands and cussed. Mumbling, he wiped them off on his uniform and saw that he had urinated on himself. Glaring at everyone, he released his harness and told everybody to get out of his way. Akio stumbled across the deck and sat next to Kim.

Steve asked the Trekachaw, "How's the family back there?"

"What? You didn't hear the parents screaming profanities? I thought I'd heard them all. Their little girl giggled the entire time and then fell asleep after it was all over. I think it's time for introductions. I'm Victis Williams.

Before merging, I was a distinguished Ryquat battleship captain. Nothing has changed except now I'm a Trekachaw captain."

It was true. All cadets knew about Victis Williams, the youngest captain ever. And if you enlist on his ship, know it comes with significant risks. But it got the most action.

Some argue Captain Victis should have been older and more experienced before being promoted. On the flip side, Victis was the wave of the future. Ready and willing to take chances others would not. His reputation opened the door for many envious young captains wanting to follow in his footsteps. But at who's cost? Perhaps the younger captains were being played. All the while, seasoned captains remained guarded because they knew better than to trust the Ryquat Council.

Steve heard plenty about Captain Victis, and it was all good. What he'd like to ask him is how he became a Trekachaw. But that could be personal. "Weren't you promoted about eight years ago? I heard about the Trinite massacre. Wasn't that about three or four years ago?"

"Correct on both counts. I took the first available assignment that I could bring my family with me. It was the new outpost on planet Trinite. That is where I learned to hate Crozins." Victis sounded cold.

"I remember hearing about the attack. No one knew much other than it was the Crozins." Steve was curious about that day. He waited to see if Victis had anything else to say. After a couple of long minutes, Victis's words made Steve wonder if he really wanted to know the truth.

"The Ukaru spared me because he enjoyed watching me suffer. And as far as the other two Ryquats are concerned, the Ukaru claimed he chose them to bear witness. Everyone else died. Everyone. It was a bloodbath. That same Ukaru is my prisoner on Captain Pify's battleship. The last thing he will see is me holding his grey heart in my hand as he did with my daughter's."

THE RETURN FLIGHT WAS UNEVENTFUL. Of course, the Crozins thought the Jager-Kis were pursuing the escaping shuttle. Anyone's guess how long it took before they realized their jets were never coming back.

Akio was better, but not so for Kim. She was diagnosed with a brain contusion and severely infected wounds caused by a Crozin's long claws. Since speaking with Victis, she had been silent. Whether it be memory loss, denial, or distraught, she hadn't spoken to anyone else. Only time would tell if she would talk about the torture she endured.

The Toogus found the letter inside Kim's pocket, where Victis had slipped it. Akio instantly recognized his wife's handwriting. For now, he would keep whatever was in the letter to himself.

All considered, the mission was a success. Four Jager-Ki jets were confiscated mid-flight without a hitch. A Special Ops pilot joined the fight. And Akio's daughter was rescued. Plus, they gained pertinent intel regarding the whereabouts of additional Special Ops.

# five

# BEHOLD ZAURAK THE NETHERWORLD

**The Umdul Language:**

DOHIEILIT UTEUMȝEⅢ BHIEO
NYBHIEȝWEIȝLIT

**PIFY** was on the mend from his third heart transplant. Despite his aging body, he was in good spirits and had resumed his chair at the helm. Phera refused to leave his side and insisted she remain on board to keep an eye on the incoming new Trekachaws as an excuse.

One unexpected matter was young Kigen. A few days before Pify's emergency, the mischievous pup came aboard. Kigen would pop out of the most unlikely places on the ship for fun. He loved to play games and demonstrate skills that no one else had. Since Kigen's first spark, Vious and Deneb had zero control over their son. There was no argument about that. And the older he got, the wilder he became.

For whatever reason, Kigen had taken a liking to Phera. At times, she found him irritating, and he was constantly underfoot. Be that as it may, Kigen had a way of growing on you. Phera couldn't help but be amused when he'd hide inside solid objects after being told to leave. Kigen would reveal only his blue eyes, believing he was invisible. She'd play along with the young Trekachaw and pretend she couldn't see him. Then it was her turn to search for him. She'd look high and low while calling out his name. Eventually, Phera would stand in front of his eyes to block his view. That is how the game would always end. She'd feel Kigen's hand trying to push her aside. Once in a while, she was quick enough to grab his arm, making him laugh hysterically. Kigen's laugh was unique and infectious, causing her to laugh too. And for a moment, she'd forget about the war.

THE NEW EARTH TREKACHAWS WERE less than an hour away. Belton sounded pleased, and if Pify heard correctly, there were over five hundred of them. Training that many with so little time would be a challenge. Still, that was a good challenge to have.

After, coms intercepted a message from Akio's shuttle. The captains on every battleship listened with bated breath. One word—*success*—was all it took to encourage those who needed a win. And though minor, it was a start.

Captain Pify requested an urgent session with Victis, Azha, Phera, Vexy, Rohan, and the new Ops at his battleship bailiwick. Victis and Azha presumed the meeting was about who, what, when, and where the next mission to Zaurak would be. And they were correct.

Pify awaited their arrival sitting in his chair on top of the table with a big smile on his face. Concerned the small chair could slide off, Victis had it permanently attached to the table. Pify liked what Victis had done for him. And it was in the perfect spot to give him a bird's-eye view of the room.

Phera looked much better too. Her stripes were green, and her yellow eyes sparkled. Victis strolled over to his salty old friend and leaned into his ear. "You have no idea how happy I am to see you."

The old salt whispered back, "Spry I am. Bask in splendor five hundred merge jibe duck soup." He patted Victis's face and then chuckled at his Earthly joke.

Confused, Victis thought about what Pify said and why it was funny. "Oh, I get it. Duck soup! Easy. Good one, Pify," chuckled Victis.

Rather than telling the inside joke to the others, Victis announced, "As you all know, Pify speaks peculiarly, and your chips do not decipher nuances. To clarify, I will translate."

Azha spoke up, "Decipher nuances? Do you mean you'll tell us what Pify's saying?"

"Yes, Azha. Shall I have someone decipher for me too?" quipped Victis with a blank stare.

Pify raised his arm to silence them. "Special Ops dire. Impel trek via Steve prowess locus Largo," Pify explained, then paused for questions.

Bewildered, Azha confessed, "I didn't understand a thing Pify said."

Vexy, Rohan, and Steve had no idea either. But rather than saying it, they were shaking their heads no.

"Seriously, nothing?" scoffed Phera.

Victis asked Phera, "Do you want me to continue, or do you want to?"

"By all means, continue," Phera replied with a snarky tone.

Victis looked over at Pify. "Are you okay with me explaining?"

Pify snorted and nodded.

Victis crossed his arms and waited for any sarcastic comments before pointing across the room. "The new guy over there is Steve. He believes Special Ops are at Largo or headed there. Until we have more Ops, our hands are tied. Trekachaws should be confiscating ships, not flying them. We need to locate the Special Ops before the Crozins catch on to what we're doing. A few experienced Trekachaws will be assigned to train the new Human Trekachaws that just arrived from Earth. With that said, basic training takes a while, so there'll be shortcuts. And we're down one of my best pilots.

"Akio will not be joining us. For now, he'll stay with his daughter. She may know more if we can get her to talk. This is what we know. During the assault on Kim, a team of Ops intervened. They killed the Crozins, but she ran away. We don't know the location of the assault. But sometime after the assault, she made it back to her residence. Of course, we don't know how long that took. So, until I have more, none of this helps. Still, we need to find those Ops and have them join us. In any case, it goes without saying what a young female Ryquat's value is to the Crozins. No matter how wrong it may feel, give them a merciful death if you can't save them."

Victis was losing his train of thought. Memories flashed in his head, seeing Narthex rip out his oldest daughter's heart and devour it like an appetizer. And the guilt. The overwhelming guilt of not protecting his wife from the Ukaru. The relentless acts of violence he must have forced upon her. How long did she hang on to the hope that he would come for her? Months? Years? What she must have thought of him when he never did. Those memories make him embrace hate.

Pify's battleship was the first to arrive at Trinite after the attack. Since that awful day, they had grown into a father and son relationship. Pify knew when Victis was falling into the dark abyss of the past. Those telltale signs were surfacing the more he spoke about Akio's daughter.

Pify interrupted Victis to create a distraction. "Veto Trinite. Forsake bygone, forthwith avenge. Sine qua non, Boo noteworthy," he spoke loudly and with conviction.

Victis stopped mid-sentence. "Ah . . . thank you. You're right; I'm off track. Okay. Boo, and Atue are currently at Trinite with what's left of the Gystfins. If you didn't already know, the Crozins and Gors attacked the Gystfin planet before Zaurak. Boo reported the Gor battleships are staging in space between Palatu and Opus. And their numbers are increasing daily. Pify heard the same thing from several of our Gor allies. They told Pify they plan on attacking Trinite once they have enough to swarm. If Gors take Trinite, the Crozins will attack the Umdul's planet. That information cannot leave this room. Not that it matters to the Crozins, but these are supposed to be the regions and zones.

"I'll try to make this as painless as possible. So, bear with me. Starting with the Crozins' planet, circle the solar system clockwise. The Gors' planet is next, and then the Gystfins' planet Gardux. After Gardux, it's the X-Region. The X-Region separates the Crozins' sector and the Fidus Achates zone. This region is a dangerous, uncharted space that accounts for one-sixth of the solar system. Continuing clockwise, these are the planets within the Fidus Achates Zone. Palatu, Opus, Trinite, Earth, and Zaurak. After Zaurak, there is another vast space called the Forbidden Zone. This zone also separates us from the Crozins. The Umduls created the Concordat, the Charted Regions, and the zones to keep the peace. This rift started three billion years ago when Mars was the Ryquats' home planet. The Crozins accused the Ryquats of defiling their sacred space. In retaliation, the Crozins disintegrated Mar's largest moon, thus causing a shift in orbit. It didn't take long before Mars was inhabitable. The planet's atmosphere was lost, and its surface became the barren red world you see today. The Ryquats were forced to leave their planet in search of a new world. Zaurak was discovered, but many lives were lost in space or perished during the long journey.

"Trinite was the Ryquat's alternate world in case the Crozins ever attacked again. We all know what happened there. We should have declared the attack an act of war. But it wasn't, and the Crozin knew it would not be. The Viceroys were already compromised. If the Crozins defeat us this time, our way of life and Fidus Achates will cease to exist."

The Trekachaws and Ryquats were staring at him. Sometimes too much focus on defeat discourages those who are trying their best. According to the look on their faces, this was one of those times.

Victis read their faces and changed his tone. "The upside is Pify already dispatched some of his ships from Opus to Trinite. We're sending twenty trained Trekachaws and three hundred new Human Trekachaws. We heard the Crozins sent most of the Gors on Zaurak to Trinite. Having them gone will make it easier for us to search for the Ops. But the Crozins have dug in and plan on staying. Our goal is to locate the Special Ops and kill Crozin Ukarus along the way. The Ruks are unorganized and will scatter without the Ukarus. We'll kill them later.

"Phera will remain on Pify's battleship. Those going to Zaurak are Azha, Cody, Takeda, Nikki, Ajax, and Duroc. Steve and Rohan will navigate shuttles. Questions?" asked Victis.

Rohan raised his hand. "Any problem with Vexy being my copilot?"

"I never thought otherwise. From now on, I'll plan on Vexy being with you."

Steve raised his hand. "Is there any chance we can check on the Ryquats I left behind? They could still be hiding in the town hall attic. It's near the warehouse where you had Akio wait with the shuttle."

Victis nodded. "After Largo if there's room on the shuttles. Remind me later."

Pify scooted out of his chair and waddled across the top of the table over to Victis. He waved his hand, motioning for him to come closer. The battle-scarred old Umdul threw his arms around Victis's neck and hugged him with all his might. Tears filled Victis's yellow eyes. The old Umdul was saying goodbye. Pify was afraid it could be the last time he'd see him. He buried his head in Victis's arms to hide the anguish on his face. Victis held on tight, not wanting to let go of the Umdul he loved. When did Pify's body become so old and frail? Phera was right to worry and be angry that no Quizan was willing to merge. He had taken it for granted that Pify would live forever. Now he was afraid too. Pify shared Victis's struggle not to cry. He wrapped his arms around the old Umdul and carried him to Phera. Victis whispered in Pify's ear, "Fear not, I will return. You have been and always will be my hero." He carefully handed Pify over to Phera and walked out. He wanted to look back but dared not. What hurt the most was when Victis let go. He knew never to forget that moment, for it could be their last.

Victis walked down the corridor and stood alone. Before taking another step, Victis had to clear his head. He must be a fearless leader. War always takes more than you fathom. And if you try to rationalize the cost, you will fail. Never forget what we are fighting for, freedom or death—nothing in the middle.

# six

# EXACERBATED TREKACHAWS

**The Umdul Language:**
OꝯЕКЗDЕВОТ ВЗОⱢЕКНIЕЕWЕЖ

**ROHAN** followed Steve's shuttle on the way down. It was a miracle they made it out the first time. This time, knowing what to expect shook him to the core. Vexy seemed unaware of the danger. She sat in front of a port window, watching the sparkling green lights of seven Trekachaws dance between the two shuttles. She recalled hearing about their powers but seeing them was another matter.

A warning sensor interrupted her entertainment when three Jager-Ki fighter jets came into view on the monitor. Vexy ran to the copilot seat and sat down next to Rohan. Since fleeing Zaurak, Rohan had drilled her on survival tactics, Special Ops skills, and navigation. She learned from the best and quickly gained confidence. Since then, she was a fighter and no longer the victim.

They were less than fifty air miles from Largo when the Crozin jets were within striking distance. Still, this far out, the shuttles were sitting ducks. Steve pitched hard and banked into a nosedive with Rohan on his tail.

Vexy pointed at the monitor, screaming, "Look at them!"

She saw the green lights flash bright purple and spiral in space. Some lights stayed with them, while others flew toward the Jagers.

"What is it? What are you pointing at Vexy?" he yelled, irritated, unable to look at the monitor while flying the shuttle in a nosedive. She refused to answer when he spoke to her in that tone. This side of Rohan she did not find charming.

Rohan shouted, "For God's sake, Vexy, what did you see? Stop with the silent treatment. Okay, okay, sorry for yelling at you. Just tell me what you saw?" He was fed up with her petty arrogance but made every effort to sound pleasant.

She sneered, "That wasn't much of an apology, Rohan."

Rohan ignored her and opened the coms shuttle to shuttle. "Did you see where the Trekachaws went?"

"No. Why?" Steve transmitted.

"I don't know. Vexy may have seen something," Rohan transmitted.

"They must have intercepted the Jagers. By now, they would have fired on us," Steve transmitted.


VICTIS AND NIKKI FLEW INTO the trailing Jager and morphed into body form behind the Crozin pilot. She gave Victis the nod, and he winked. Victis grabbed the Crozin's head and snapped its neck. She had a strange look on her face he did not recognize. What she did next made Victis smile. She held her nose while removing the harness one-handed and then pushed the Crozin out of the seat onto the deck.

"Are you okay, Nikki?"

"Yeah. They stink so bad. It's hard not to gag. Doesn't the smell bother you?" Nikki choked, looking down at the dead Crozin with a scrunched face.

"If you think about it, the stink is a good thing. You can smell Crozins long before you see them. And the stink lingers after they're gone. Didn't know you had a squeamish side, Nikki," Victis teased, raising his eyebrows.

"Normally, I'm not. But your point is well taken." She covered her nose and mouth with her hand while dragging the Crozin with the other to the back of the ship.

"You okay, Nikki?"

"No worries," she replied, flopping into the pilot seat.

"See you later in Largo," he grinned, then flashed out of the shuttle in green energy.

Victis circled Takeda, signaling it was time to take the Jager flying center formation. This Crozin pilot appeared to be just as clueless as the first one. But they were wrong. When Takeda peered over its shoulder to look at the navigation systems, the Crozin spun around in the pilot's chair. Face-to-face, they were equally shocked. Victis grabbed the Crozin by his ears and slowly lifted him out of the chair until the harness cut into its shoulders. The screech that came out of his split nose-mouth made your eyes water. The Crozin swiped at Victis with its sharp claws, missing every time.

Victis had grown to enjoy killing the vile beasts. He thought about the pain Crozins caused as he slowly twisted its head. He felt the snap and let go.

Takeda unharnessed the Crozin and shoved him onto the deck. "Damn, that was ruthless, Victis. Wow, that thing stinks. I was sprayed by a skunk on Earth and thought that was bad. Compared to this, a skunk smells like perfume."

Victis laughed out loud. "Human Trekachaws sure don't care for Crozin stench. You'll get used to the smell. If you're good, I'm out of here."

"Don't tell anyone. Okay?" asked Takeda, holding up his thumb.

Victis turned into energy and flew into space; two down, one to go.

He circled Azha to follow. Victis was surprised to find such an old lead pilot. He looked frail from a vicious past and seemed oblivious to the take-over of the trailing Jagers. One of his ears was missing. And his skull was disfigured and scarred. Could the war have taken its toll more than he previously presumed? The old Crozin touched the console to activate the weapon systems and locked lasers on both shuttles.

"Stop him!" yelled Azha.

Victis grabbed the Crozin's hand to prevent him from engaging. It wasn't afraid when he saw the Trekachaws. He stared defiantly at them and hissed, then bit down on Victis's arm. The pain was excruciating. As much as Victis wanted to, he could not let go or turn into energy. If he did, the old Crozin would disintegrate the shuttles.

Azha and Victis punched the Crozin in the head over and over. But it hung on and bit down even harder. Victis grimaced in pain rather than cry out. The only thing left was to bite it back. Victis sank his teeth into the Crozin's sagging skull and spit out a chunk. Nothing seemed to faze it. The Crozin curled its scaly nose and turned its head to glare at Victis. Fluid oozed from its skull, and bloody saliva dripped from the corners of its mouth over Victis's arm. A strange gurgling noise came from its throat that sounded as if it was laughing. That couldn't be it. Victis could have sworn Crozins weren't able to laugh. The nasty old thing gurgled again and violently shook its head to shred Victis's flesh.

"Azha, get him off me. Get him off!" screamed Victis.

Azha punched the Crozin in the eye, and it moaned and acted dazed. That gave Victis a chance to free his arm from the nasty hole. He stumbled away, holding his arm in agony.

Azha caught the crazed Crozin by its one good ear. Victis never fought a Crozin like that before. But then, he had never seen a Crozin that old.

The skinny thing spun around until its ear Azha was holding twisted off. That must have hurt, but it didn't act like it. Azha tried to grab the Crozin as it lunged for the weapon systems. It was old but fast and almost touched the screen before Azha could slap its hand away. That made it flip out into a fit of rage. Its eyes bulged, and it swiped back, shrieking. Before it could try again, Azha shoved the vile thing back into the chair. Victis was no help. He was unsteady and looking at his mangled arm. His words were slurred, but Azha understood he was cursing for not killing the Crozin the instant they boarded. Azha looked away for a split second, but that was all it took. The old Crozin sank its teeth into Azha's arm. The pain was excruciating. Azha buckled and got dizzy as if poisoned. That gave the Crozin enough room to squirm out of the pilot's seat and slither to the deck floor, dragging Azha along with him. As Azha fell, the Crozin wrapped its legs around his waist. The vicious old pilot was hanging on to the Trekachaw for dear life.

He had profoundly underestimated the old alien's tenacity. The toxin in the Crozin's bite was finally wearing off. Victis turned into energy and flew into its vile head. The faster he fried its brains, the better. But he stopped when he heard the Crozin's thoughts. Hesitating is what got them into this mess. Even so, he had to make sure he heard right. The Crozin knew death was inevitable. Yet it didn't fear death or feel sorry for itself. What it felt was remorse and guilt for the lives it took. That was not possible for a Crozin. He had to find out. Victis told it to explain its guilty thoughts. The Crozin refused and concentrated on chewing off Azha's arm and destroying the shuttles. Victis surged his energy, and the Crozin screeched in pain. Victis repeated the question.

The alien's thoughts were difficult to accept. It could feel remorse and guilt. And it had something to do with the Gors. Victis told the Crozin to let go of the Trekachaw and explain. But it refused to answer. Victis surged his energy again as a warning. The Crozin gurgled and spewed but hung on to Azha's arm. Whatever hint of decency was gone and replaced by vile thoughts.

Victis surged enough to kill, but not instantly. He flew out of the Crozin's head and morphed into body form next to Azha. Even as it was dying, it refused to release Azha's arm. The old Crozin made a last-ditch effort to swipe Victis with its long claws. The fight became less and less until it twitched a couple of times and then was no more.

Victis pried the old Crozin's jaws apart. Free at last, Azha pulled his arm out of its mouth and stood up dizzy.

Azha was rotating his arm, trying to see all the Crozin bite marks.

Victis wasn't much better off; his arm was shredded too. "Guess we misjudged that one."

Azha could not let that one go. "Not *we*, Victis, *you* did, not me! You're the reason my arm got chewed to pieces," Azha growled, counting the bite marks on his arm.

"Yep, but you kept it distracted," praised Victis, checking out Azha's bite marks and then looking at his own.

"What? Asshole. So glad I provided my arm as a chew stick!" fumed Azha.

"Whoa, whoa, whoa, that was a compliment. And what's with the Human stink mouth? I thought we made a deal not to cuss anymore?" crowed Victis.

"You're lucky—that's all I have to say," snarled Azha.

"No, you're lucky I killed it, or it would still be attached to your arm. I could blame you for not learning how to fry Crozin brains?"

Staring at each other with menacing glares, they started laughing.

"I hate Crozins more than anything. How they got so powerful is beyond me. And what's with the old Crozin's bite? I've been bitten before, and it didn't make me sick and dizzy," frowned Victis.

"I wonder if the old Crozins get some kind of venom, or their mouths get that nasty when they're older than dirt." Azha thought about looking inside the Crozin's mouth but didn't want to risk it. He'd seen them come alive when he could have sworn they were dead.

Victis bent over to get a better look at the old Crozin. "I don't know. Too bad Pax can't examine it to see what's in there."

Do you think it's true some of the Ryquat Viceroys were double-dealing with the Crozins?" asked Azha.

"What brought that up? Are you tired of talking about the Crozin? What's double-dealing? Is that an Earth thing?" smirked Victis.

"Seriously? You've never heard the expression *double-dealing* while watching Earth's cinema movies?"

"Cinnamon? Is that a spicy movie?" mocked Victis.

"Oh, now that's real mature, Captain. Since you started this, it's not *stink mouth*. It's stink eye or potty mouth. Cinema is a movie theatre, and cinnamon is an Earth spice. Double-dealing means acting in bad faith—deception, like pretending to be on the Ryquats' side but selling out to the Crozins. There you have it. You'd be better off sticking with the Ryquat language.

"If we're done, I'd like to talk about the Viceroy traitors. My question would be who survived? Smyth's not a Viceroy, but he's a good start. We know he's a traitor. Everyone thought he died with Choan on his battleship. But according to what Phera learned from Narthex's thoughts, Smyth is alive. Phera thinks he's somewhere on Earth holding Choan's energy captive. Let's go back to Earth when this is over. Smyth murdered thousands of Quizans. I will enforce poetic justice and cut off his head," swore Azha.

Victis did not understand what poetic justice meant, but he understood Azha's hatred. Smyth was addicted to Quizans' grey-death energy. And the only way to feed his addiction was to kill for it. But that wasn't why he was a traitor. He used his addiction as a diversion and an excuse to get sympathy. Before becoming an addict, he had conspired with the Crozins for many years. Zaurak should have been invincible, but greedy Ryquats like Smyth sold Zaurak to the enemy. And as far as the Viceroys' participation, they joined the Crozins willingly. They sacrificed Ryquats' freedom for tyranny. The cost of their greed for wealth and power was war and death. The only justice is that most of the traitors are dead. Ironically, they were killed by the same Crozins who made them promises.

STEVE BRACED AS THE JAGERS came within striking distance on the monitor. As a last-ditch effort to save one of the shuttles, he transmitted to Rohan, "Get outta here. I'll distract them. Fly low—you're almost there. Wait, wait, Rohan! Cody's light just turned into his body next to me." Steve howled, "Hoorah! Cody told me the Trekachaws are flying the Jager-Kis. Follow me down."

The jets flew over. "Shadow jets to shuttles. Acknowledge—shadow jets to shuttles. Confirm designation. Click twice to acknowledge."

Two clicks, then another two, brought a smile to Victis.

Victis watched the shuttles bank starboard toward Largo. He recalled the hostile planets and battles he had encountered over the years. Perhaps in a cruel way, those prepared him for this one. But the more he understood, the more he wanted the answer to one question. Why, at every crossroad in history, have miracles occurred? Who or what orchestrates the balance in the cosmos? He was beginning to believe nothing was by chance. Since meeting Pify, his path seemed predetermined to become the Trekachaw leader. He had stepped into that role without question. Why? Now he had two questions.

ON THE OUTSKIRTS OF LARGO, the two shuttles landed first, followed by the three Jager-Kis and two Trekachaws. If you weren't aware of the invasion, standing under palm trees overlooking a blue seascape, you'd never know it existed.

Rohan and Vexy walked down the shuttle ramp and met Steve, waiting for them next to his jet. He asked Rohan and Vexy if they felt like kissing the ground they stood on. That was Steve's way of saying they were lucky. Instead, Rohan picked a long blade of grass and smelled it. For him, the scent was home. Steve put his hand on the side of his jet and nodded. These simple connections eased their minds. Vexy had been crying and was running her fingers through her hair. They were okay now. The worst was over. They agreed to look for the Trekachaws and where the Jager-Kis landed.

Not far away, they stopped on a grassy knoll. What they saw beyond the sleek Jager-Ki fighter jets they'd never forget. Seven magnificent creatures stood with their arms stretched toward the sky, slowly turning in circles. Their stripes were a brilliant green, and their spectacular bodies glistened under the sun. Seeing them on the planet embracing nature was a sight to behold.

The Trekachaws closed their eyes and knelt on the ground as celestial lords from another realm. Transfixed, they listened to the creator speak or perhaps the beating heart of a planet. Were these creatures created by a higher power beyond the understanding of Ryquats or Humans? If that were true, what were they called before Trekachaws?

# seven

# LARGO

The Umdul Language:
LIEȝOGI

**STEVE** heard someone call out his name. He turned an ear to the trees and listened. It could have been the palm leaves moving in the ocean breeze. He thought he had heard his name again. Steve tapped Rohan on the shoulder. "Did you hear that?"

"Yeah . . ." Rohan looked in the same direction and slowly pulled his laser out from his belt.

Steve made a circle motion with his finger. "Cover me." He then cut between two Jagers.

Four Special Ops Ryquats watched Steve sneak toward their location. They were getting a kick out of it, betting on how long it would take him to figure out it was them. It had been years since they'd served under his command. Seeing Steve was a welcome sight. Of course, the chance to give him a hard time was too good to pass up.

"Hey, over here," yelled a Special Ops leaning on a tree. "Took you long enough to figure out we were watching you."

Steve threw his arms up and waved back at Rohan, giving him the A-OK sign.

"What a sight for sore eyes. I should've known you'd make it out alive," Steve shouted, holstering his Neco laser.

Rigdan swaggered over to Steve and gave him a bear hug. Three more of his Ops team were leaning on trees whistling, "Damn, you got grey. Good thing we found you."

"Come over here and say that again, kid. The snow on my head comes from experience, pure gold. I know something you won't believe unless you see it. They're the most powerful creatures in the galaxy—Trekachaws. Then let's see who's glad to find who."

"Deal. Where are these Trekachaws?" Rigdan asked, scratching his chin through his scruffy beard.

"They're on the other side of the Jagers. Let's take a walk, and I'll introduce them to this ragtag squad. I'll catch you up on the way. The Umduls were able to stage another fleet in this sector. And the Trekachaws have been stealing Crozin and Gor jets in flight. Anyway, I have a few questions. Do you know how many Ops are at Largo? And what about medical staff?" asked Steve.

Rigdan smirked, "All joking aside, explain how they stole jets in flight? Hold that question. I want the long version explanation. Pilots? I'm guessing about a hundred. A few more are getting patched up. And about a hundred Special Ops that are hardcore Crozin fighters. We have forty Mic-10 jets. Eight more can fly, but that's about all they can do. A dozen or so experienced engineers and enough medical staff to run a small hospital. By the way, your timing couldn't be better. The Crozins will attack soon, and we're running out of supplies. Umdul

battleships, you say. Hmm . . . maybe we have a chance after all." Rigdan scratched his beard, relieved.

The war-torn soldiers walked up the hill beyond the Jagers, where the palm trees lined the ocean. In that perfect setting of peace and nature's beauty, they witnessed the mighty Trekachaws. Awestruck, they stopped dead in their tracks, wide-eyed with disbelief.

"Are those things friendly?" Rigdan stammered.

Steve grinned. "Yeah, I felt the same way. They're a Quizan mixed with a Ryquat or Human."

Rigdan looked stunned. "This takes the wagsham. I thought you were joking. Wow, I hope they're friendly."

"They're friendly enough. The blond-haired one is Captain Victis. He's in charge. Over there, that's Azha. I'd guess him to be second in command. Supposedly, he was the first Trekachaw and a police officer on Earth. The slender one is Takeda. Trust me; I'm still learning about who's who," Steve said quietly.

Victis overheard their candid conversation. Rather than wasting time, he would address the scruffy Ops himself. Victis turned into energy and landed behind them.

"Steve, introduce them to me," asked Victis in his authoritative voice.

Rigdan and the three Ops spun around. Steve couldn't help but laugh. "Guys, close your mouths."

According to Victis, Rigdan was the most competent. The others looked rattled. Victis stepped toward Rigdan, and his yellow eyes narrowed. "Rigdan, I have no patience for small talk. That said, we're here to rescue Ryquats and Ops in Largo. What I want from you is information," snarled Victis.

Rigdan was equally insulted and intimidated. But he'd make sure no one else knew it.

"Good. I don't like small talk, either. We've been fighting in these sectors since the Crozins invaded. You could learn a lot from us."

Victis cocked his head and leaned over face-to-face at Rigdan. "We'll get along just fine. Steve, brief him on our mission."

Victis threw his head back and roared. "Today, we are victorious. Onward to Largo!" The new Ops stepped back and cursed a disparaging reference to a mother.

Victis and six Trekachaws turned into energy and circled above.

Rohan and Vexy saw the impact Victis commanded. Vexy could not see the slightest hint of the Victis she once loved in this strange creature. He may have his memories, but that was all. Her heart broke, and she felt herself start to cry. She was foolish to dwell on a love that was one sided. It was time she let go. Rohan took her hand as if he knew what she was thinking.

Rigdan walked away, glad the Trekachaw encounter was over. He took a deep breath, exhausted by the overwhelming anxiety he felt and the self-restraint it took to hide that fear.

THE SPECIAL OPS CHOSE WELL when they selected a coastal city. Largo's sandy white beach stretched for miles, thus providing a perfect site for an airdrome landing and a saltwater defense. It is well known salt water will burn Crozin skin. Even the ocean air can cause them to blister. This knowledge was passed on from Mars to Zuarak billions of years ago. Some Ryquats still carry salt water with them for this very purpose. Another advantage was Largo's thick terrain, making it difficult to breach and restricting ground access with one-road access into the city. Strategically, Largo provided an excellent location for a defensive stronghold.

Victis conjured up ways to flood Largo with salt water. The Crozins couldn't be far behind. If they didn't know before, they knew now. The jets flying to Largo were a dead giveaway. Victis ordered everyone to gather on the beach to mitigate confusion. The new Ops kept their distance from the Trekachaws, and the Trekachaws kept an eye on the new Ops. Victis found this awkward moment to be humorous but remained stoic. Nonetheless, the ocean breeze and invigorating ambiance were intoxicating. It would have been easy to let go and laugh. But that would have made him their equal. And that was not what they needed. They fought with no hope of winning and would have rather died than submit. All eyes were on him to fix this war with the words he was about to say. If they only knew he was just as nervous. He did not have the answers, but this role he'd play to give them strength.

"The evacuation of Largo is paramount. The children and their parents go first. Board all aircraft to capacity except for one jet and one shuttle. When you're clear of Crozin intercepts, contact Captain Pify's battleship to confirm which ships can accommodate Ryquat families. Return to Largo as soon as you've offloaded. Steve, find Ops with any experience flying a Crozin Jager-Ki jet. We don't have nearly enough pilots. In the meantime, the Trekachaws and I will acquire additional jets. Rigdan, work on getting the roads and buildings flooded with salt water. You won't have much time, so get it done," ordered Victis.

"Why flood Largo with salt water?" questioned Rigdan.

Victis's eyes narrowed, and his stripes turned red. "You don't know? Disappointing! Salt water acts like acid on Crozin skin." Victis turned to the other Trekachaws and cursed, *"Unko baka yarou."*

Nikki whispered to Azha, "Is Victis cursing?"

Azha whispered into Nikki's ear, "In Earth's Japanese, *unko* means shit and *baka yarou* means stupid asshole. Or at least that's what he told me. I guess Victis thinks it's better to curse in that language. Sounds just as bad when you know what it means."

Victis turned his back to the new Ops so they couldn't see him wink at Azha. However, Nikki and Cody saw it. His wink was a reminder of the special bond he had with Azha.

And though unspoken, Azha, Phera, his daughter Tilly, and Captain Pify were family. Everyone else was treated according to their integrity and diligence.

Victis raised his hand, and like magic, the Trekachaws flashed into bright lights and streaked into the sky.

A STONE'S THROW FROM LARGO, the Trekachaws encountered a band of Crozins. Over fifty of the vile aliens were swarming farmhouses. Circling above, four low-flying Crozin Jager-Kis searched for Ryquats fleeing on the ground. There were too many to kill, so taking the four Jagers first made sense.

Victis morphed into body form, and the other Trekachaws followed suit. From the look on his face, something was bothering Victis. "I mistakenly underestimated an old Crozin pilot, and Azha's arm got chewed up. Mine too. Anyway, don't do what we did. Kill the Crozin as fast as you can. Here's the plan. We'll take the four Jager-Kis. I'll be with Duroc. Nikki, you're with Ajax, and Cody, you're with Azha. Takeda, you keep an eye on the ground Crozins. Ready?" Victis asked, rocking back on his heels.

Azha had a question. "Can Cody and I go first? After we secure it, I could join you and Duroc to take the fourth jet."

Victis jokingly asked, "What's the matter? You think I'll get in another tangle with an old Crozin?"

"No. Well, maybe?" Azha replied, shrugging it off.

Victis pointed at Cody. "As long as he gives you the good to go, I'm okay with that. Let's go get the Jager-Kis."

Azha and Cody morphed into body form behind the pilot. Cody reached out to grab the Crozin, so Azha stood back. The Crozin never saw it coming. This was an easy one. That's why what came next startled them.

They heard muffled voices. Cody acted fast to secure the jet. He pushed the dead Crozin out of the pilot's seat and took control of the Jager. Azha motioned for him to stay there. It was up to him to see whatever or whoever was on the jet. But the threat was short-lived. Azha listened to mournful cries coming from the shadows. Whoever they were had suffered the cold hands of a Crozin.

The girls were young, not more than eighteen years old. One had long, stringy, blonde hair. The other had dark, short curls that hung in a tangled ponytail. A crude metal device cuffed the two girls' bruised wrists together. And a harness bound them to chairs. One of their legs was tethered to anchor in the deck floor. The bindings were extreme and most likely used to cause them pain. None of these ancient torture devices were necessary. There was a solenoid brig on board. To top it all off, the sadistic Crozin had stuffed a ball device in their mouths.

They were filthy and malnourished. But at least they were alive. Azha took a step closer to get a better look. Whether drugged or listless, they were slow to raise their heads to look at him. Their swollen eyes told Azha more than words. He could see the hurt and fear on their young faces. *What must they be thinking?* Yet another terrifying monster was standing before them. The girls leaned away, and the pain it caused was evident.

Azha squatted to make himself appear smaller. He reached out with one hand as a gesture that he meant them no harm. The blonde-haired girl's eyes softened, and she grunted, trying to spit the ball out of her mouth. Azha pretended to take a ball out of his mouth; she nodded yes. He stood up slowly and reached around her head to unlock the device. She winced when he pulled the ball out and coughed several times. The dark-haired girl was terrified. She recoiled and watched him with wild eyes. When she saw Azha remove the ball, her expression turned into desperation. Azha reached around, unlocked the device, and gently pulled the ball out of her mouth. She coughed and sputtered as she turned away, sobbing.

Azha looked at the other restraints. The cuffs required a sensor to release the device. Whereas the harness had a quick release. He removed the harnesses first and then rechecked the cuffs. He must have looked puzzled when he turned her wrist to look at the sensors. The blonde pointed at her ankle and wiggled her toes. If she was afraid of him, it didn't show. As soon as her leg was free, she reached out to the dark-haired girl with her free hand. When she tried to stand, she collapsed to one knee. Azha thought about catching her but held back. Most likely, his good intentions would be misinterpreted.

It was good Azha did not intervene. When the blonde stumbled to one knee, she jerked the brown-haired girl out of her chair. But neither one cared. Looking up at Azha, they giggled. That was the best sound he had heard in a long time. To think, at their young age, they had the fortitude to rebound from such atrocities.

The blonde rubbed her throat to soothe her raspy voice. "The sensor is on the Crozin's strap belt." She motioned for him to get it.

Azha did as she asked and flipped the Crozin over. Not sure which device was the sensor, he removed all the items from the belt and slid them across the floor one at a time. She shook her head *no* until Azha slid the correct one. Holding it up for him to see, she smiled. Azha watched the two interact. They weren't that far apart in age, but mentally they were years. Freeing the dark-haired girl first showed Azha the blonde had taken on the role of a surrogate mother. And the dark-haired girl was grateful for it. She quickly hid behind the blonde and refused to look at him. From what Azha saw, the dark-haired girl was submissive and bashful. But no telling what had happened to her since being captured. One thing was sure: she only trusted the blonde.

Azha spoke to the blonde. "I am Azha. And who are you?"

"Skylon, and she's Ella." Her voice was still hoarse but sounded better. How rude not to have offered them water. Since becoming a Trekachaw, he didn't think of such things.

"Are you thirsty?" he asked, keeping his distance.

Skylon nodded. "Yes. Thank you. Food would be nice too." She reached behind and touched Ella's leg.

"No problem. I'll see what I can find." Azha stepped away backward until he was across the cabin, then turned. He opened several stations and found water packs and hydro food. And like before, he slid them across the floor to Skylon. She grabbed one for herself and opened another for Ella. "Thanks a lot! We haven't had anything to drink or eat for a while."

After gulping down the water and devouring the food, they sat in the chairs that had previously bound them.

Skylon spoke for Ella. "She's from Earth. That's about all I know. She doesn't talk much. When we first met, she wouldn't say anything. Ella and I met on this jet. This is my third Jager. Every time, I thought, here goes, I'm toast. When they touched me, I acted dead, even when they clawed me. I guess I'm a good actor. I don't know what they did to Ella. She has a translator chip because we can understand each other. Maybe she'll talk to you," Skylon turned around and hugged Ella.

Azha's Human half insisted on speaking with Ella. It was best to listen to him this time. Cole's soul rose with angry thoughts and mixed messages. Memories of Earth flooded their mind, along with vivid flashes of his wife. Ginger died because of a jealous mistake of identity. Azha had second thoughts about succumbing to Cole. But they needed to know how she got there.

Azha looked and sounded the same to Skylon and Ella, but Cole took control of the conversation.

"Ella, what I'm about to say won't make sense. I have two souls. You spoke to Azha first. My name is Cole, and I'm from Earth too. I was a police officer in California. Do you know where that is?" he asked, sitting on the floor in front of her.

Perhaps Ella sensed the alien was of Earth. Her eyes locked onto his, and her fear faded away.

"Yes, I know where California is. I want to go home. I live in Jasper Highlands, Tennessee. My mom and dad own a horse ranch up the road from the second waterfall outside town. Please take me home. I want to go home."

"I'll try, but it may take a while. How did you get on a Crozin ship?" He wondered if she understood how lucky she was they found her.

"I thought I was having a nightmare. I'm not, right?" Ella covered her face with her hands.

"This is real, but you'll be okay," Cole assured. On the contrary, Azha was reluctant to make such promises.

Ella let out a big sigh. "I was riding my horse, and the air felt heavy like before a tornado. Guess you'd have to be near one to know. Everything sounds flat, except this was different. The sky was blue, and there were no clouds anywhere. My horse got spooked and just stopped. He was squealing but couldn't move. I tried to get off, but I couldn't move either. Something was holding us, and I started floating out of the saddle. Then I shot up above the trees and watched my horse run away. It sounds like a lie, but it's the truth. That's the last thing I remember. When I woke up, a monster like that one on the floor was on top of me. I tried to fight, but it kept touching me. It forced my mouth open. It was awful. I think it was, you know. I bit it. That's what my mom told me to do if anyone ever did that. I know it hurt because it shrieked. Another monster choked me until I let go and shoved that ball thing in my mouth. I don't want to talk about the rest." Ella's face grimaced, and she began to cry, shaking her head in disgust.

Azha was sorry it happened, but Cole was furious. He knew what the Crozins did.

Cole asked Ella and Skylon to secure their harnesses for the flight. Azha was proud of Cole, but it was time to switch back. Azha walked away and sat in the copilot's chair next to Cody. From the portal, he watched a thin blue beam sweep across the farmhouses. Victis chose to eradicate the Crozins along with any living creature in the beam's path. Azha was glad that Victis could make the tough decisions. If ever forced, he would ask Cole for strength. Left on his own, he doubted if he had the resolve.

THE TREKACHAWS PROCURED ADDITIONAL CROZIN Jager-Ki jets without a hitch. In the coming days, Largo was evacuated. And, as promised, Steve was told he could rescue the stranded Ryquats in the attic.

On the way there, Steve talked about the group he'd left behind. A week or two before Akio landed the shuttle on the street, Steve and the other Ryquats constructed a makeshift fortress to elude the Crozins. They used mattresses as sound buffers and furniture to conceal the town hall attic. The attic has two access doors. One on the first floor, at the east end of the building. The other is on the third floor, west end of the hall-way. They shoved heavy floor-to-ceiling armoires to block and hide the doors. To complete their facade, the panels on the back of the armoires were removed to provide hidden access. And to prevent the Crozins from opening the armoire doors from the outside, locks were installed on the inside. Unless the Crozins caught a fresh Ryquat scent, they would not bother to look further.

What Steve had the group do next most would consider outrageous. He explained how the Crozins track Ryquats by their scent. A good trick was to overwhelm the Crozins' noses. The best way to do that was for them to urinate on the walls and floors of the town hall. This task included outside areas and other buildings in the town to confuse the Crozins. The group made haste and did a great job. Steve was confident the hideaway was safe. But watching the Crozins swarm the streets full of Ryquats meant certain death for those in plain sight. If any Ryquats survived, the attic was where they'd be.

The streets were deserted, but that was to be expected. Steve ran down the ramp and across the road into the town hall lobby. "Hello! Anyone here?"

He ran to the far east end of the first floor. "Hello! Anyone here?" Faint voices were coming from the other side of the armoire. Steve kicked open the doors and pushed aside mattresses blocking the attic. Hiding in the shadows, he saw mothers clinging to their babies. And children were peeking out from behind young adults. The Ryquats running in the streets had sacrificed themselves to the Crozins to save the few. Thirty Ryquats were not what he'd hoped for; still, it was better than none.

ROHAN WAS GRATEFUL THE EVACUATION of Largo was behind them. A day or two of rest away from prying eyes was overdue. The area was free of Crozins, and they could pretend there was no war for a while. Until now, surviving seemed unlikely, and not talking about it or dwelling on the future made the inevitable tolerable. That premonition had changed, and she had changed. For years, he hoped she would see him as more than a bodyguard. This place and moment in time was theirs and theirs alone.

Early in the morning, Rohan awoke next to Vexy. Watching her sleep, he remembered her words the night before. Those three words meant everything. Before the invasion, he questioned her flirtatious sincerity and kept his feelings at bay. He dared not trust her until she let go of the infamous Captain Victis. But no matter how high the wall she built to hide behind, his commitment and admiration for her never wavered.

She was different since meeting the new Victis Trekachaw. However, the war altered their roles and status, allowing them the freedom to be themselves. The truth is, the only one who changed was Vexy. But last night, she was his for the first time.

Content to let the world go by, he stretched and rolled over, thinking about going back to sleep. But the morning was growing short; soon, they should pack up the last supplies and leave Largo forever. Mulling over the list in his head, he thought about the items Victis mandated. That order was impossible; the shuttle was too small. For now, a few more minutes would not make a difference. He touched Vexy's arm and wondered if anyone dared tell her how loud she snores. Rohan dozed off beside the woman he loved.

HOW LONG HAD HE SLEPT? It wasn't morning any longer. Vexy rolled to her side, pulling the covers over her head. Not to awaken her, he slowly slid one foot from beneath the sheets and then the other before sitting up. He took a deep breath; the air was fresh with a hint of a warm ocean breeze. Searching with his eyes, he saw his clothes across the room next to the nightstand. Quietly, he got out of bed and tiptoed across the floor. He glanced back at her and felt young and pure happiness. He'd get dressed and sneak outside to start loading the shuttle. By the time she awoke, they'd be ready to go. He sat in a chair and was putting on his boots when he heard the noise outside. A noise that sent chills up his spine. Where did he leave the Neco weapon? Last night, getting his clothes off was all that mattered. He quietly crossed the room toward the clothes strewn about on the floor. *Why now? We should have left yesterday.*

A shadow crossed the window, then another and another. God help them; there were Crozins outside. Vexy stirred and sat up.

He snapped his fingers to get her attention, motioning *shh,* and pointed at the door. Rohan found his Neco under the clothes and removed it from the holster. Vexy was petrified and fixated on the window. Her body trembled beneath the sheets, and she took shallow breaths so the monsters would not hear her. Rohan saw a Crozin staring at her through the window. Death was near, and they both knew it.

Before he could get to her, a loud crash broke the door, splintering it into pieces across the room. The Crozins were in a frenzy, pushing and shoving through the doorway to be the first to rape her. He shot three, maybe four of them, but dozens more outside were screeching to get in. Vexy was hysterical. She jumped out of bed naked and stood against the wall. He thought about what she begged him to do. With seconds left to fulfill his promise, Rohan aimed his Neco at her. She looked at him, scared and confused. But then a calm came over her, and she opened her arms.

He fired; he shot the woman he loved. Rohan collapsed beneath the weight of the shrieking Crozins and felt their claws rip his body apart. But in his mind, he was free and blind to the pain. He focused on Vexy's beautiful face across the floor and what their life could have been. With his last breath, he watched her eyes fade. He saved her.

# eight

# REVENGE IS NEVER ENOUGH

**The Umdul Language:**
ʒOVONYOGO AⱮ NYOVOʒ
ONYIUMOGHIE

**THE** incoming Largo shuttles awaited docking instructions. Akio requested notification if his wife and two sons were among the rescued. With each passing day, his optimism faded. On the sixth day, Largo's last passenger shuttle docked. Azha reminded Akio that Largo Ryquats were not the only survivors on Zaurak. But Akio didn't want to hear it. He knew locating survivors outside the searched area was a long shot.

All of it had become emotionally exhausting. But Akio knew better than to assume anything. Sometimes you're lucky enough to beat the odds. And sometimes the odds are not in your favor. For instance, his family was alive. But the odds were against him the day he rescued Steve in the middle of the town. Little did he know, Mya and the boys were hiding inside the hall attic. That was indeed unlucky. And another time when Steve returned to rescue the attic Ryquats. Worse than bad luck, everyone assumed Mya was Mark's wife and the boys were his. Even

Steve had made that assumption. As far as everyone knew, there was no connection between Akio and Mya.

Steve received docking instructions to transfer the attic survivors to an Umdul battleship. Typically, the Umduls would not accommodate Ryquat civilians. But then again, nothing was routine since the invasion. This Umdul captain just so happened to be the eldest son of Captain Pify. And one of the most recent ships to arrive from Opus. Per his father's request, Pubney agreed to house the Ryquats.

During the trek to Zaurak, Pubney's ship remained in Bogtu-urp silence to avoid detection. Thus, Akio's request regarding his family was never received. Adding to the confusion, Mya had given up trying to find Akio. She heard rumors that Crozins had destroyed his battleship. Initially, she didn't want to listen to the lies. But time can crush hope. And the cruel stories become believable.

Not long after the first attack, Mark Keller swept Mya's building look-ing for survivors. He told her the city was unsafe and that it was best for her and the boys to leave with him. But that meant if Akio came home, they would be gone. As a testament, she wrote a letter to Akio and left it on the nightstand. The letter was her way of admitting guilt to herself and saying goodbye. But it also meant she was leaving behind a sliver of hope. As much as she didn't want to go, she told herself this was her only way out. Granted, Mya was grateful Mark found them. Still, she would have stayed if not for the boys. But there was another reason not to go. Mya would be forced to accept another cold reality—her daughter's fate. Kim must have died when she sacrificed herself as bait to save them from the Crozins. Hearing stories about what happens to young women became unbearable. She refused to talk about Kim. It was too painful, and she hated herself for being a coward. All Mark needed to know was that she swore to protect her sons no matter what.

A loud noise on the shuttle rattled her, and she sat up. They had docked and were unloading. Mya never thought she would see an Umdul battleship, much less board one. What she wanted to do was stop being afraid. Maybe now she could. And though overjoyed at making it out alive, she still felt worthless and empty inside. The boys and Mark made haste to the galley for real food. They had been eating nonstop since they came aboard. She was relieved to be free of them, to have a moment alone.

Mya couldn't help but daydream of the recent past. She recalled carrying Benji in her arms for days with Wren glued to her side. Fearing every second a Crozin would catch their scent and eat her boys while she was raped and forced to watch. Night after night, she closed her eyes. But short naps were the best she could do. It's strange the things you remember as being important. She took comfort in listening to Benji and Wren breathing while they slept on the ground next to her. Mark always slept with one eye open. She wondered how he did it.

How long had it been since leaving Cape Parrish. She couldn't even guess. But traveling the back roads never got any easier. Somewhere between towns, they crossed paths with another group with a Special Op. Together, Mark and Steve were always one step ahead of the Crozins. The group would have been slaughtered on more than one occasion if not for them. She wanted to introduce herself to Steve and ask about Akio. But she chose not to because it would make it real if he said the lies were true. Besides, Mark claimed her as his wife, and she said nothing to the contrary. And as far as anyone knew, Mark was the boys' father. More than that, the boys acted like they were his sons. Who could blame them? Akio was a stranger because he was always gone.

For one reason or another, Mark and Steve chose a small town to hold up in. A couple of weeks after settling in, a shuttle landed on the road and flew away with Steve. Crozins swarmed from every direction. She picked up Benji and ran, dragging Wren behind her. But she wasn't going to make it back to the attic. Mark ran across the road and picked up Wren, yelling at her to follow.

She heard the Crozins screeching but did not look back. And then the awful screams of Ryquats being slaughtered. Mya couldn't take much more. Benji and Wren were crying because they were terrified and hungry. Their living conditions were horrible. Food was scarce, and now this. At that moment, she considered asking Mark to mercy kill them. It was better than watching her boys starve to death or be eaten by Crozins.

Mark rushed them into a building across the street and down a staircase into a room that led to another hidden room. He had kept this place a secret in case this were to happen. He shoved several mattresses to block the door and then pushed a large dresser against them. The room reeked of urine, but she knew why. Mark carried the boys to the far corner of the room and sat with them. He spoke softly, telling them they'd be okay. And to play a game with him of how good they were at whispering. She saw he had stored bottles of water, canned food, and several blankets in an open cabinet. They waited and listened. Nothing—the Crozins were duped. Once again, she owed Mark for her life and her boys.

They were alone for the first time, and the boys were fast asleep. He was never pushy, but she knew he wanted more. She pretended it was mutual and did nothing to stop him. Akio was dead. So, she wasn't doing anything wrong. But it felt dirty. And now that it had happened, he wanted her often. Why bother saying no now? Days later, they left the hidden room together. She walked behind Mark and her boys to the attic across the street. If only Akio and Kim were alive. Things would have been different.

Mya gazed out a porthole and quietly grieved the loss of her husband and daughter. She needed to stop thinking about what her life was and accept what it had become. Little did she know Akio and Kim were on the battleship she was looking at through the portal. And soon, her time on Pubney's ship would be cut short, along with coming so close to finding them.

Mya, Steve, and the boys boarded shuttles with other Ryquats en route to Cape Parrish. The battleships were preparing for war. And they were no longer safe for civilians. According to recent reports, the city was the best place for them. Packaged food was abundant, and the power had been restored to buildings with minor or no damage. The most crucial detail, the city was finally rid of the Crozin infestation. Those reports were grossly misleading. Hundreds of nests lay in wait. Cape Parrish was a death trap.

VICTIS WAS THE FIRST TO notice Vexy and Rohan had not checked in. Azha and Clyde agreed something must have gone wrong. They volunteered to go with him to Largo. Victis welcomed the company. He had a bad gut feeling. And his gut was right. The Crozins were swarming Largo, and the shuttle had been ransacked. Victis hoped the supplies strewn across the road had kept the Crozins busy long enough for Vexy and Rohan to escape. The Trekachaws' light orbs floated above the grizzly scene.

Rohan's mutilated body was face down inside the doorway. Vexy lay nude on the floor next to the bed. She must have been looking at Rohan when she died. Her eyes were open, and the expression on her face Victis had seen before. There was a time when she looked at him like that. It was love. He floated over to her and morphed into body form. The Crozins had not touched her. Rohan spared Vexy by shooting her before they could rape and rip her apart.

Victis raged purple. He threw his head back and roared. The Crozins scattered in all directions. He pried the Neco from Rohan's cold hand and gave it to Azha. The demons did not get far. Most were cut in half by lasers. A select few suffered at the will of Victis. He looked for those soaked in blood and took his time. One after the other, he flew into their brain while in energy. Victis told them who he was and what he was going to do to them. Azha and Clyde watched the Crozins screech in agony until they passed out. When Victis could not revive them, he killed them. When the last Crozin stopped breathing, Victis returned to Vexy.

Victis knew Vexy well enough to know she would want to be with Rohan. He would bury them next to each other in the same grave. Victis's stripes had faded to a sickly blue, and he sounded broken. "Azha, I need you to look for excavators or shovels in storage." Victis did not look up. His ring was on her finger.

Azha found the shovels and headed back. Victis did not deserve this heartache. Vexy was one of a long list of deaths that had touched Victis. Azha stopped in the doorway. Whatever happened while he was gone had made matters worse. Clyde was spooked as if he'd seen a ghost. Victis's stripes had faded into a waxen grey—the color of death. As a Quizan, he was close to the final stage before ascending to Aeon Devotio.

Azha dropped the shovels and stepped over Rohan's body to grab Victis, "NO, Victis! Don't do this!"

Victis did not hear him. He was in a place not of this world. If it were possible to will oneself to ascend, Victis was doing it.

"Victis, stop!" Azha screamed, shaking him.

"I can sense the others." Victis sounded as if he were speaking from the other side.

He was searching above with his eyes, but there was nothing there. Azha tried to understand who or what Victis was seeing. That was not possible. Victis had embraced a world beyond death, where past souls beckoned him to cross over.

"Can't you see them?" whispered Victis.

"No. See what?" pleaded Azha.

"The souls of Quizans," whispered Victis. "They're beautiful. Rodia and Zith are waiting for us. I share Zygo's need to go home. His soul is ancient and wise beyond my Ryquat's birth. My god, how old is he? I can feel my creation from the beginning when we were young. I see Earth blanketed with snow and the fiery volcanoes of our past. Azha, I understand now. This is not over; I know what we must sacrifice and why Zygo chose me to merge. Our preordained cast was by design. It is and always has been our Holy Grail. Their calling is strong. Remember what they say.

"The creator is the beginning and end of time and space. We have seen beyond this cosmos. The trials forced upon our Quizan ancestors must continue their journey. In every realm, there is a balance. They are the balance. Some among us came here with no soul. Such evil plagues the good and is cleverly disguised as beings. Crozins have no soul, as do those Ryquats and Humans who choose to have no soul; rise *fin de vital elan* to be spared. Evil spreads hate, lust, greed, and power when free to reign.

"Zygo knows. We are Paladins of our time. I accept my destiny and sacrifice, *initium bellorum*, no matter what form evil takes," Victis roared, raising Vexy's limp body above his head.

Clyde was overwhelmed by what he had witnessed. *Are we angels?* His Human half was faithful to God. His Quizan half was at peace with the words spoken. *What are we? If Trekachaws are angels, then why do we die? Is a Paladin the same as an angel? Can Victis see Heaven?* Clyde wanted to know what he had become.

Azha didn't know what to believe either. But for now, distracting Victis from joining souls on the other side was more important. He gently nudged Victis out the door into the sunlight, and it worked. The glorious sun revived his stripes, and his souls returned to the living. Never in Azha's Human or Quizan life had he been more disturbed. Perhaps finding Earth as a Quizan was part of what Victis was saying. But why Cole, of all Humans? Could it be Cole's courage and strength? Azha had to stop thinking. Maybe he wasn't meant to understand.

Vexy and Rohan were laid to rest on a grassy windswept bluff. There was no gravestone or words said on their behalf. Few knew them, but those who did would not forget.

Clyde was the first to walk away from the gravesite. His mind was racing, trying to understand what he witnessed. Clyde thought about the dead soldiers left behind on Earth's battlefield. Were their souls saved? War never gets easier. With every loss, it takes a piece of you. Clyde understood what Victis must be feeling. If it was ever in question, do Trekachaws have a heart? He could feel his ache. Eventually, the pain becomes more than one can bear.

Victis and Azha threw a handful of dirt upon their grave. They looked toward the ocean, turned into energy, and flew away.

PIFY WAS PLEASED WITH THE number of jets the Trekachaws hijacked. For his own reasons, he told them not to take any more. Plenty had changed since last meeting with Victis and Azha. Pify had kept secrets from Victis and was eager to share the news. Without further ado, all were to convene in Pify's bailiwick.

The old salt looked healthy and bright-eyed, sitting on top of the oval table in his designated chair. A couple of surprises brought smiles to Victis and Azha. Boo and Atue strolled into the bailiwick, followed by two new Umdul captains. The Umduls tried shoving the tall Trekachaws aside to walk past them. When that didn't work, they poked Boo in the behind to get his attention. That worked—Boo bent over, and the Umdul captains walked between his legs.

Pify rolled in his chair, belly laughing. Victis's stripes turned bright green, and the other Trekachaws roared. Today was a good day, but every day was a good day with Pify. Before getting down to business, Pify introduced everyone around the table. When he got to the last one, he reversed the introductions. After all, that was the Umdul way. He raised his stubby hand, motioning for the meeting to begin. Exaggerating his pronunciation, Pify tried his best to articulate the words so there would be no misunderstanding.

"Boo vis-à-vis Myosis. Gystfin aberrant erring dyad spar to balance. Anew enliven guardian spirit Boo. Amiss spawn inherits nefarious soul

Myosis. Trekachaw Boo jointly presents battleship captains, Trekachaw Atue engage planet Trinite. Atue elite past Einstein Ryquat engineer. Declare benefit duo Trinite front Captain Jifney. Asperser Gors link covets defect acquit vilifier, Crozin quibbler yes. Unforeseen feted wave our favor. Declare Zaurak Captain Pubney fleet. Honor usher eldest indigenous Umdul planet Opus sons. Solicit inquiry presession?"

The new translator chip was useless. And, as always, no one understood a thing Pify said, aside from Victis and Phera. Strangely, Phera was not at the meeting. Victis looked around the room at the perplexed faces and decided to take charge of the translation. He scooted his chair back and walked over to Pify. The old Umdul waved at Victis to come closer and whispered in his ear, "Phera occupied? Parley Azha expedite."

Victis heard the concern in Pify's voice, and he agreed; Phera's absence was unusual. Azha was sitting close enough to eavesdrop and stood up. Victis nodded toward the door, and Azha promptly exited the bailiwick to search for Phera.

Victis whistled, "I need to check on something with Pify. Stay here; we'll return soon." Victis picked up Pify and carried him out of the bailiwick.

Whatever had to be clarified must have been complicated; they were gone for a long time. Atue suggested that Boo should go find out how much longer. After that, everyone chimed in, saying Boo should go. Just as he stood up, Victis entered the bailiwick carrying Pify. No one would have guessed who would return with them—a Gor.

Chairs crashed against the wall and the oval table was shoved out of the way. Trekachaws glowed purple, and their yellow eyes narrowed. The Gor hissed at them, clicked its jaws, and rolled into an armored ball. Victis stood Pify on the end of the oval table to free his hands and yelled at everyone to stop. The old salt waddled across the table and scooted into his chair before speaking, "NO! Repeat misinterpretation. Arbiter Captain Victis depict enlightenment."

All eyes shifted to Victis. "I was just as surprised as you to see a Gor on the ship. But, after hearing the whole story, I was, well, let's say, even more surprised. Pify has been busy. Sit down, and I'll explain.

"Until now, we thought the Gors were related to the Crozins. We assumed they didn't look alike because the Gors evolved on a different planet. We also thought the Gors fought as equals alongside the Crozins. But that couldn't be further from the truth. The Gors are not Crozin allies; they are enslaved. So, what is a Gor, and when did all this start?

"Here goes from the beginning. The Crozin elites told the lower-caste Crozins they needed a pathosis transfusion for a pandemic viral cure. The transfusion was used as a ruse to experiment with synthetic DNA. Eventually, all lower-caste Crozin births received the transfusion. As the Crozin infants grew, their bodies mutated. It was too late to reverse the damage even if they stopped giving the transfusions. Eventually, they evolved into the species we know as the Gors.

"Since then, a transfusion has been required every five years. If not, the virus spreads, and the Gor dies. At the age of thirty Earth years, the elite Crozins deem the Gors less productive and expendable. Without exception, the last transfusion is a five-year death sentence. The Crozins control every aspect of the Gors' lives. They have no rights and are considered slaves. If a Gor resists, the consequences are swift and brutal. For example, a Gor who protests is hunted down and forced to witness their family slaughtered. After that, the Gor is displayed and dissected as a deterrent. To the contrary, if a Gor dies while defeating adversaries in combat, that is considered a final act of loyalty. In penance, the Crozin Maomarx law allows the Gor's family a one-time pardon for a violation.

"Look, I never thought this could happen either. But Captain Pify has done the impossible. He allied with the Gors, who were willing to defect from the Crozins' bolshevism. He provided them with a hermitage on the cold side of planet Trinite. For now, the Gystfins occupy the warm side of Trinite. Yes. I can see your loathing expressions and skepticism. However, I do not doubt Captain Pify when he says the situation is under control. Not that it excuses their violent past, but the Gors didn't have much choice.

"That said, we're still learning bits and pieces from the Umduls. Like, the actual life cycle of a Gor and traditions. Captain Pify's Toogus suspects ninety Earth years on average. Another unexpected discovery, the Gors are religious. Of course, Crozin laws forbid religion. That, too, is enforced by the death penalty. From the sounds of it, the Crozins took pleasure in killing the Gors. Guess they're no different than any other species the Crozins have encountered in the galaxy. After learning about them, the idea of Gors defecting is reasonable."

The Gor uncurled and stood by Victis's side.

No one had ever seen a live Gor for any length of time. They were either fighting or curled up in a ball. Gors were strange-looking creatures, and even Victis felt uncomfortable being so close to one.

He took a step to his right and then continued. "Pify's Toogus has a new transfusion called Ectype that neutralizes the Crozin virus. The transfusion is available on Trinite and Opus. Ever since, the alliance of Gors has steadily grown. They will join our fleets stationed between Trinite and Opus. To protect them and the Ectype secret, they will identify themselves by a coded transmission known only to Pify, Phera, and myself. When the Crozins learn of the Gors' intention, they will do everything in their power to destroy them. If all goes well, we will prevent the Crozins from ever attacking this sector.

"With that covered, if you wondered why we had little resistance during our rescue mission on Zaurak, this is why. The Crozins believe Zaurak is defeated because that is what our Gor allies are reporting. But we should remain diligent. The Crozins on Zaurak are reporting the opposite. Lucky for us, the Ukarus are arrogant and confident that we are not a threat. They have dispatched most of their battleships and Jager-Kis en route to planet Trinite. We will intercept them with our Mic-10 jets, the jets we hijacked, and the

Umduls' new friction-energy Mic-12s. With the Gors on our side, we have a good chance of defeating the Crozins.

"Before I forget, Captain Pify's two eldest sons have joined the war. Captain Pubney is with my fleet, and Captain Jifney will be at Trinite with Boo and Atue. Also, the Crozins had a couple of eradicators, but they no longer function. And they couldn't repair or duplicate the device. In conclusion, anyone not assigned will receive orders before the end of duty. Dismissed."

Victis waited for the bailiwick to empty and sat in a chair next to the Gor. He had his doubts if he'd ever get used to the alien. Captain Pify, on the other hand, slid out of his chair and waddled across the tabletop toward him. Victis was about to grab Pify when the old salt reached out and asked the Gor to help him off the table. Never, ever did he think a Gor could be gentle or friendly.

Pify wiggled out of the Gor's arms and chuckled, "Expat noble worthy. Laissez-faire inauguration triumphant. Epithet interpret propose, Olypo!"

The Gor responded by bobbing its head up and down, and its eyes blinked in sync. Victis watched the two dumbfounded, and when it finally dawned on him, he asked, "Oh, the Gor's name is Olypo?"

Boo and Atue crashed into the bailiwick, spooked as if they'd seen a ghost. Boo pointed at the Gor. "Stay, Atue, protect. Myosis attacked Phera and Kigen at Narthex detention."

Victis scooped up Pify and ran out of the bailiwick with Boo running by their side.

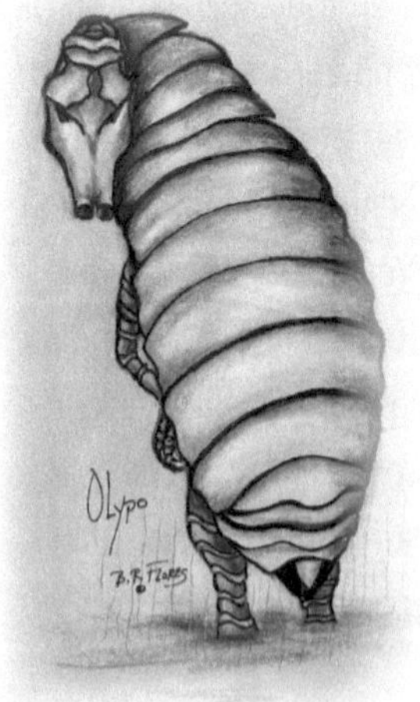

PHERA WANTED TO INTERROGATE NARTHEX before the meeting to find out if he knew anything about the Gors defecting. If so, their future plans could be a trap. If he didn't know anything, she had to be careful not to ask questions that could raise suspicion. Phera preferred that Narthex cooperate; probing his thoughts was disgusting. Regardless, this was the best way to confirm his knowledge one way or the other.

Kigen tagged along with Phera on the way to detention. She told him not to follow her because it is where they keep the bad things. He refused to obey, giggling and disappearing into the wall when she stopped to scold him. "Kigen! I know you're there. You can't go with me. That bad thing is a Crozin. Pify and I have already spoken to you about this. Some places you can't go. Detention is one of them. Go back to the bridge!"

Before opening the detention door, she looked for Kigen, acting like he was still there. But, for all she knew, he could be on the bridge. "Okay, last warning: do not follow me," she said sternly, trying not to laugh.

Kigen's blue eyes appeared on the wall next to the door.

Phera wagged her finger at him. "I mean it, Kigen! Go!"

Kigen giggled and stuck his hand out of the wall, wagging his finger back at her.

"Kigen, I'm serious," she demanded, putting her hand on her hip.

Kigen stepped out of the wall and scrunched his face, nodding yes.

"That's much better. But what's with that frown? What if your face got stuck like that?" Phera teased affectionately. "I won't be long." Phera gave Kigen a big hug. He was almost as tall as her. One would think he was an adult until he acted like a goofy child.

Kigen hugged her back and disappeared into the wall. Phera waited a few moments longer, testing Kigen's resolve before opening the detention door.

Narthex's cell was dark, making it difficult for her to see where he was. From the shadows, he crept toward her. The light sensors lit the cell, and he was exposed. Narthex was standing dangerously close to the charged particle field face-to-face with Phera. She couldn't help but notice his split nose was wrinkled. She glanced over at the red symbol to confirm the security was active. Phera questioned his defiance—a wrinkled nose is how a Crozin mocks or hunts for prey. Narthex had posed to show his lack of fear and disrespect. He knew something.

Phera did not see it coming. A stabbing pain pierced her head. Her back was on fire, and she could feel herself fall to the floor. Someone was attacking her, but who? Phera tried to focus on a blurred shape standing over her. She heard screaming but couldn't understand a word. Pain swept down her side. It felt like Crozin claws. She told herself to stay conscious, knowing she was too weak to turn into energy. It was on top of her now. She tried fighting the heavy body that straddled her, but it was too strong. Myosis? It was Myosis on top of her. And it was Narthex who was shrieking in a frenzy, "Kill her! Kill her!"

Knowing she was too weak to fight him, Phera struggled to escape. But Myosis's crushing weight made it impossible. He hurt her just enough to keep her from turning into energy. The beast lowered his body to lay flat on top of her. He curled his lips and bared his yellow fangs inches from her face. Every horrific fear she had as a Quizan returned. Myosis was going to bite her head off. She kicked her legs and tried to roll, but the beast was too strong. Thick saliva dripped on her face making her gag. He slowly turned his head sideways, and she felt the sting of his fangs piercing her neck. She screamed for help, but Narthex shrieking was all she heard.

A flash of red light streaked between Myosis's fangs into his mouth. He gasped, choked, and spit Phera out. Then stood up, grabbed his neck, and collapsed to the floor. Phera crawled away on her stomach, leaving a trail of blood. Myosis had shredded her flesh, and her head ached from the holes left by his fangs.

She had a chance if she could make it to the door but feared it was too far away. Myosis was spitting and ranting and had gotten off the floor. With all her strength, she crawled faster. Myosis lashed out and grabbed her ankle, crushing her bones. The room began to close in, and she struggled not to faint. He yanked her off the floor, spinning her in circles while roaring with pleasure. Phera reached out for anything she could grab, but the room spun faster and faster, and all went dark.

Her Quizan soul knew what was about to happen. Myosis would smash her into the wall as his final act of torture. So many times, she watched the Gystfins kill Quizans in the same way. Being a Trekachaw, she thought she was safe.

A purple light slammed into Myosis's chest and knocked him to the floor. He scrambled to his feet, raging that whoever hit him would die. The purple light flashed above his head and disappeared into a wall. It was Kigen! Phera could see him looking at her, but his eyes were not blue—they were red.

Myosis saw Kigen's red eyes and swiped the metal wall with his claws, leaving long slashes. But the mysterious red eyes did not disappear. Myosis beat his chest, and his stripes flashed bright purple. Phera tried to turn into energy, but she was too weak. Kigen shot out of the wall into the back of Myosis's head. The beast grabbed his head and shrieked. She saw Kigen streak out of Myosis's head and back into the wall. She saw fear in the young Trekachaw's eyes.

Myosis flashed into energy and streaked into the wall where he last saw Kigen. Seconds later, he flew out, spitting and screaming profanities. Narthex was shrieking at Myosis to stop chasing the light and disarm the security field. Kigen's eyes appeared in the wall again, and Myosis went mad. Kigen was brilliant; he had learned how to taunt Myosis without getting hurt.

Phera tried turning into energy again. This time she rose above the floor, free at last. On the other side of the detention door, she morphed into body form and collapsed onto the floor.

She took comfort in knowing Kigen would be okay. As her mind faded into darkness, she thought of Pify and her love for him.

# nine

# TRINITE

The Umdul Language:
BȝANYABO

**UMDUL** Teepug soldiers were the first to arrive. Their transmission was dire. "Acute, Captain Phera. Nonce Trekachaw Kigen. Detention incog Crozin internment."

Victis needed to get there before Pify to assess Phera's condition. He worried the old salt couldn't take the shock if she were dead. Victis ran with Pify in the corridor but handed him off to Azha halfway. He turned into energy and streaked ahead.

By the time he arrived, several Umdul medical Toogus were huddled over Phera. They were blocking his view of her upper torso. But from what he could see, her stripes were pale grey. And her legs had been shredded. Kigen was kneeling by her head, and she had not moved.

A light streaked into the corridor and morphed into Clyde. He looked at Phera and then at Victis. He flashed back into energy and disappeared into Phera's body. Victis yelled at the Toogus to move. They shuffled away to give the Trekachaws room to do what they could not.

Kigen glared at Victis with red eyes. He wasn't going anywhere, and Victis knew he could not make him. The young Trekachaw scooted in closer to her side and held her hand. Victis wanted to ask Kigen what happened, but now was not the time.

Phera had not changed, and standing by helplessly was gut-wrenching. He worried they were too late to save her. Victis could kick himself for not learning how to transfer energy. But for one reason or another, he never did.

Azha stopped cold in the corridor when he saw Phera on the floor. Pify gasped, and Azha turned to shield Pify's eyes. But he was too slow. Pify saw her and was kicking and screaming. He demanded that Azha put him down.

As fast as his short old legs could waddle, Pify ran to her and squatted on the floor. He touched her face, begging Victis to do something. His hands were shaking, and he couldn't catch his breath. Pify wobbled, then rolled over flat out on the floor. Victis dragged him away from Phera, yelling at the Toogus to get over here. Just as he suspected, Pify's heart could not take the shock. His eyes were closed, and his body was limp. Several Toogus scrambled to Pify's aid and began emergency medical care to save the old Umdul.

During all the chaos, Clyde's faint light arose from Phera's chest. He morphed into body form, lying on the floor next to her. Victis ran to check on him. He would recover, but what he had to say was not good. Clyde whispered, "Phera won't make it. She needs more energy. Pax and Zeta know how to transfer energy. Find them."

Victis knew seconds could be the difference between life and death. A call to all battleships was sent. *Trekachaws with the knowledge to transfer energy respond immediately.*

Clyde waved his hand at Victis. "It was Myosis."

Pax streaked through the walls and descended into Phera.

She had not moved. Victis wondered how it must have looked when Myosis bit him in half. No one thought he'd live. At least Phera was still in one piece.

Victis watched for a hint of change. How long had it been? She needed natural solar light. That could make the difference. Pax had been inside for a while now. This was taking way too long. There! There it is. Her lips have a tinge of blue. One more Trekachaw and Phera would be okay.

Another Trekachaw energy flew toward them in the corridor. Zeta morphed into body form and sat on the floor next to Clyde. "Are you hurt?"

He pointed to his cheek. "I'm fine, but a kiss wouldn't hurt."

Zeta laughed and slapped his arm. "You're definitely okay."

The Toogus were surmising, examining, and fussing over Pify. Though no one could understand them, it seemed Pify was feeling better. As for Phera, her stripes were pale blue, and she moaned in pain. Any sound was better than nothing.

Pax's energy floated out of Phera and morphed into body form. He had learned more about what had happened. "Phera told me Myosis attacked her from behind while Narthex distracted her. Myosis bit the top of her head and clawed her back before she realized what they were doing. That evil Crozin helped Myosis. Phera said he was screaming at Myosis, 'Kill her!' She wanted everyone to know that if it weren't for Kigen, Myosis would have killed her. Kigen pestered Myosis long enough for her to escape."

It was Zeta's turn to help Phera, but she refused. Clyde lowered his voice so that no one else could hear him. Of course, that didn't work. Every Trekachaw in the corridor listened to every word loud and clear.

"Zeta, I fired first. I'm more guilty than she is. Phera didn't fire a laser. It was Azha and me. We all thought Ginzal was Myosis. You need to forgive them."

Zeta stood up in a huff. "Don't remind me of what you did. And I don't need lecturing! I forgave you because those two said Ginzal's red energy was Myosis. You were stupid enough to listen to them. Why did they assume she was Myosis? Did you ever ask yourself that? If they weren't so promiscuous, Ginzal would still be alive. Cole would have stopped them. But Azha keeps Cole's soul buried. They murdered her, and nobody cared. If you're listening to us, this is Beverly speaking, not Zeta. I will never forgive either one of them. Look at how they dote over her. It's disgusting. Phera will be fine, just like always. First, I'll speak to Cole. Then I'll leave. Or do I need permission from Phera and Azha for that too?"

Kigen's stripes were purple, and he glared at Zeta with red eyes. Worried about what Kigen might do, Victis nonchalantly sidestepped next to him. If Kigen attacked Beverly, Victis wasn't sure if he could stop him. Victis wished Zeta would rise and take charge of Beverly. Regardless, after hearing Beverly's rants, they had to go. But nothing is ever that simple. Beverly stomped over to Azha and demanded to speak with Cole. Before he said a word, she called him a soul thief.

Grunting and groaning, Pify pushed the Toogus away. The hard part was getting to his feet. Kicking his short legs up in the air, Pify got the momentum to roll forward and sit on the floor.

"Must I interpose? One's seat does not pause gratuitous tone accede?"

However, Pify need not intervene; Victis had had enough. In a tidal wave of profanity, Victis spewed Japanese curse words. Or at least the way he said them: "*Damare! Baka yarou fuzakeruna! Doke busu!* Zeta! Beverly! Not another word. Beverly! You are his Earth mother. I am Azha's captain and yours as well. You'd be dead if it weren't for Azha taking Cole's soul. Can't you understand if not for Azha, the Crozins would have conquered us. We've all lost loved ones and will lose more before this war is over. Ginzal died because of her jealousy. Did you know Azha knew Phera when they were quieys on Palatu? He's loved her his entire life. He didn't want to owari bond Ginzal. Guilt—that's why he did it. Ginger and Quetzal were strangers. Your anger and resentment ends here. Return to your ship and stop spreading hate."

Beverly's stripes were bright red. "Yes, sir! No problem!"

Victis's yellow eyes narrowed. "Clyde, she is a problem. Beverly is a danger to all of us. You know what I will do. I need to know if Zeta can take charge."

Clyde warned Beverly. "I would do almost anything for you. But you're wrong, not them. Don't keep doing this, or you're on your own." Clyde waited, hoping Zeta would rise and say something. But she did not. Beverly yelled at Clyde, calling him a backstabbing doormat. Clyde shook his head and walked away. Victis told Azha to make peace with Cole. If Beverly continued to disrupt, he would end her.

Captain Pubney waddled-ran down the corridor, yelling about an urgent message. "Jifney conveys imperative besiege Opus, Trinite, Kikis exigent. Mikado Kiki Thude dies at Crozins' wrath!"

Pify rolled to one side and stayed like that for a couple of seconds. Then he struggled to get his knees beneath him and got stuck in that awkward position. Victis wrapped his arms around Pify's rotund belly and lifted him to his feet. After a quick once-over, Victis brushed off the old salt's rumpled suit. He held on to one of Pify's hands just in case he got dizzy again.

"Are you okay? You gave me a good scare."

Pify leaned back as far as his squatty body and stiff neck allowed. He smiled, showing his big white teeth. *"Uketotta."*

Azha had made a habit of avoiding Zeta. That was not going to work this time. Letting Victis fight his fight was the coward's way out. Azha asked Beverly to speak with Cole before leaving. Besides, having Cole present to deal with his mother was fine by him. Cole surfaced and spoke, "Mom, it's me."

"Is it really you?" asked Beverly, trying to contain her emotions.

"Yes. It's me, Mom. I wish you weren't so angry. Azha had no clue the red energy was Ginzal. I should know. I was there. And it's been my choice to let Azha be dominant. I've learned Azha's soul is a good one. And about what Captain Victis said. He's right. If we fight among ourselves, we will lose this war. He's right about you too. You were dying of cancer. As for Phera, she is strong and brave. Do not judge her indiscretions. You know nothing about her. Please make peace with them for me," asked Cole, kissing her cheek.

Beverly touched her cheek. "Can you visit me now and then?" Beverly hugged Cole, but his body tensed, and she knew Azha had returned.

"Yes. That would be good for Cole too. I hope you can forgive me. I meant no harm to Ginzal." Azha took a step back. Confidence replaced Beverly's disturbed expression. Indeed, Zeta had returned.

Pify pulled on Victis's hand to bend over. Whatever he whispered made Victis smile.

"Azha, you're with me. Pify is following Phera to the infirmary. Pubney will be there, too, until Phera kicks them both out. Pify made me laugh. He said Pubney wanted to go with him because he was sick of hearing Beverly moan. Okay, enough with Beverly's drama. Back to the business of war. The Crozins are en route to attack Opus and Trinite. We have fifty-plus Trekachaws on standby that will intersect and hijack their ships. Better yet, I have Pify's blessing to probe Narthex's brain."

"Why now? Is it because of Phera?" asked Azha.

Victis slapped Azha on the back as he walked past him into the detention room.

"Are you coming or not? Who cares why? I've been wanting to do this for a long time. Three things he will tell me: what he knows about the Crozins killing Kiki Captain Thude; if they destroyed Thude's battleship; and third, well, whatever I want."

Narthex screamed, and his nose split when they entered the detention room. "It was Myosis, not me!"

He crouched in a shadowed corner of the cell. He did not want to be alone with Victis and Azha.

"Get over here!" yelled Victis.

Narthex leaped out of the corner, then paced in circles hunched over. The sound of his hooves reminded Victis of when Narthex ripped out his daughter's heart and ate it. The same dreadful noise when he walked up the ramp after tossing her body away like trash.

Victis growled, "Azha, cut the security field."

Narthex took a stance, exposing his claws.

Victis taunted him, "Try it! I'll rip your claws off and cut your throat with them!"

Narthex cringed, and he lowered his arms.

"Do as I say, or I will fry your eyes first, then your brain. I'm going to ask you questions. If you lie, I can justify killing you to Pify. Until now, he's the only reason you're alive. Let's go down memory lane, you evil demon. I still see you ripping my daughter's heart out and eating it. But no, that didn't satisfy you. Did it? You tossed her body to Ruks, and they shredded her to pieces. You stole my pregnant wife to mutilate and raped her hundreds of times. When my youngest daughter was born, you kept her as your pet to control my wife. What you did to my family is worse than death. So, how shall I punish you? With great pleasure, I may add. Today, however, is still your choice. Do we have an understanding?" Victis tilted his head with a smirk.

Narthex shivered, and his nose curled into a ball. The sight of his exposed mouth was disgusting. From the hole, he sprayed a mist that reeked.

Victis ignored him and turned into energy. He circled above Narthex to torment him. As he descended into his head, the alien collapsed unconscious. That was unexpected, but conscious or unconscious was moot—Narthex could not hide his thoughts.

Azha watched Narthex's legs stiffen and then scissor freakishly. His nose uncurled and became straight and rigid. Whatever Victis was doing was causing quite the reaction. The alien shrieked, jumped up, and began pounding the sides of his head with his hands. He bent forward and defecated, then fell to the floor. His eyes rolled back, and a snaky tongue flickered in and out of the hole he calls his mouth.

The image of an Earth demon flashed in Azha's mind. If Cole saw that image again, Azha would insist on Cole keeping his hellion memory to himself.

Narthex stopped displaying his distemper and opened one of his eyes. Azha kicked the alien to see if he was cognizant. Narthex hissed and swiped at Azha with his claws. It was what Azha thought. Narthex was putting on quite the show.

Victis flew out of Narthex and morphed into body form next to Azha. The nasty Crozin lay motionless with his eyes closed, and his snakish tongue hung limply between his split nose.

Victis roared, laughing, "What a buffoon. Is he pretending to play dead? Hey, Azha, look, half of him is outside the field. Activate it, and he'll pop up."

Narthex rolled over to clear the field and acted dead again.

"You're not fooling anyone. Narthex, open your eyes. You're going to clean up your own stink. What do you think, Azha? Should I go back in there and rub his noses in it?"

Azha was shaking his head and laughing at Narthex. "Did he tell you what you wanted to know?"

"Uh-huh, that and more. Myosis was supposed to take Narthex with him. The double dumb ass was too busy trying to kill Phera and catch Kigen. Narthex was told the Crozins couldn't take Thude's ship because of the biometrics code embedded in the ship's AI cerebellum. Of course, the Crozins slaughtered her crew, trying to find out how. I know where the battleship is; you'll never guess. The Crozins hid it inside a hollow moon. They plan on returning after they invade Opus when they have more time to figure out the AI. Well, that's not going to happen. Oh, look who's awake and giving us attitude? Narthex, you mucky crud, sit down, or I'll come back in."

Azha wished Victis had burned Narthex's eyes out, but that was for another day. "Victis, let's go. He's pathetic."

They could hear Narthex screeching as they walked down the corridor.

Victis was talking so fast that Azha found him confusing. One thing was clear to Azha: Narthex was unaware of the Gors on Trinite.

Phera and Pify were waiting for Victis inside the infirmary. The old salt was in good spirits and feeling a bit better. Pify knew Narthex had kept secrets. Knowing what they are gave them an advantage.

Pify was sad to hear that his old friend had died, but he tried to warn her. For the Kikis, Thude's death was the utmost betrayal. All negotiations ended. They're back with a vengeance to fight with the Umduls. They learned a tragic lesson—never trust a Crozin.

# ten

# KOGBOR SURVITE

**The Umdul Language:**

ꟽIOGDIƷ ЖUMƷVOABO

**EVEN** though this meeting was necessary, Victis was dreading yet another one. Azha sat next to him at the far end of Pify's bailiwick.

Kigen's presence was unexpected. Of course, his unexpected should be expected by now. No one ever knew when or where he'd pop up. The young Trekachaw often hid in solid objects and eavesdropped on private conversations and meetings. Perish the thought of what he'd seen and heard. This misbehavior had been addressed many times, but Kigen learned at a young age no one could stop him. Given what just happened, perhaps this time, he was worried about Phera.

Some of the faces from the last meeting were missing. Most likely, they had been deployed. Pify sat in his chair affixed to the top of the oval table. Phera announced with reservation in her voice that Pify had another new chip. This revised chip was supposed to provide clarity. Victis never minded translating for Pify. As a matter of fact, he felt special being one of only a few that understood Umduls. But it pleased Pify, so this was a good thing.

Pify scooted to the edge of his chair, then rolled over onto his belly. He dangled his legs until he felt the tabletop with his feet and stood up. This was new. Perhaps Victis needed to cut the chair legs shorter. Pify straightened his rumpled jacket and cleared his throat to get everyone's attention. When everyone was quiet, he walked with a wobble around the top of the table, speaking loudly and with conviction. Victis was a nervous wreck watching him.

"Umdul virtuoso translate and paraphrase simplistic comprehension complicated Umdul argot." Pify winked and pointed to the device attached to his wrist.

"Welcome, Victis plus one; Umdul clarity hence ends questions, correct? Satisfactorily, not perfect. Cohort Gor, Olypo, thwart Crozin tyranny. Toogus Oiba aborts Crozin efficacies transfusion Ectype. Free Olypo plus Gors align Fidus Achates. Conclude.

"Boo plus Atue one Captain Jifney son en route to Opus and Trinite. Second Pubney son mission, orbit planet Zaurak. Proxy asset Roon science proficiency unites Umdul Pubney warriors. Fitting balance. Probabilities sons perish light-years divide. Crozins' celebration such death plus relish my dismay.

"Versed. Thude Kiki captain, Umduls' ally bird, odious assassins nefarious. Reject furtive Opus siege. Warned self-martyrize loyal sacrifice. Crozin's perpetual, vile cast vetted. Fate theories crew plus battleship. Victis rifle Narthex dome, enlightenment pro atrocity?"

Victis repeated what Pify said, "Narthex knew where the Crozins hid Thude's battleship."

Pify reached out and patted Victis's arm. "Super. Victis, son of another mother. Partake mission anon hollow moon. Umdul clarity, wrist *Tranvice* advantageous. Succeed, *inter nos Uketotta*." Pify motioned for Victis to help him down.

He lifted Pify from the table and carried him out the door. Pify spoke so others could not hear. "*Inter nos Uketotta* translated?"

Victis whispered, "Yes, the meetings and missions are secrets shared with no one outside this bailiwick."

Pify smiled. "Opinion required. Translator improve?"

"I understood you just fine. Maybe I should clarify the fine points. Besides, if they have questions, they can ask me." Victis set Pify down on his feet and let go.

He followed slowly behind Pify, who was shuffling down the corridor.

"Notably, fine points!" Pify balked, scratching his head. Diligent as ever, Pify's pet tit Fizz parted Pify's hair to peek out and investigate what caused Pify to be flustered and why the Trekachaw was following so closely.

Victis noticed the two little eyes glaring at him. He'd never seen the body of a tit and thought this might be a perfect opportunity. Closer he came, leaning in to get a better look at Fizz. All the while, Pify was humming a familiar tune. *"Here, there, eyes, keep watch. Beware to dare a tit you see. The sting it brings will make you flee!"*

"There you are, little girlie. I see you're watching Pify's back. Good job!" praised Victis while trying to see the rest of Fizz's body. Victis was not listening to the words in Pify's song.

Fizz stuck out his tongue at Victis. His antenna eyes stiffened, and he stomped his feet and disappeared.

Pify stopped humming and shifted his weight on one foot to pivot with the other. "Underestimate Fizz, poke out eye. Avert sting, walk side by side. Fizz protest Victis brass ruse. Scandal I neglect to correct. Fizz iron-heart he-tit. Perceived dainty manifests anger."

Victis thought about Pify's warning. "Okay, did I get this right? Fizz will poke out my eye if I get too close. And Fizz is not a female. Wow, he's a male."

*"Uketotta!* Fizz mighty legend Noggin-Stomp."

Fizz peeked out and grinned at Victis.

BRIGHT LIGHTS STREAKED ACROSS THE galaxy, giving solace to all those aboard battleships. Not so on Trinite. Boo, Atue and Umdul Captain Jifney received overlapping transmissions requesting reinforcements from the Gors and Gystfins on the planet. The Crozins were attacking, but that was Pify's plan. The fact is, he gambled on it. So far, the Crozins were unaware of the incoming Trekachaws and the Gystfin incursion. More important than that, the Gors' were willing to sacrifice themselves to live in a world free of tyranny.

Sitting in his chair at the helm came second nature to the Umdul. This battle was no different. He knew the transmissions meant there were losses. Who they were and how many were unknown. With all that, he knew he was selfish when assigning Victis to recover Thude's battleship outside the battle zones. Still, he couldn't bear the loss of his Trekachaw son. Besides, Victis was the future, not him. Selfish or not, this battle was pivotal in the war. The outcome would determine the fate of the galaxy.

A TREKACHAW'S ENERGY FLEW ONTO the bridge of Pify's battleship. As the light was morphing into body form, it divided into two, and they collapsed to the floor. The victims of war were becoming real.

Pify recognized Clyde; the younger one, he did not. Clyde was bloody and had survived a living hell. He cried out, asking for Pax or any Trekachaw that could transfer energy. Deep laser cuts and burns covered the younger Trekachaw's body and face. Clyde crawled across the deck on his hands and knees to check on him. Bowing his head in grief, he choked back the tears. The young Trekachaw was Vious, Kigen's father. No one came to save him, and Clyde knew he did not have the strength.

He wrapped his arms around Vious and held him. Soon, he would ascend to Aeon Devotio. His Quizan grey-death energy would leave this world to join his ancestors and embrace the evolution of eternal life. For Vious to ascend, he needed to find his way to the portal. The eyes were the window of souls. If he could not find his way there soon, Clyde would slice off the top of his head with a laser.

Clyde asked for a laser and steadied his hand. Being forced to do such an unspeakable act to Vious was gut-wrenching. There had to be another way.

He lowered the laser and spoke to Vious. "If you can hear me, follow my voice. Your body is but a vessel that no longer holds you at bay. Aeon Devotio is calling you home. Follow my voice until you find your way. Look for the lights. Your eyes are windows where your souls are set free."

Vious's yellow eyes turned grey, and a whiff spiraled into the light. His souls were free. Clyde tried to touch Vious's grey-death energy, but it wafted into random puffs around his hand. He watched it entwine and float above until the spiraling souls vanished to Aeon Devotio.

Pify sent word to Phera to keep Kigen busy until Vious's body was moved to sick bay. He was worried Kigen might try to retaliate and get hurt or die. But Kigen did what Kigen wanted to do. Pify's good intention only piqued his curiosity.

Kigen stepped out of the bridge wall as Vious's grey-death energy disappeared. He cried out, "Papay, don't go!"

But Aeon Devotio had claimed Vious in the afterworld. Kigen's stripes turned a pale blue, and he looked lost. Pify waddled over to the young Trekachaw and reached up to hold his hand. Kigen looked down at Pify. "Manany dead too?" Pify turned to Clyde.

"Deneb was alive when I left. Several Human Trekachaws and Vopar came aboard to assist her. That's all I know. I can't even tell you who's on a battleship or flying a jet. The Trekachaws are going where they're needed. Can we talk alone?" Clyde was exhausted and needed to rest.

Pify waited for Phera's arrival on the bridge before letting go of Kigen's hand. She seemed better, but her injuries from Myosis's attack were horrible, disfiguring, and still painful.

### *Three hours earlier . . .*
*ВНІЕЗОО НІЕІУМЗЖ ОЕЗАОЗ*

THE FIRST WAVE OF CROZINS to attack the planet was not a surprise. What came next? No one saw it coming. Boo and Atue's battleship became ground zero. Nonetheless, it did make sense, considering Boo was the Gystfins' liaison. Destroying his ship would disrupt communications between the Gystfins and their allies.

Myosis was another reason. He loathed Boo for reporting the rogue Gystfins on Palatu. Killing him went beyond a strategic plan. It was a personal vendetta.

From the onset, nothing was going as planned for Boo and Atue. The only advantage they had was their battleship was faster. But they were being shredded by lasers on all fronts as they fled the Crozins. And firing back was not an option. As far as they knew, the Trekachaws had breached several Crozin battleships to kill the Ukaru captains. Which ones they did not know.

Something had gone terribly wrong. The lead Crozin battleship should have been the first hijacked ship. But it had yet to deviate as planned. And a trailing Crozin battleship advanced to join the pursuit. A barrage of laser strikes aimed at Boo and Atue's battleship hit their mark. The flash blinded the monitor. Then, another flash lit the black space.

The damage was significant. Sections of Boo and Atue's battleship spiraled out into space, creating a chain reaction of destruction. Deneb and Vious's battleship was in the direct path of the wreckage. The bridge took a substantial hit. Deneb screamed at the navigator to pitch hard and bank starboard, to avoid incoming shrapnel. It was too late. They collided with spinning projectiles that cut into the bow and the bridge. Their battleship was dead in space and an easy target.

To Deneb's relief, the Crozins did not disintegrate her ship. The bridge was on fire, and her crew was screaming for help. They would die from smoke or burn to death if she didn't act fast. She tripped over the bridge wreckage, following a wall with her hand. The billowing smoke blackened the air, and the heat from the fires scorched her face. She no longer heard her crew calling out for help. Her hand was getting burned, touching the wall, but she was afraid of being disoriented without it. A couple of steps more and she bumped into the console edge. She ran her hands over the virtual interface, blindly searching for the life support sensor. A light appeared that displayed the image. Deneb was overwhelmed that she had found it. All nonessential systems were diverted to extinguish fires and filter the smoke into clean air. Until that moment, she did not feel her hand. Her fingers and palm were burned when she followed the wall. Now her pain was significant. She saw herself in the reflection of a metal plate and took a second look. From what she could see, her ear was scorched, and that side of her hair was gone.

The main monitors on the bridge and communications were down. Deneb checked the observation screens and found one functional. Her allies had surrounded the battleship to protect her from the Crozins.

After assessing the damage, Deneb was grateful to learn the lower decks had minimal repairs and no casualties. Now that medical and engineering were on the way, she searched for Vious beneath the charred wreckage.

The crew was injured worse than she had suspected. Their burned bodies lay twisted beneath layers of jagged metal. Some died quickly, while others must have succumbed to smoke. But there were a few miracles. A hand reached out from beneath a stow locker. Several more Ryquats called out. Most likely, they survived because they were under large thermo-panels that provided air pockets and blocked the smoke and fire.

Deneb lifted a panel and tossed it to one side; Vious was underneath, unconscious and shredded by shrapnel. She screamed in desperation and tried to lift the heavy carbon deck grid that had him pinned to the floor. She tried to lift the corner, but the weight was too great. She tried pulling on it, but it would not budge. She searched for anything to pry up the grid, but there was nothing long enough or strong enough. She felt helpless and feared that by the time help arrived, Vious would be dead.

From the corner of her eye, she saw a Trekachaw. The light orb morphed into body form next to her. Clyde had come to rescue Vious from death. But the battle had also taken its toll on Clyde. He was hurt and bleeding.

"Can you help Vious? I heard you know how to transfer energy. He can't die! Please, Clyde, I can't lose him," cried Deneb, touching Vious's face.

"I'll do my best. Pify's out of the battle zone. If I can transfer enough energy, I'll get 'em there. Deneb, your crew needs ya. Stay strong. There's a Ryquat battleship comin' real soon. They'll help take care of your injured crew and do what they can to get your ship patched up. Ya know, this ship is in pretty bad shape. Right? Do what they tell ya, okay? If you gotta leave the ship, you do it. Some of those ships out there been keepin' those Crozins off ya can't stay too much longer. We're right in the middle of fightin'. You gotta get up and take care of your crew."

Deneb kissed Vious and shook her head *no*.

"Com-on, get up. I'll take care of him." Clyde pulled on her arm until she stood up.

Her stripes were red, and the look on her face made him pause. He couldn't describe it. But he had seen it on Earth's battlefield when death was no longer feared.

Her yellow eyes shifted from him to the crew carrying the dead from the bridge. "Don't worry about me. Save Vious."

ATUE'S BATTLESHIP SPIRALED IN A controlled dive toward Trinite. Boo was giving a play-by-play account of what the pursuing Crozins were doing. The battleship skimmed the edge of the Trinite atmosphere, and the Crozins veered back into space. Grunting was Boo's way of laughing at their predicament. Flying the massive battleship out of a spiraling dive into the planet's atmosphere would be ambitious, to say the least. Fifty percent of the navigation systems were damaged, and the ship's hull showed signs of stress. Soft or hard, they had to land the battleship on the planet's surface. Too fast, they would burn up. Too slow, the ship's hull would break apart.

Atue shouted at Boo, "Get over here and help me kill us! We're coming in too fast. Tell me if I vary more than five degrees, one way or the other. At this speed, the gravity drag will burn us up. Tell the crew to hang on; I'm flying in on a belly flop to lose velocity. It's gonna get bumpy, but this should cut the heat."

Boo yelled, "Not built contort!"

"Unless you've got a better idea, shut up!"

"Level out starboard!" yelled Boo.

Atue screamed, *"Deus vult!"* and pitched the battleship starboard until Boo thought for sure the ship would vibrate apart. Grinding carbon metal twisted and buckled to the breaking point to counterbalance the force. The battleship couldn't take much more before ripping apart.

Boo yelled, "Four degrees port!"

The mighty battleship held together.

"Three degrees starboard!" Boo yelled, hanging on to the flight seat.

Atue focused on the stabilizers while maintaining a steady speed. The deck began to rattle, causing anything not bolted down to bounce across the bridge, including several unharnessed Ryquat crew.

Boo roared, "Level out, level out! I see Trinite!"

No sooner than he said those words, a melee of fighter jets in combat formation came into view. V-Jak Gor jets were firing on other V-Jaks who were firing on Ryquat Mic-10s and Umdul Mic-12s. And from what they could see, the Crozin Jager-Ki jets were firing on any craft other than their own.

Boo shouted, "Incoming port side, five Gor V-Jaks, and two Krof Gystfin jets!"

"Try to raise the Gystfin Krof jets!" screamed Atue.

"Krof, Boo of Gardux requesting assistance. Confirm Gor V-Jaks' status ally. Relay aerodrome site, need air support?"

*No response.*

"Try again, Boo. They're flying in fast," shouted Atue.

"Krof jets, Boo of Gardux requesting assistance."

"Request granted—V-Jaks allies. Air support affirmative. Landing site open level aerodrome, no docking space available."

A Krof jet sped past them, taking the lead. "Boo of Gardux . . . Kogbor Survite. Per mandate directive, mark location, airspace secured. Do not disembark battleship landing site—ceasefire on all land advances. Do not engage Crozins," ordered Gystfin Kogbor Survite.

Boo transmitted, "Acknowledged," and thought, *Did Boo hear right?*

Atue waved his arms in the air to get Boo's attention. "What did he say? Not to defend ourselves against Crozin ground attacks? Fat chance of that happening!" cursed Atue. And then questioned Boo if the coms were off, rethinking his response. His "*Fat chance of that happening*" could have been broadcasted.

Checking the coms, Boo whispered, "Think so. No matter; we've no ship lasers. Hope Survite right, not mistakes."

Flying over the planet revealed a world barely explored. The surface was filled with splendor and beauty. No wonder the Ryquats kept it classified. Rolling hills covered with breathtaking majestic white flowers seemed to go on forever until a small clearing appeared. Survite's coordinates marked that spot as the landing site. Curious as to why there? The flowers ended a stone's throw away, and for as far as the eye could see was an open grassy field. It did not make sense, but Survite was specific.

Boo asked, "Think Kogbor Survite thought flowers conceal battleship?"

"Ah, no. Can you smell it?" Atue replied, releasing his harness to walk over to the observation port. "The flowers smell like a fragrance I gave to one of my . . . well, that was another life when I was a Ryquat. Anyway, *no* to your question. Survite knows better than that; I haven't a clue why he had us land here."

Boo walked over next to Atue and looked out at the field of enormous white flowers. "Wasn't Captain Victis told story about flesh-eating flowers on Trinite?"

"Yeah, now that you mention it, he did. Do you think that's why Survite told us to stay on board? Then why not land in that open field over there?" Atue wondered, shaking his head.

"Strange. We dire for ship lasers?" Boo said, getting nervous.

"At least eight hours; I don't like this at all. We're in the open, with no way to defend ourselves and barely enough reserves to take off and land in that field. What do you think?" Atue asked, frustrated.

"No, understand logic. Ask me, stay here. Trust Survite. Neco lasers suffice ground fighting, nothing more, nothing less," Boo said, sounding uneasy.

"Oh, frickin! Is the sensor data correct? No way. The data shows over a thousand Crozin Ruks and Gors in this area. Are the Gors friendly or not?" Atue choked, dancing in place while looking closer at the data.

"Too many to fight," Boo snarled, tightening his fists.

"Arm all crew with as many Necos as we have on board. IQR2000 frequency to destruct at 50 percent registered life. If half the crew is still alive after this, dying in an explosion is better than being Crozin snacks, agree?" asked Atue.

"Yes. Crozins breach ship, energy we kill Ukaru, next Ruks," growled Boo.

The two Trekachaws' stripes were glowing purple as they watched hundreds of the Crozins enter the white flowers. Closer they came, waves of them trampling the beautiful flowers in their path until the field beyond was empty.

Atue gasped, "Did you see that?"

Boo's eyes widened. "Jaaju, flowers killing Crozins. They eat legs, next body. Flowers communicating? Yes, under petals, they talk. Pretend plants till surround Crozins, ambush smart. No! No! No! Flowers leave dirt. Look, see moving!" Boo's voice was shaky.

Atue pointed at the massacre. "They move faster than the Crozins. Geez, it's a bloodbath out there. They're devouring them from their legs up. I hate Crozins, but this is brutal. The flowers are every bit as ruthless. No wonder Survite told us not to leave the battleship. He knew the flowers were going to kill the Crozins. Glad Survite is on our side. When this is over, I want to meet him. Unbelievable, did you see that? That one leaped into the air and landed on the Crozin's back. Eww, it bit through the saggy part of the skull, popping it. Ugh, they eat everything. Look, look there; I can see its stems or legs or whatever you'd call that. They're running into the open to chase down the Crozins who made it back to the field. Nope, no way, eww. They're not getting away. There goes, that was the last Crozin. Wow, did you see the six-inch fangs under those petals? Unbelievable. The Crozins didn't have a chance. I don't think they got off more than a couple of laser blasts, do you?" Atue asked Boo, thoroughly disgusted and in awe.

"Couple Boo see. All Crozins dead," Boo said, taking a step closer to the edge of the observation window. He leaned forward and looked straight down beneath the docking port.

Boo stumbled backward. "Flowers crawl up landing gear! Inside ship? Boo no turn energy, leave crew behind, flowers eat. Hundreds, too many. What do Atue say to Boo?" Boo was hyperventilating. He paced across the bridge, talking to himself about the flesh-eating flowers.

Atue looked down and jumped a little himself. "We have the advantage of knowing what they can do. Don't let this rattle you. If necessary, we'll fight the flowers just like any other alien. Okay? We'll be fine," Atue assured Boo while trying not to hyperventilate himself.

Atue still thought the flowers were beautiful despite them being ruthless and deadly. But ruthlessness did not make up for advanced weapons. Under most circumstances, the flowers would not stand a chance. That didn't seem to comfort Boo. He was terrified, more than Atue had ever seen him before. His stripes were red, and he wasn't calming down.

Atue shook Boo to get his attention and then looked to the sky. "Two fighter jets are inbound; focus on them, Boo. Snap out of it!"

The jets flew close enough to recognize—one a Gystfin Krof and the other a Gor V-Jak ally. Side by side, they landed in the field just beyond the flowers.

Boo panicked. "Flowers attack? Warn, stay out! Tell them!"

Atue covered his ears with his hands to block Boo's hysterical screams while looking for the correct ship-to-ship frequency. "Warning. Warning. Do not enter the white flowers. They can attack, lethal. Do not enter the flowers," transmitted Atue.

Boo was screaming and walking in circles.

"Boo, shut up! I can't hear when you're screaming!" screamed Atue louder than Boo.

"No! No! No! They walk to flowers. Atue repeat!" growled Boo, getting within inches of Atue's ear.

*No response.*

"Tell flowers, not in dirt!" shrieked Boo, waving his arms in the air to get their attention.

Atue had to duck twice to avoid getting slapped. "Boo, stop screaming. You're hurting my ears. Stop it; they can't hear you!" Atue repeated the warning. He pronounced each word slowly and exaggerated, *"The white flowers will KILL YOU and EAT YOU. Go back, do not enter!"*

Boo dropped his arms to his side. "What? NO! NO, understand. Wave back at me. Boo not watch; this *plochoi!*" Boo said, defeated, shaking his head in disbelief.

"Do you think they understood me?" Atue questioned.

"Sad. Boo no save Gystfin. Enter flowers trap they go." Boo resigned himself to the inevitable. Refusing to watch, he turned away.

Atue put his head down on the console. "I'll try to warn them again." Atue looked up,

"Wait, what are the flowers doing? I don't believe it. Boo, look!" Atue urged, shocked at what he was seeing.

"No, Atue. Bad," scowled Boo.

"It's not what you think. Turn around and see for yourself. The flowers are not attacking. Uh, they're pulling their roots out of the dirt to clear a path. For real, turn around. You need to see it to believe it," howled Atue.

Boo was stubborn, and Atue knew it. To get his attention, Atue slapped Boo's face. More curious than angry, Boo peeked over his shoulder to see what Atue was willing to slap him over.

"How possible? We go, find out. Open lower docking port," Boo howled with laughter as he ran across the bridge and out the door, yelling, "Atue slap Boo face again, punch you out."

Unbeknownst to Boo and Atue, the crew assigned to the bay had received specific instructions from Kogbor Survite that no Ryquats be present upon his arrival.

The hatch door slid open before Atue could address this unorthodox request, allowing Survite, a Gor, and one flesh-eating flower to enter.

Boo's growl was unintentional; his primitive Gystfin instincts were taking control of his emotions. The Gor hissed and coiled into a ball in response to Boo's aggression. That triggered Boo's Gystfin soul. He had encountered a coiled Gor while in a fight to the death too many times. Lowering his stance to attack, Boo bared his fangs.

Atue was watching a colossal misunderstanding spiral into a disaster. The flowers were dangerous enough, but a hissing Gor too? It became apparent to everyone in the bay that throwing these two enemies together provoked the wrong response.

Given the Gystfins' history with the Gors, they deserved Boo's hate. They hunted, killed, and harvested Gystfins for food. And most recently, the Crozins and Gors invaded and destroyed his home planet.

Survite postured, baring his fangs. "Captain Boo, muzzle self. Gor, my guest and ally!"

Atue understood Boo's trepidation, but controlling his anger would not be easy. On the flip side, the hissing Gor had cause to defend itself too. Dare say, when a half Gystfin Trekachaw loses self-control; it's a grisly scene. Atue spoke up, hoping his diplomatic intervention would distract from the volatile situation.

"Welcome aboard. Let's start over with introductions. I am Captain Atue, and this is Captain Boo. We welcome our new allies." He directed his question to the flower. "And how may I address you?"

Captain Survite purposely cleared his throat, which was his way of telling Atue to be silent. The gnarly old Gystfin relaxed his upper lip and began talking.

"No translator chip for flowers. Unique language complex as Umduls. Ersatz failed—Umduls design prototype. I advocate for my Gor, Klop, and flower. Captain Pify informed Crozins enslaved Gors. Why necessary I explain Gor's allegiance? Do you question Captain Pify? Captain Pify plus first Gor, Olypo, reason Gystfins survive. Gors sacrifice by thousands. Crozin-led bolshevism servitude death when disobedient. Tyranny concurs galaxy and beyond. Past gone, we unite, act as one. Understand—Captain Pify, Gors, and Survite join forces on Trinite."

Survite pointed at Klop. "Crozin slave Gor 579114; Umduls removed exoskeletal Gor tag. My Gor from old generation. Captain Pify's reverse transfusion frees Gors to defect. Gors with flowers support natural harmony. Flower called Ikiniku is prominent Mejou. Planet Shirai is what flowers call Trinite.

"Mejou flowers mortal enemy Cerbalus spider on planet. Same look, not same Drutgak spider indigenous on planet Gardux; five times size. Gors hunt spiders, prefer meat. To Gor, better than chewy Gystfin. Rude words, good news. Unknown how Mejou flowers and Gors communicate. Strange sounds, not words. Flowers reap Gors' Cerbalus spider appetite. Natural harmony." Gystfin Survite rubbed his leg and sat down on a container. Boo and Atue knew most of Survite's information, but neither cared to interrupt.

After calming down from the shock of a hissing Gor and Mejou flower, Boo noticed Survite's fur and clothes were disheveled. He looked thin and older than expected. His aging body was a disadvantage, but his wisdom was invaluable. He was one of only a few Gystfin Kogbors alive. The Gystfins had suffered more losses in the recent war than all the other species combined.

Being half Gystfin, Boo felt the loss and was sad that he would never see his home planet again. He'd miss the thrill of climbing steep mountain cliffs to the crest, where he looked down at the layers of vivid green jungles. That thick, humid air growing up as a young Gystfin made him strong. Gardux was quite beautiful, and the thought of evil Crozins spreading their filth sickened Boo. He vowed to find a way and rescue Gystfins who may have survived the invasion. In truth, returning to Gardux was unlikely. The Crozin planet was on the same side of the galaxy and in close proximity.

Boo sat next to Survite. "Heard from Captain Pify since battleship entered war zone?"

Survite appeared to be frowning, which could mean nothing because it had been like that since he got there. "Cannot understand Pify. Trekachaw Phera translate. Phera says war now our favor. High cost. Trekachaws die seizing Crozin battleships. Phera brief, preparing hyperbaric shock wave to stop advancing Crozins."

Survite tilted his head, listening to the transponder in his ear. He stood up and motioned for Klop and Ikiniku to follow him. Survite spun around and said nothing until whoever was talking in his ear finished.

"Captain Pify transmit clash, I go. You repair battleship fast. Gor V-Jak fighter jets protect the sector. Do not engage V-Jaks with frequency FIOXRAD 6000. Must use code, ship to ship."

Atue thanked Survite. "One question before you go. Why did you request no Ryquats down here?"

Survite spoke earnestly, "Flowers insist no Ryquats here. No Ryquats on Trinite. Ryquats ate them. Don't forget; they won't. Must go, fend Captain Pify." He walked over to Boo and placed his open hand on Boo's chest. Boo bowed his head and put his open hand on Survite's chest. The feud between them was over.

# eleven

# CRESCENT BE THY HARBOR

**The Umdul Language:**

КЗОЖКОNYВ DO

BHIEYI HIEЗDIЗ

**WHY** Pify insisted on the Kiki battleship being a priority made no sense to Victis. Azha agreed. If the moon coordinates were not exact, they'd hikari speed to the Trinite war zone.

Akio asked Victis to come over to his station. According to the rondure trajectory, the moon should soon be visible on the bridge monitor. What came into view was a crescent, not a moon. Being in the path of asteroids for eons had etched deep, pitted craters shaping the moon into a dark, barren rock. Why the Crozins would hide a Kiki battleship in such a volatile place was suspicious. There had to be more to this story. Possibly another hoax that Narthex and Myosis concocted to distract them from the war? Rather than risk his battleship, Victis would check it out in energy.

"Hold your course mark 8-35 and stay out of hyperbaric range. Azha and I will let you know if it's a Crozin trap. While I'm gone, you're proxy in command. Akio, above all, protect my ship—Keijo-alert lockdown."

Soaring through space felt good. A freedom that only a Trekachaw could know. Victis reflected on his brief life as a Ryquat compared to a Trekachaw. He almost died, never knowing what he would have missed. But at the time, Azha decided for him. Azha found a wise, old Quizan who chose to merge with him on death's door. If not, he would be but a memory. He cherished Zygo's soul; they were the perfect match.

Quite the opposite, Victis worried about Azha; he stole his Human soul. From the looks of it, Cole would never find peace. But life is not always what is fair or just. Sometimes you do the best you can with what you have. Azha was an excellent example of fortitude. And Victis respected that.

Azha hesitated when they reached the crescent moon. Victis circled back. "What are you doing?" Azha seemed reluctant to enter the craters.

"This doesn't feel right, Victis. Nothing about the Crozins leaving a Kiki battleship here feels right. Aren't you the least bit suspicious?"

"Yeah, I'm suspicious; I never trust anything a Crozin says or thinks. But we're here, and Pify sent us for a reason. Let's check it out so we can head back, all right? You worry too much, Azha."

Azha flickered in protest, and Victis led the way. They flew slowly into fissures and crevices, lighting the rocky surfaces along the way. Deep inside the abyss, they found caves and catacombs that intertwined. It wasn't long before they became disoriented. At every turn, they questioned if they had just been that way.

Ahead, they saw a rainbow of shimmering colors appear. It was beautiful how it reflected against the jagged walls of the catacombs. Inside was a Kiki battleship, waiting to be rescued. They had found the ship, but what of the crew? Witnessing the victims of Crozin cruelty was always dismal.

True to their nature, the Crozins left behind a trail of bloodshed. Dozens of Kikis in the corridors were sliced and mangled. They were in such a killing frenzy that they didn't consider or simply forgot an important detail: the

Kikis' unique battleships require a minimum number of live bio scans to engage the ship.

Victis and Azha headed for the bridge. It was worse. Feathers and body parts were strewn everywhere. Their arms and legs had been ripped from their bodies. Some even had their beaks bitten off. The Kikis had been brutally tortured. And the Crozins took their sweet time killing them. Seeing this was a grim reminder not to be captured.

A shock wave crossed the bridge and ended with a boom. A split second later, a hard jolt shook the battleship, followed by another blast. A barrage of explosions hammered the Kiki battleship where the catacomb did not protect it.

Akio broke Keijo silence. "Six Crozin Jager-Ki jets fired lasers on your coordinates. Threats eliminated, six disintegrated. Sensors detect no Tajat Rakta Crozin battleships in this sector. Confirm your status."

"We are aboard the Kiki bridge, *ansen' na tabi endo dens.* Stand by."

Only a few Kikis on the bridge survived the Crozin attacks. One of them recognized Victis and chirped to get his attention. The Crozins had taken their time, pulling out almost every feather and slicing his skin with their long claws. Without medical attention, he would die. Victis asked how he could help. The bird whispered, "Cargo deck five, Kikis are hiding. Cifrons are there, Kiki doctors. I'll rest until you return." His eyes closed.

If Victis remembered correctly, deck five is at the front end of the battleship's stern. Given enough time, the Crozins would have found the hidden Kikis. That is, if it weren't for an unexpected twist. Myosis had planned on breaking Narthex out of detention. But then, Phera showed up. The faux pas was telling Narthex about Thude's murder and the location of the Kiki battleship.

Still, more than half of the crew were slaughtered before the Crozins realized what they had done. The birds sacrificed themselves to ensure the Crozins could not engage the battleship's biosensors. Of course, that angered the Crozins. They took pleasure in forcing Thude to watch as they tortured her bridge crew.

The hidden Kikis must have been watching Victis and Azha on a closed circuit because dozens of them ran onto the bridge moments later. The injured Kiki opened his eyes and grinned. "Now, we'll make the Crozins pay for killing Thude."

Several Cifron Kikis whisked the valiant warrior off the bridge. They moved fast, zipping about the stations to repair the ship. Victis asked several Kikis zipping by who was in charge. Zilch—he got nothing—not a glance, not a word, those onara birds.

Victis ran out of patience and grabbed a Kiki by the neck as it whooshed by him. "Who can answer my questions?"

The Kiki squawked and pecked Victis in the face. "Let go! Watoto is Mikado Thude's adjutant."

Victis flicked the bird's beak. "Fine, where's Watoto?"

Azha reached over and smoothed the Kiki's feathers with his hand, then asked nicely, "Where can we find Watoto?"

"Don't touch me! The mean one already spoke to Watoto," he chirped, pointing at Victis.

Victis scowled at the Kiki. "Well, Watoto is no longer here. So, who do I talk to?"

"Watoto is not dead! Go ask Watoto!"

Azha nicely asked the next question, "Where did they take Watoto?"

"Follow Bibet!" screeched the angry Kiki.

"And may I ask, what is your name?"

"You may. Tubet," squawked Tubet, pointing up at Victis again.

Azha tried not to grin. "Thank you, Tubet. We shall follow Bibet."

"I've had enough of these birds," grumbled Victis, glaring down at Tubet.

Bibet fluffed her feathers and led the way. Down one corridor, then another, and another, they walked behind her. Four, maybe five times, Victis forgot to step lightly and bounced up, hitting his head on the ceiling. But who's counting? Azha was. He had bounced more than a couple of times himself. The low gravity was not funny anymore.

Twenty minutes later, Victis figured out Bibet had led them around in circles. Finally, Victis got it. She was flirting with Azha and didn't want it to end. Azha was dumbfounded and had no idea how to react to the flirty bird.

No surprise, Azha's predicament amused Victis. He'd let this drama ride out a little longer. It was worth watching Azha squirm.

Fluffing her feathers to get his attention, she'd pause and gaze up at him, cooing and blinking her eyes. Azha's stripes had turned some weird turquoise color. Without being offensive, he was desperately trying not to encourage her. But the jig was up. And though she would've liked to continue the charade, they had arrived at the infirmary.

With a seductive look and a melodramatic one-finger touch, Bibet pressed the button and sashayed sideways, making way for them to enter the room. Watoto appeared much better, and he was sitting up in a swing cot of some sort. He waved at them to come over, assuring the Cifrons it was okay.

Bibet fluffed and plumed her tail feathers, cooing for Azha to bend over so she could whisper in his ear. Distracted by her seductive teasing, Victis and Watoto stopped talking to watch. Whatever she told him made him blush in all kinds of colors. Victis would find out later what she said to make him blush Trekachaw style. Whatever she said had to be good.

Watoto choked a bit when he realized what she was doing. "Bibet! You're shameless. Stop courting Azha."

Bibet's beak twisted, and she frowned with a pretentious glare before storming out of the room.

"My apologies, Azha. Bibet is broody and preening. She is smitten and wants you for her mate. I'll make sure she doesn't bother you anymore. Enough about Bibet. What about my ship?"

Of course, Victis had that familiar wise-guy smirk on his face. And it would be impossible for him not to tell an irritating joke. But, to Azha's surprise, Victis did not.

"As much as I enjoy this Bibet crush for Azha, I need to know how we can help you get your battleship on its way."

Watoto swung the cot around to face Victis. "Captain Pify is the reason you're here, correct?"

"Yes, that's correct."

"I will let you in on a well-kept secret. All Kiki mikados have one trusted confidant with the code to their battleship biosensors. Captain Pify was Thude's confidant. Now that the ship is secure, Pify will give you the code. After you enter it, you must change it. From then on, you will be my confidant. Never tell anyone but me the new code. If your death is imminent, pass the code to someone you trust and have them contact me. Go to the bridge and request the code from Captain Pify. I will meet you there to assist in the process." Watoto motioned for a Cifron to help with a waft.

Despite all the safeguards of a Kiki battleship, such as an AI with memories and emotions that only specialized Kiki engineers understood, Victis did not trust the communication systems. The Crozins may have compromised the artificial intelligence software with their technology. Until he knew otherwise, the battleship was not secure.

"I'm returning to my ship to retrieve the code. It shouldn't take me too long. Azha will accompany you to your bridge, where I'll meet you with the code." Before Watoto could resist, Victis flashed into energy and disappeared.

By now, Akio thought a Trekachaw's energy streaking into the bridge would not startle him, but he jumped anyway. "Welcome back, Captain."

Victis morphed into body form, sitting in his chair. "Ship to ship, advise Captain Pify; I need a secure line to ascertain information."

Akio received a disturbing response: "Captain Pify unavailable. Crozin Tajat Rakta engaged besiege. Jager-Ki intercepts engage strikes at Umdul battleship. Will advise when available." Transmission ended.

Victis felt numb; even if he left now, he would not make it back in time. Pify was second to none during warfare, but even the best can succumb when outnumbered.

Akio shouted, "Captain Victis, I have a secure line." Victis entered a binary sequence on the console of his chair to activate a frequency that only he could hear. "Transmit code."

An Umdul spoke, "Confirm once received." Akio turned in his chair and stared at Victis. He looked scared.

Victis listened to the message again. Umduls were screaming, and Captain Pify was shouting. Laser blasts drowned out the voices; these were familiar sounds of a battleship in combat. The transmission failed, and in the silence that followed was dread. Victis could only hope that if Pify were to fall, Phera would be by his side. Neither one was whole without the other.

Victis waited for a response; he tried again, no response. Whatever else was necessary to get the Kikis on their way, it had better be quick. Victis flashed into energy and flew out of his ship toward the Kiki battleship. Victis would give Watoto the code. After that, they were on their own.

# twelve

# OLD SALT

**The Umdul Language:**
ILIT ЖELIB

**PIFY** waddle-ran over to navigation and sat next to his best Umdul pilot. He wanted to assist with the ambush. As planned, Pify had all systems shut down, making it look like they were out of commission. The captain of the lead Crozin battleship took the bait and closed in for the kill.

The narcissistic Ukaru couldn't resist it when he saw the famous Captain Pify's battleship alone and powerless on the perimeter of the war zone. When he broke ranks, that weakened the Crozins' strong front. The Ukaru made another grave mistake. He assumed this would be an easy kill and did not use basic defense protocol. The arrogance of the Ukaru is what Pify was counting on, and the old salt was not disappointed.

Pify's son Captain Jifney and twenty Trekachaws waited out of sensor range until the Crozin battleship had no means of escape. The new Umdul friction-energy battleships were twice as fast and could fly circles around the Ukaru's battleship. Indeed, the Ukaru was blind to his impending dire situation.

The old salt transmitted a message to the Ukaru: "Foolish Crozin, submit or perish. Offering one to live, second to vanish. Death awaits. Wise to accept."

The Ukaru demanded a ship-to-ship visual. Pify opened channels and listened to what he had to say just in case he had misjudged the Ukaru's intent. But there was no mistake. The Ukaru sat at the helm, boasting, "Ask yourself, Captain Pify, who's the fool? I will conquer you and this galaxy. You submit, not me. My V-Jaks and Jager-Kis surround your ship, old fool," mocked the Ukaru.

Unbeknownst to the self-righteous Ukaru, the Gor V-Jaks were allies of Pify and part of the ambush. The Trekachaws had already killed his Crozin pilots and commandeered their Jager-Kis. The jets were Pify's sword to wield. And soon enough, so would the Ukaru's battleship.

The Ukaru transmitted orders for the jets to fire on Pify's battleship. His nose split to display his contempt. But to his dismay, the jet pilots did not respond. The old salt couldn't help but chuckle and snort when the Ukaru's nose slapped close and twisted, enraged by their insolence.

Pify cut the visual. He regretted what was about to transpire, but the time had come. This was war, and the Ukaru was beyond redemption. Pify signaled Captain Jifney to ready position for the ambush. Then, with all his skills and wisdom, the old salt flew his Umdul battleship across space toward the underbelly of the Crozin Tajat Rakta battleship.

The Crozins fired a hyperbaric shock wave followed by laser strikes. Pify banked hard starboard, clearing the incoming shock wave, and circled back, dodging the laser strikes. At full hikari speed, the Umdul ship flew over the Crozin battleship taunting the Ukaru into the trap.

Captain Jifney was staged and waiting to sterilize the enemy. The two battleships passed the point of no return, and a blue beam crossed the path of the Crozin battleship. The Ukaru and his crew ceased to exist in a matter of seconds.

The Umdul crew snorted, squealed victory, and bounced across the bridge in celebration. Captain Pify sighed and slowly stood up. He had not grown too old to fight but had grown old enough to regret the fight.

"Death torments. Haunt those who prevail. Phantom evil takes, bequest virtue of one's spirit."

Pify was a hundred and ninety-four years old. His heart was failing, and the mental stress of wars had taken its toll. Before meeting Phera, he planned to resign and spend his senior years on Opus with his three wives and eight scion heirs. He cherished his wives, but love was seldom the reason to pali-otos. Propagating scion heirs was the priority. But in his twilight years, he found Phera, the love of his life. The thought of not being with her broke his heart. If only a Quizan would merge with him, he could spend centuries with her. But for whatever reason, not a single Quizan was willing.

Today was a good day for Pify because evil did not win. Besides, the crew's joy was infectious. Pify smiled and belted out his song: *"Umduls, we do celebrate. Pluck those Crozins out of space. Can't run from yer fate; we will exterminate."*

The old salt bounced ever so slightly to the music as he shuffled back to his captain's chair and hugged Phera. Watching Pify made Phera laugh. He was by far the funniest, brightest, and kindest creature she'd ever met.

Vopar, Clyde, and Zeta joined the Human Trekachaws that had boarded the wayward Crozin battleship. They had to act fast; the ship was in the direct path of a meteor shower. Vopar morphed into body form as he slid into the pilot's chair. Nothing was coded or damaged, making it easy for him to fly the battleship.

Ship to ship, Vopar transmitted, "Captain Pify, I am in control."

Pify transmitted the same words that Victis always said to him, *"Anzen'na tabi.* Safe journey, my friends." He watched their new Trojan horse veer toward the battlefront.

Pify patted Phera's hand and adjusted his chair. "Caw-caw Crozin junk ship to Opus hasten behest. Spruce for cohort Gor Olypo," transmitted Pify.

Vopar shrugged his shoulders at Clyde and Zeta. "Did you understand any of that?"

Zeta shook her head no. Clyde was thinking out loud. "Sorta?"

"Well then, what did he say?" Zeta asked, surprised.

"I think he said fly the ship to Opus for repairs instead of Trinite. And a Gor called Olypo gets the ship. Not sure about where we go from there?"

Vopar transmitted, "Confirm battleship to Opus. Pending orders?"

Pify chuckled. "Unfettered Trekachaws embrace vital befall. Chary way paved, Opus promptly expecting nasty bird."

"Clyde, did you understand that? Didn't Pify get a new translator chip?" Vopar asked, baffled.

Clyde nodded. "Yep, got a new chip. But he sounds the same to me."

Zeta's stripes were turning a woozy blue. "I'm glad you understand him. All I hear is, *Blah, fetter caw-caw, nasty bird?* Can't the rest of you smell the Crozin stench left behind? The whole ship stinks. It's making me sick."

Clyde and Vopar agreed it was terrible. The sooner they depart, the sooner they can get off that battleship. Full speed ahead, they set coordinates to Opus.

VICTIS WAS GROWING SHORTER ON patience by the minute. And the Kikis were taking their sweet time repairing their battleship. If he couldn't confirm Pify's status, they were leaving.

"Akio, contact Pify. If you can't raise him, try every battleship from Opus to Trinite. I want confirmation right now!"

Pify acknowledged Akio's transmission. "Plethora relay. Phera amend status at bay."

Hearing Pify's voice was a blessing. "You had me worried. The last thing I heard was Umduls screaming. What happened?"

Phera leaned over and kissed Pify's cheek. He smiled and opened communications so she could talk.

"Victis, it was great! They weren't screaming; the crew was cheering and bouncing. You know that little dance they do? Watching the Umduls makes me laugh so hard I hurt. I wish you could have been here. Not one casualty, and we sterilized the lead Crozin battleship. Pify and the Umduls are amazing. Anyway, enough bragging. The Crozins figured out there's a Gor resistance. A Gor spy contacted us just before you did. He said the Crozins are outraged and have vowed death to all Gors involved and their families for as long as it takes. I can't wait until the Crozins figure out we have a transfusion to counter their five-year injection.

"Also, Olypo told Pify that every V-Jak Gor pilot who came here under Crozin control has refused to go back. They've joined the resistance on Trinite. He warned us that since the Crozins failed to take Trinite, they're in a mass exodus to Zaurak. We need you and the Kiki battleship to return to Zaurak immediately. Pify and Jifney's battleships are faster and can rendezvous with you at Zaurak before the Crozins can get there. Captain Pubney and five other battleships are currently at Zaurak, but they won't be able to hold off the Crozins for long.

"One more thing, the Gystfins have no food resources on Trinite and are forced to leave. As you well know, there's nothing worse than a hungry Gystfin. Kogbor Survite will contact you regarding locations Pify arranged for the Gystfins to settle on Zaurak. In the meantime, Pify supplied the Gystfins with a food supplement. We both know the Ryquats will not understand this decision. But we need them just as much as they need us. Remind everyone how hard the Gystfins work; that should make them think twice. *Anzen'na tabi!*" Phera ended the transmission.

VICTIS MET WITH AZHA AND Watoto on the engineering deck regarding the Umduls' victory at Trinite. And Pify's request to rendezvous with them at Zaurak. For some reason, Watoto did not care to comment on the positive news.

"Am I the only Kiki battleship?"

"Why?" asked Victis, telling himself not to assume the worst. He knew the Kikis had made a deal with the Crozins behind Pify's back. What made no sense was why the Crozins assassinated Thude. But he'd like to know.

Victis got to the point, "We need to go."

"My engineers have not completed repairs." Watoto was nervous and stalling.

"How much longer?"

"Why should we engage Crozins to protect Zaurak? Kikis do not regard Ryquats as allies. That is Umdul choice," chirped Watoto.

Victis's suspicions were correct. The ungrateful Kikis would have died if not for Pify.

He felt his stripes turning red. "I don't care who you do or don't regard. I saved you and this ship from the Crozins. Fight with us or against us. I give you three minutes to decide."

Watoto's feathers ruffled, and he stretched his neck to make himself look menacing. "Is that how you negotiate? Kikis don't take well to threats. Why should we die for Ryquats? Answer that question, and I'll answer yours."

Victis's yellow eyes narrowed, glaring down at Watoto. "Thude made that mistake and died. The Trekachaws and Umduls do not fight for Ryquats alone; we fight against the Crozins to protect this galaxy. We lose, and your galaxy is next. Until now, we have been your allies, but that ends if you don't fight in this war. I answered your question; now answer mine."

Watoto's feathers smoothed. "You speak wisely. I can see Captain Pify has taught you well. But you need to improve your delivery."

Watoto was going to be a pain in his rear. "Quid pro quo. I find you obnoxious and manipulative, and your opinions are grandiose. One question.

How long before your ship is ready? And from now on, you contact me, not Captain Pify," Victis scowled.

"Concur, lizard. My ship's repaired," hissed Watoto.

Victis resented the ungrateful Watoto. How Pify managed a diplomatic relationship with the Kikis was remarkable. It seemed Pify could charm anyone.

During their heated debate, Bibet snuck into engineering, looking for Azha. She perched atop a stair lift to get a clear view of everyone. Every so often, she'd wave at Azha and fluff her feathers. Azha tried not to encourage her, but Bibet was impossible to ignore.

Azha asked himself, *Where does she think this is going?* Look at her. She's relentless, even after being ordered to stop flirting. She's cute, but that's it. A relationship between a Trekachaw and Kiki could never happen. But then, who'd guess Phera and Pify would find love? Maybe he shouldn't be so narrow-minded. Phera had pointed out that supposed flaw in him more than a couple of times. And surprisingly, his Human half, Cole, liked the little bird.

Azha waved back at her before turning into energy. She chirped, giggled, and flapped her wings to bid him farewell. Victis was so angry at Watoto that he didn't notice Azha circling her before flying into space. Azha told himself he'd talk to her if they ever crossed paths again.


CAPTAIN PIFY AND JIFNEY WERE already between Trinite and Opus. Even if Victis flew at hikari speed, Pify would reach Zaurak before he could.

Akio received a ship-to-ship transmission from Pify: "Watoto fret sought intervention. Kikis demurred quarrelsomely. Unite concertedly."

"Confirm. Are you saying we stay here near the moon?" asked Victis.

*"Uketotta!"* transmitted Pify.

Victis assumed Watoto had contacted Pify to complain. Therefore, Watoto didn't listen when he said not to. So be it; the bird was not worth the aggravation.

Watoto was dragging his chovo feet to have an excuse not to go. But the Kiki battleship came alive, and he had to launch. It shimmered iridescent colors and snaked in and out of the moon's lunar tubes finding a path into deep space. As much as Victis didn't want to be impressed, he was mesmerized by its beauty.

Watoto and Victis were waiting for Pify, side by side. Their ships were nothing alike. The contrast was as apparent as their differences in opinions. If ever there were an awkward moment, this was it. Neither one wanted to be there.

They didn't have to wait long. Captain Pify and Jifney's battleship streaked across space toward them. Someday, Victis would ask Pify to retrofit his battleship with the latest Umdul friction energy. But for now, his ship was the next best in space.

Pify opened a view monitor to update and answer questions before departing. Watoto's arrogance was astounding. Before Pify could get a word in edgewise, he insisted on being addressed as Mikado Watoto, and that a Kiki battleship fleet is called a pasha. To top that, he required a Jagnar's approval before flying to Zaurak.

Phera sounded irritated. "Trekachaw Phera speaking. I will answer your questions and address your demands as per Captain Pify's request. Umduls recognize you as a Mikado and a Kiki fleet as pasha. However, others have no obligation to do so. The Crozins destroyed Thude's pasha. Therefore, you have no pasha. You are under no obligation to assist us. However, the trek to your galaxy will be dangerous. The Crozins occupy that sector. You are one ship flying alone. That is not wise unless you deviate and navigate in uncharted space. Standby; Captain Pify wishes to speak."

Victis and Azha spoke at the same time, "Can't wait to hear this!"

Akio spun around in his navigation chair and smiled.

Phera opened the view monitor. "Mikado Watoto. Captain Pify wishes you a safe journey. Being inexperienced, you should refrain from engaging in this level of warfare. Captain Pify will contact Trinite Gors and request an escort through their sector. However, Pify recommends you wait it out near Opus. Furthermore, Captain Pify will advise your planet Kowok and the appropriate Jagnars regarding Thude's death and your location. We await your response."

Dead silence. Surprise, surprise, how would Watoto react to being rejected?

Phera transmitted, "What is your decision?"

Watoto did not look well. He cut the live monitor and transmitted, "Contacting Kowok and Jagnars unnecessary. As Thude's adjutant, I respect the long-standing relationship with Captain Pify. I request to join the Umdul fleet and continue to Zaurak."

The other battleships listened in on the conversation with bated breath.

Phera transmitted, "Captain Pify has reconsidered; he welcomes your request. Your flight position will trail Captain Victis to Zaurak. Both battleships will land near Cape Parrish to engage in ground warfare upon arrival. The Crozins have reclaimed the city. Extinguish them before reinforcements arrive. Captain Victis is in command, with you being second in command. Captain Pify requires an answer regarding the status of your rank."

Victis's mouth dropped, and he cursed in Japanese, *"Ahoka! Baka yarou baka warugaki. Nai, nai, nai."*

A few of those Earthly Japanese words were new. "Sounds like you've been expanding your vocabulary," laughed Azha.

"I saved the *goman mueki tori* from the Crozins, and now I'm stuck babysitting him. This stinks," growled Victis.

"Huh, care to share what you said in Japanese?" smiled Azha.

"What do you care as long as I'm not cussing?" scowled Victis.

Watoto transmitted, "Captain Pify, I agree with your terms. If I may, can I transfer an experienced coveys as my liaison? Perhaps she can educate the crude lizard about our refined traditions. Presently, his respect is lacking. I offer her in all sincerity."

Phera sounded surprised. "Captain Pify agrees; however, Captain Victis must accept your offer."

Victis rolled his eyes at Azha. "What do you think?"

Azha didn't know what to say. But for selfish reasons, he was hoping Bibet was the diplomat.

Azha asked Victis to ask Watoto who he was sending. "No, I will not," barked Victis, shaking his head at Azha.

Victis transmitted, "I agree with the transfer. Docking bay eight, stand by for shuttle entry."

Watoto's reply, "May our differences lessen, and our united forces prevail. Bibet volunteered. She is at the end of molting and has vowed not to molest Azha. Do you accept her as my Kiki liaison?"

Without asking Azha, Victis smiled. "I welcome Bibet. I will treat her as one of my own."

Watoto seemed genuine. "As one, we are powerful and will defeat the Crozin affliction."

Victis had second thoughts; he may have been wrong to judge Watoto so harshly. Of course, talk is cheap. He'd take the high road and try to keep an open mind.

Bibet's transport docked as Azha and Victis rushed into the bay to meet the new crew member. The shuttle was fascinating. It shimmered and snaked like the Kiki battleship. The long cylindrical body was nothing like any craft in this galaxy. On the way back to the bridge, Victis thought how strange the technology was a mere thirty million light-years away.

Pify announced the final countdown. The battleships engaged, and Victis gave the order: "On to Zaurak. Watch your six, Kiki!"

HUNDREDS OF JETS AND BATTLESHIPS shadowed Cape Parrish as they flew over the grim destruction below. Victis felt a knot tighten in his stomach. Seeing the devastated city before did not make it any easier to see it again. Memories of Vexy and Connie came to mind. Like this city, they were in his past. A life that was fading into a dream. If he thought about it too long, he'd go to a dark place that would consume him with hate and guilt. They had come so far. A new future was within reach. That thought brought hope. And with that, understanding his role was a means to an end. Green fields were ahead, untouched by the spoils of war. Whatever the sacrifice, Zaurak must not fall to the Crozins.

Rigdan and Steve were waiting on the field in front of their Mic-12 jets. What a sight for sore eyes. Victis wasn't the least bit surprised they had beaten the odds again. They were resilient and as tough as they came.

Victis ran down the ramp. Azha, Bibet, and Akio followed but came to a screeching halt halfway down. Painful-looking chest bumps and slaps on the back were not inviting to them. Bibet was stiff, wide-eyed, and she quietly tiptoed behind Azha to peek out.

The war was still brutal, if Steve and Rigdan were any indication. They were thin, unshaven, and their uniforms had seen better days. After the hoorah rush, Steve lost his vigor, and his long face returned.

"If you've already heard any of this, tell me. Boo contacted me about the Gystfins. You were rescuing a Kiki battleship. And Pify was ambushing a Crozin battleship while negotiating with the Mejous and Gors. Busy Umdul, wouldn't you say? This is what I know. The Gystfins are in transit a day or two out on a cargo ship. Boo and Atue are with Kogbor Serlof, Tysug, and Survite. Pify sanctioned the northern continents here on Zaurak as their new home. I heard the Gystfins have nothing to eat on Trinite. They tried to eat the Cerbalus giant spider, but it made them sick. I guess the Gors hunt and eat the spiders. It turns out the only enemy of flowers is spiders. Not much else on the planet to eat. Boo said there was another problem. The flowers think the Gystfins' odor smells bad. Guess with all that considered, Pify relocated the Gystfins here. Ya know, it's not a bad idea. Half of the Ryquats population is gone. Zaurak is in ruins, and we could use the help to rebuild. Can't argue there's not plenty of room on the planet. Atue went over our laws with the Gystfins. They agreed to comply and wanted to prove their worthiness as loyal citizens. Sounds good if you ask me. Boo said if we don't take the Gystfins in, they'll have to leave this galaxy. They don't have the resources to do that. And they can't return to their world as long as the Crozins control that sector.

"Now for the wagsham of all wagshams. Here goes. That traitor captain called Smyth contacted us a couple of days ago. He claims a Crozin Ukaru warned him and the Viceroys on Earth to leave. Supposedly, they're coming back to Zaurak to occupy the planet. After that, they'll invade Earth. I thought all the Viceroys were dead. Guess not. They slithered off to Earth. I asked Smyth why he'd help us now. And if he meant it, give me the names and locations of the Viceroys on Earth. He said he would tell you. He told me to tell you something else. It didn't make any sense to me, but Smyth said you'd understand. Choan is alive and contained. Smyth wants to trade Choan for his safe passage and return to Zaurak."

Victis looked surprised. That was the best news he'd heard for a while. "Choan is a Trekachaw and a lot more to me. If Smyth contacts you again, tell him he is welcome on Zaurak and find out where he is going. Lie. Do whatever it takes to get information out of him and contact me immediately."

"He also claims the Viceroys are still communicating with the Crozins on Zaurak. Supposedly, our shuttles were used to transport more Crozins to Cape Parrish. Thousands of them. Smyth swore that's all he knew. He might be telling the truth. He thinks the Ukarus will kill him and the Viceroys once they are of no use to them. He sounded scared.

"If it helps you, I do believe the story about the Crozins. I just lost more Ops in Cape Parrish, thinking we had cleared them out. If the Ukarus don't kill the traitors first, we need to do it."

Victis pictured how proud Vexy was when elected to the council. He never thought, in a million years, the members would sell out to the Crozins. But they did and still are. As much as he would've liked to have enjoyed the serenity of the green fields for a while longer, he had questions that could not wait.

"Steve, did you get any hints of where the Viceroys or Smyth could be hiding on Earth?"

"No. He wants to talk to you about a deal." Steve moaned, trying not to draw any attention when he shifted his weight to ease the pain from a wound days old.

"Okay. Give me an estimate of how many Ops and Crozins are in Cape Parrish. And can we wait for everyone else to arrive before giving your Ops support?" asked Victis.

"They can't wait. The last count earlier today, thirty-eight Ops are hunkered down in the heart of downtown Cape Parrish. They're low on lasers and won't survive if we don't get them out tonight. The best time to go in is just after sundown. As you know, the Crozins' night vision is poor. That gives us a slight advantage. After we get the Ops out, about fifty stranded civilians are on the top floor of a high-rise building on the north side of the city. The stranded Ops were trying to rescue the civilians when they got ambushed. One more thing, do you know where Akio might be?" Steve shifted his weight to his other leg.

Akio heard his name and got up. He had been resting on the grass behind a jet. "Hey, Steve, over here. Did you miss me?"

"Are you hiding back there? Get over here. I have some good news for you. I would've told you this before if I'd known who your wife was. Mya and your two boys have been with an Op I know since the first attack at Cape Parrish. I can vouch for him. His name is Mark Keller. They were on an Umdul battleship for about a day, but then transported here. We thought the city was safe. Your wife and boys might be with the group we're rescuing tonight. Don't worry. We'll find them if they're not with that group," assured Steve.

Victis never saw Akio show this much emotion. His face was white, and he had a hard time standing. Azha caught him as his knees buckled. The shock of confirming Mya and his two boys were alive was too much to take.

As fast as Akio dropped, he struggled to stand. Azha helped steady him until he felt better. Victis waited until Azha let go to give the order. Akio was not going with them. He was too emotional.

"Akio, you're staying with your daughter on the battleship until we know more. I need you to take care of my ship while I'm gone. Let Captain Pify know what we're doing and that I'll return as soon as I can. I won't transmit, nor should you, unless it is crucial. The Crozins can use our transmissions to locate us. Come to think of it, that gives me a great idea. I want you to transmit fake messages all over the city to confuse the Crozins. That should keep them busy," grinned Victis.

Akio pushed Azha away. "I'm not going back to the ship! That's my wife and two boys out there. I need to eat, that's all." Akio was putting on a tough act even though his legs were still wobbly.

"No, you're not. I can't take the chance of you jeopardizing the rest of us. Have Pax check you. Trust me; it's better this way. I need you to take care of my ship. Can you do that?" Victis's tone meant it was final.

From the corner of his eye, Victis took a double take when he saw Kigen sitting on the nose of Steve's Mic-12 jet. "Kigen, get down from there! What are you doing here?" yelled Victis.

Kigen stepped off the jet's nose and glided over to Victis. The young pureblood Trekachaw was enormous, with brilliant stripes and piercing blue eyes. Victis would never admit it, but Kigen was intimidating.

"The Crozins killed my papay. Captain Pify told me I had to learn from you to hunt them. I think he worries too much. Myosis tried to kill me. He failed. I saved Phera from Myosis, or she'd be dead. I can do things no one else can. You know, accepting or refusing rules is my choice. No one can force me. I listen to Phera, Pify, and my manany only because I want to." Kigen stared down at Victis.

Victis's stripes flashed red. "Being defiant is immature and annoying. You annoy me. That attitude will isolate you from others. I know about your encounter with Myosis and that you were brave. But you were also lucky. You're not impervious to lasers. Feeling the slice of a laser is not the same as seeing someone else cut by one. Fearing death makes you sharp and stronger. Believing you're invincible makes you reckless. I will not sacrifice others so you can boast superiority. Before you embarrass yourself further, change your attitude or leave, I don't care. If I allow you to stay, I am your captain. My team, my rules, no exceptions, understood?"

Kigen took a step back and noticed they were not alone. "Understood."

"Akio, find out if Pify, Phera, or Deneb knows he's here. A no is one click. A yes is three clicks." Victis glared at Kigen.

Akio nodded and walked away to his jet. He was shocked to see how big Kigen was and that he spoke like an adult. Not all that long ago, the purebred was a child. Akio engaged the shuttle and rose above Zaurak. As much as he hated it, he knew Victis was right. In war, arrogance, emotions, or desperation cannot be tolerated.

# thirteen

# CAPE PARRISH DO OR DIE



**CAPTAIN** Pify preferred that Kigen learn the meaning of fortitude from Victis. The problem was, he wasn't sure if Victis would be willing to take on the mischievous Trekachaw. Phera suggested it first. She had tried to discipline him, but the young purebred wouldn't listen. Kigen's behavior was tiresome, and he lacked respect. After Kigen saved her, Phera told Pify she could not ask him to follow the rules. If he had listened to her that day, she'd be dead. They agreed Victis was best suited to enforce tough love.

Victis heard three clicks. He would have rather heard one. But it was three. Victis told Kigen he could stay if he understood the rules. No one there was his babysitter, and to keep his attitude in check. Follow his command or go back to the ship. Kigen's grandiose attitude toward Steve and Rigdan didn't last long either.

Kigen's nasty smirk at Steve was all it took. "I'll only tell you this once. None of us will die for you. Now get in line and don't crowd me. Standing over the top of me shows just how stupid you are. Being tall does not impress anyone. Tall is a target. Your melon will be the first to get lasered. Know this, until you prove you're worthy, you're nothing but a pain in the ass," Steve barked as he motioned at Kigen to get away from him.

Since no one respected the cocky kid, Kigen wound up trailing the pack. He thought about leaving, but pride and Victis kept him there. No one fought better than Victis or knew the Crozins' weaknesses more than him. Pify had the most experience, but age and health limited his strength and abilities. He'd listen to Phera, but she was glued to Pify, knowing his health was failing. Then there was his manany. She lacked experience, and her mind was full of grief over losing papay. And even though Victis seemed just as arrogant as him, Kigen knew he had earned it. Someday he, too, would deserve the respect of a great warrior. He'd follow Victis into battle and learn what it takes to lead and fight to win.

Night fell, and they began the trek into the ruins of Cape Parrish. They didn't get far. Kigen had to learn how to control his stripes from glowing before the team could continue.

Victis ordered Kigen to stay close and do nothing until told otherwise. Whispering in the dark, Victis handed him a laser. "Have you ever fired one of these?"

"No, but I've seen Ryquats and Trekachaws fire them," whispered Kigen. He was getting a taste of reality and his rank as the team's novice. Victis showed Kigen the basics and told him the most important lesson—not to shoot him.

The air was dirty and stunk the closer they got to where the Ops last reported bunkered down.

Kigen had never smelled such an offensive odor. It was heavy and seeping into his skin. Victis got his attention and pointed at things partially lit by the moonlight on the street. Whatever those things were, they covered the road at the intersection. Kigen focused on it and felt sick. Those things were hundreds of Ryquats left to rot. Some were rat infested with their faces gone. Others were laser cut into pieces. And then those who looked asleep if you didn't know better. Kigen had his first taste of the spoils of war. Victis touched Kigen's shoulder and felt the young Trekachaw shaking.

Speaking in private, Victis told him it was okay to be disturbed by death. Kigen was beginning to understand why Ryquats and Trekachaws were willing to follow Victis into hell.

Bibet heard a noise. She pulled on Azha's hand to get his attention. "I hear Crozins."

She was right; the Crozins had surrounded them. Azha gave Bibet his laser. "Go! Follow Steve and Rigdan into that building."

The night sky was ablaze with streaks of light. Bibet ran with the Ops, dodging lasers until they took cover behind a doorway. Rigdan's arm was bleeding. And he was shouting at them, asking if anyone else had been shot. He rolled up his sleeve. "It's nothing but a flesh wound," he mumbled, pulling the bloody sleeve down to cover the cut.

Steve yelled at Bibet and Rigdan to get down. A door behind them crashed open, and Crozins rushed them, firing lasers. Bibet returned fire, slicing two Crozins as Rigdan dove behind a cabinet. Steve ran in the opposite direction, firing lasers at the Crozins clawing their way in. Bibet was fast. She bounced off a wall and shot several more Crozins.

The three Trekachaws flashed into energy. The Crozins would regret starting this fight. One red light orb stood out among the others. Fast as lightning, it streaked across the night sky, disappearing into Crozins' heads one after the other.

Victis was amazed by the young Trekachaw's speed. But he questioned the scope of Kigen's capabilities. With such power, could he turn into a monster if left unchecked? Kigen circled above, watching the Crozins die and screaming in agony. Their pain did not seem to affect him. Perhaps he had already grown to be callous. Or was it an act to impress Victis? Kigen knew Victis saw what he could do. But he did not solicit praise or act arrogantly. He had learned that much.

A light streaked through the wall and morphed into body form next to Bibet. Azha grabbed a shrieking Crozin running toward her and snapped its neck. Another light streaked past the doorway and disappeared into a Crozin's head that had reached over the cabinet and cut Rigdan with its long claws. Steve fired from across the room and sliced a Crozin in half.

Finally, the Crozins were dead, and all was quiet. Kigen flew into the room and landed in body form, wide-eyed and shaking. "You left me out there alone! Five Crozins fired at me. I could have died!"

Victis grinned. "But you're not dead, are you? Next time, stay with me."

Kigen's stripes flashed bright purple. "What? Look, I was cut by a laser," pointing at his leg.

"You're fine. Stop whining. How many Crozins did you kill?" smiled Victis, curious if Kigen was ready to tuck tail and fly back to Pify's ship.

"Twenty-seven. How many did you kill?" he shouted in anger.

"Not that many. Guess that makes you part of the team now. Next time, you won't make the same mistake. Pay attention when the Trekachaws leave."

Typically, Kigen was not at a loss for words. He wanted to scream but chose not to. Victis was the first to intimidate him. Pify was right when he insisted on Victis being his mentor and not him. At the time, he thought Pify's rationale was ludicrous. All he understood was rejection from his surrogate parents. He was wrong to doubt Pify.


THE COVER OF NIGHT WOULD soon end with the light of dawn. Azha found Bibet sleeping, perched on the top of a broken table. She chose that spot because it provided an unobstructed view in both directions. He startled Bibet when he picked her up, but she did not resist. Azha felt her body relax and the coolness of her beak nuzzle against his neck. For whatever reason, he cared about the little bird.

Steve was outside, checking for Crozins lurking in the shadows. He signaled them to follow him out of the building with a hand wave. At the next intersection, they turned right, expecting to find more Crozins. After a quick check, the streets were clear. With a bit of luck, no one would die tonight. He remembered those same streets when they were filled with bustling sounds of prosperity. Now they were in a war zone, scarred by lasers and lined with buildings reduced to rubble. No Ryquats walked the streets freely. They lay dead in the streets. Steve was impervious to the spoils of war. He never counted on surviving. One day at a time. That was his goal.

With less than two blocks to go, Victis wanted Azha to stay with the group inside an enclosed breezeway until he returned. He told Kigen to turn into energy and go with him. Kigen's stripes were glowing red again, making everyone nervous. Victis shook his head and flashed into energy. Kigen flashed red and disappeared into the night sky with Victis.

Flying with the famous captain made Kigen feel special and afraid. The last time he was alone with Victis scared him enough that he wanted to go home. Kigen missed his familiar battleship world. He did not have the same desire as others to be on a planet. More often than not, the odors were offensive. And the ground was unpredictable and usually dirty. The battleship was clean and orderly, unlike this frustrating planet.

Beneath them, fifty or more Crozins had swarmed an area leading into a subway. Victis circled, searching for the Ukaru. That did not take long. The Ukaru was easy to spot with his arcane Ruks at his side. Flickering at Kigen to follow, Victis flew atop a roof and landed in body form. Kigen landed next to him, worried about controlling his stripes. Victis could change the color of his stripes to blend with the night sky, except for his yellow eyes. This was new for Kigen. He would need practice to become as skilled as Victis. He thought about asking for tips, but Victis had that look on his face.

"I will kill the Ukaru. You enter either one of the Ruk's heads standing next to him. Position yourself in an eye so that you can see the Ukaru. Do you know how to do that?"

Kigen did not want to do what Victis was telling him to do. "Yes. No. I mean, Phera had me explore different areas of the brain."

"Follow the light, and you will find the eyes. Do not kill the Ruk. If I can control the Ukaru, I will have him command the Crozins to leave. After that, the Ukaru dies, and we will use the Ruk to control the Crozins. When you see the Ukaru drop, leave the Ruk's eye and go to his brain. Tell the Ruk he's next to die unless he does exactly what you tell him to do. By then, another Ruk will have touched the dead Ukaru, giving me a chance to transfer into him. From there, we kill the next one that touches the body we are in until they are all dead or the Crozins run away. Okay, here's Plan B. If the Ruks do not comply, kill the one you are in and transfer to a live one every time one touches the dead Ruk you possess. If they figure out not to touch the dead, just start killing all of them like I saw you do before. I'd guess fifty down there. Are you ready?" Victis asked. But really, he didn't care. Ready or not, they were going.

"Yeah?" Kigen was thinking about how much he missed Pify and Phera.

Victis flashed into energy and dove inside the Ukaru's head. Kigen spiraled, then decided to fly into the Ruk's head, standing nearest the Ukaru. After probing random brain areas, Kigen panicked. He could not find the Ruk's eyes. Considering his limited options, he decided to fly out of the Ruk's head and re-enter through an eye. Kigen flew out of the Ruk and saw the Ukaru convulsing on the ground. The Crozins had surrounded him and were making groaning noises.

A Ruk shrieked, "Trekachaw!" pointing up. From every direction, the Crozins were firing lasers at him. He streaked away, searching for somewhere to hide. But then he remembered, Victis was counting on him. He felt the laser's heat as he streaked into the Ukaru's head.

"What happened to our plan?" snapped Victis.

"I couldn't find an eye; I tried. I'm sorry." Kigen's light was flickering. He was terrified and had overestimated himself in so many ways.

Victis laughed; he did not expect that.

"We're okay. Let's go to Plan C. Whatever I do, you do." Victis sounded like he didn't care about his screwup. Kigen stuck to Victis so close that his shadow was crowded.

The Ukaru stopped shaking. Victis told Kigen to listen, not to talk.

"Welcome back, Ukaru. How does it feel to almost die? Shall we start over?" mocked Victis.

The Ukaru's thoughts reminded him of the hollow sounds he'd heard while exploring the belly of Pify's battleship.

"Trekachaw! Who are you?" demanded the Ukaru.

"Doesn't matter who I am. What matters is what I can do. The pain you felt is nothing. My question is, will you command your Ruks to leave?"

Victis flashed his energy inside the Ukaru's head to remind him of the pain. The Ukaru's ear-piercing shrills vibrated inside his brain. Victis was testing the Ukaru's resolve. His body collapsed and lay motionless, and he had no thoughts.

"Is he dead?" asked Kigen.

The Ukaru's brain pulsated, and he screeched, "Kill me. There are two Trekachaws inside my head!"

Victis yelled, "Kigen! Follow me, or you'll die!"

Kigen did not hesitate. He followed Victis into a Ruk's brain who was firing a laser at the Ukaru.

The young Trekachaw was afraid. Not of the Ukaru, but of Victis. Too much to learn, and Victis was too fast. He didn't know if he could keep up.

It looked like they were inside the area of the brain Kigen was familiar with. Victis spoke to the Ruk, "I am the Trekachaw who tortured your Ukaru. Do as I say, or you're next!"

The Ruk screamed, "The Trekachaw's in my head!"

Victis yelled, "Kigen, get out!"

Kigen streaked out of the Ruk's head with Victis and dove into another Ruk's head.

Victis was laughing. "This is perfect. The Crozins are killing their Ruks, chasing us. Keep close, Kigen; let's see how many times we can play this."

"Ruk, you have two Trekachaws inside your brain. Cooperate, or I will kill you. If you tell them we're in here, your Crozins will kill you. Don't talk; I can hear your thoughts."

*Don't kill me,* thought the Ruk.

"Excellent choice. You will feel us moving inside your eyes. Do not react or rub them; it could draw attention. Kigen, this is how you find the eyes." Victis zigzagged until he saw the light and followed it to the eyes.

"That's how you do it. This Ruk better not act rattled, or he'll get lasered. Too late—I told him not to rub his eyes. Geez, he's slapping his face!" shouted Victis as he streaked out of the Ruk's eye and into another Ruk's head with Kigen on his tail.

The Ruk stopped slapping his head and ran away, screaming, "Don't shoot me, don't shoot me. They're gone. NO!"

The Crozins sliced him into pieces.

Victis was growing tired of head charades. He'd spell it out for the last standing Ruk. "You're the new prize genius with two Trekachaws inside your brain. Do as I say, or you'll die like the others. Don't talk, don't move your mouth, slap yourself, or rub your eyes. I can hear your thoughts."

The Ruk thought, *Don't kill me. I'll do what you ask. Why aren't you dead? I heard lasers can kill a Trekachaw while in energy.*

"Clearly, you have been misled. If you're a smart Ruk, you'll make it out alive. That's up to you. As long as you cooperate, I will remain in your brain pain-free. I want you to get the Crozins to leave. Whatever it takes, do it."

This Ruk seemed to take instructions better. *I will do as you say. The Crozin standing next to me is important. I ask that you spare her. I was told a Trekachaw dies if the Ruk dies with you inside.* The Ruk's thoughts were beginning to waver.

"I will spare the Crozin. You should not ask me a question like that. But if you really want to know, I'll tell you and then kill you. Do you still want to know?"

*No!* The Ruk was holding his breath.

"Kigen, choose any Crozin to kill other than the one the Ruk wants alive. If the Ruk fails me, kill her. If they start lasering each other, fly straight into space and don't stop. I'll meet you up there." Victis sounded cold and calculated.

The Ruk shouted to get the Crozins' attention, "I am the last Ruk and your leader. Lower your lasers."

A large, older Crozin yelled, "Quiet, defiant dreg."

Kigen chose well. The Crozin standing next to the older Crozin shrieked in agony and fell to the ground. The older Crozin stumbled backward and dropped his laser. Kigen streaked out of the dying Ruk's head, one heartbeat away from death.

The older Crozin screeched when he realized a Trekachaw had entered his brain.

Kigen parroted Victis, "Do nothing, say nothing. Agree with the Ruk you called dreg, or I will kill you. I can hear your thoughts."

The old Crozin trembled. "Lower your lasers. Flurg is a Ruk. I am not."

Flurg looked surprised, wondering if the old Crozin had a Trekachaw in his head too. Victis told him yes. And from there on, the old Crozin would keep his hole shut or die. Ruk Flurg spoke to the Crozins, "The Ryquats are in our nest. Food for later. Our Ukaru died honorably; we must join the others and celebrate his reign."

The old Crozin yelled, "Homage to Ukaru! Elites await, body to honor."

The Crozins screeched and lifted the dead Ukaru into the air.

Kigen found the old Crozin's eyes and watched Flurg until he saw Victis streak out of his head. Before joining Victis, he told the old Crozin, "You're alive because you obeyed me. Spread the word. The Trekachaws are coming for the Crozins who fight us. Our wrath begets no end for those who rage war!"

BIBET AND AZHA STOOD OUTSIDE the breezeway, taking in the beautiful night sky. Azha yearned to be free among the vast stars. Whereas Bibet was content anywhere as long as she was with the Trekachaw she adored. Azha was no longer star gazing. He was searching the night sky for his friend. Victis and Kigen had been gone longer than he was comfortable with.

Among the twinkling stars, Azha saw them first. He waved, welcoming their safe return. Bibet chirped and flapped her wings, running after Azha into the breezeway to share the news.

Victis and Kigen circled the group and morphed into body form. Despite their dangerous encounters with the Crozins, they appeared none the worse for wear. Victis was calm, and you could see he was pleased. But Kigen had changed. Though unscathed, years of affliction had etched his face. The young, cocky Trekachaw was gone. What transpired between the mentor and his apprentice was their story to share, if ever.

Beyond the breezeway, the streets leading to the subway were free of Crozins. With the morning sun rising, they descended into the dark subway tunnels.

Speed-rail tracks disappeared into the concrete tunnels that iron trains once traveled. Since the invasion, those rails were of no use. As well as the dusty train cars left to rust. Without conductors, they were anchored in place by tons of dead weight.

Victis was getting a bad feeling about being in the subway. If they walked into a nest of Crozins, the Ops would be trapped. Besides, they could use the break. "Azha, Kigen, and I will find out what's down the tunnel and come back for you. Sit tight. We won't take long."

The three Trekachaws flashed into energy and flew into the dark. Bibet did not blink until their lights disappeared. She was not pleased with Victis's order. Fuming, she fluffed her feathers and perched on a ledge with a view of the tunnel.

Not far into the subway, a small, ragged group of Ryquats were walking toward the Trekachaws. Victis did not want to frighten them, so he motioned for Kigen and Azha to return to the entrance and get the others to head this way. This group of Ryquats was not doing well and couldn't take many more surprises.

Bibet flapped her wings and stood up, alerting the others of the Trekachaws' return. Azha morphed into body form, glowing green.

"Half a mile down the tunnel, we found live Ryquats. Steve, you and Rigdan lead the way. They need to see you first. Don't tell them about us until you explain who we are. Also, ask them if there are more stranded Ryquats down here and if they've seen Crozins."

Finding the Ryquats was incredible. How they survived was remarkable. Steve and Rigdan picked up their pace and headed into the tunnel. Bibet heard them first. "I hear whispering Ryquats. Call out to them."

Steve shouted and heard the echo of his voice, "Hello-Hello, I'm Steve-I'm Steve, from the forty-first Ops-the forty-first Ops."

A Ryquat with a raspy voice called out, "You're a godsend-godsend. We were giving up-giving up on anyone ever finding us-finding us."

The silhouettes of Ryquats came into the light from the dark tunnel. One after the other, exhausted women carried babies and small children. They had not bathed for some time. And their clothes were soiled and torn, yet you could see hope in their eyes. Behind them, men and women dragging makeshift cots, cradled the severely injured.

Steve and Rigdan opened their packs and handed food and water to them. Some began to weep, while others were listless and aloof to suffering. The Ryquats dragging the wounded carefully laid the cots on the ground. After taking a drink of water, they identified themselves as Ops.

Steve explained to the group that the lights flickering above should not be feared. They were aliens who could change into bodies. Whether or not the group grasped what Steve was saying, they didn't seem to react. However, Bibet's presence triggered an alarming reaction. The Ryquats were salivating and smacking their lips. One of them asked if she was a new breed of chovo.

Naturally, Bibet was disturbed by the comparison. Their loud whispering and innuendos suggesting that she might be their next meal terrified her.

Azha caught the Ryquats gawking at Bibet and wondered why. When he realized what they were saying, his stripes glowed red. He knew that a chovo on Zaurak was equivalent to a chicken on Earth. Although he never understood the comparison. To him, chickens were cute. But a Kiki looked like a graceful egret. Azha restrained himself until Victis finished introducing the Trekachaws. At least it gave him time to calm his stripes before speaking his mind.

"Bibet is not a chovo. Stop looking at her that way! She is a Kiki from another world, and she is my bird. No one touches her!" Azha terrified the group. If anyone considered eating Bibet, that thought was gone.

Victis walked away from the tongue-lashing Azha was giving to hear a garbled incoming message. He tried several times to communicate, but the thick subway walls interfered with the signal. Kigen's keen ears heard Victis and volunteered to fly with him to the subway entrance.

What little Victis understood was that he was out of time. The Crozin battleships were inbound, making his ship the priority. But considering the declining health and dire situation of these Ryquats, Victis felt obligated. All were malnourished. And some wouldn't survive without medical aid. Leaving them in the Crozin-infested subway was not an option. If he did, their chances of survival would be zero.

The best course of action would be to risk flying a shuttle to their location. But that decision could be a death trap for the pilot.

Wishing he had never gotten himself into this predicament was mute. It is what it is. He'd make it work. Victis motioned at Kigen to follow. In a flash of light, they streaked toward the subway entrance.

Because of Bibet, Azha didn't mind staying behind with the Ryquats. It was a good thing he did. Not long after Victis left, an Op told him some disturbing information. They may have heard Crozins talking. And it sounded like it was coming from the next entrance. Nowhere inside the subway was safe, but that was too close. If even one Crozin caught their scent, they'd all swarm to that area. In that event, a swift death would be merciful.

Azha picked up Bibet and walked away before telling her his plan. He would sneak away and check the next couple of entrances to see if the Crozins were there. Bibet's eyes got big, and she asked him not to go. Azha told her not to worry and sat her down. She puckered her beak and asked him to hurry back. Off he went again, leaving her alone with the Ryquats.

Bibet watched Azha disappear into the dark. Not pleased, not one bit, she found a good spot to perch and stood guard. She kept her distance from the chovo-eating Ryquats. A couple of them watched her perch, making strange, creepy faces.

Every so often, they'd glance her way. Bibet stretched her neck and fluffed her feathers to make herself appear bigger. If Azha didn't return soon, she'd make a run for the entrance.

Azha's energy searched the subway tunnels until he caught the scent of the familiar Crozins' stench. He stopped when he saw their ghastly shadows dancing on the curved walls. To Azha's advantage, he had no odor while in energy. It was worth the risk to fly closer.

Then he heard the awful sound of hooves and claws scraping the walls and ground. There were more Crozins than he had initially thought, and they were dangerously close. The slightest breeze through the tunnel in the wrong direction would alert them. The Ryquats had to move. If Victis and Kigen had not returned by the time he got back, they would head for the entrance they came in at.

Azha streaked back and morphed into body form next to Bibet. He picked her up and spoke quietly into her ear, "There are Crozins at the next terminal—a lot of them. Everyone needs to get up. We're going to the entrance we came in at."

Bibet looked scared. "I'm faster than Crozins. Promise if they find us, you'll turn into energy and go with me? Don't die for them. Promise me!" Azha stroked her neck and set her on the ground. He walked over to the group of Ryquats and snapped his fingers to get their attention.

"You need to listen and do as I say. There are Crozins within spitting distance in that direction. We can't stay here. Everyone, quietly get ready to go."

No one said a word as they packed their broken suitcases and bags. The adults picked up the small children while the Ops checked on the injured. An Op waved at Azha to come over and pointed at a cot. The Ryquat had passed on. No one held his hand. No one said a prayer. He left this world peacefully in his sleep.

An older woman stopped folding blankets and gasped when she saw them standing over the cot. She covered her mouth to muffle herself and ran to him. She must not have realized that he had died. Her pain was excruciating and unbearable to watch.

Azha placed an old pillowcase over his face. But that angered her. She grabbed it and threw it at him. Her outburst toward Azha was not anger. It was grief. Through the sobs and moaning, she apologized to Azha and walked over to a bag. Her old hands trembled as she pulled out a handmade blanket. It meant something significant, something to hold that was good. She kept the blanket close to her chest and carried it to the man. Looking down upon him, she wept and struggled to her knees to touch his cold face. Her fingers trembled, and she shook her head in disbelief. There she stayed by his side, as hollow as the man she grieved. She carefully placed the blanket over his head and unfolded the rest to cover his body.

Azha listened to her whisper goodbye. The man was her husband, the father of their dead children, and the love of her life. Refusing to leave his side, she held onto his hand.

The Op, who had cared for the man, was struggling to. He resisted showing grief and told himself there was nothing else he could have done. The older man was easy to talk to. They'd swapped stories and laughed until he was too sick to laugh anymore. Days turned into weeks, and keeping him and his wife safe became personal for the Op. He hung his head to hide his tears. But Azha saw his anguish before he walked away from the cot. For some strange reason, Azha felt compelled to follow the Op into the tunnel. He witnessed what he had struggled not to do. The Op let go and lowered his armor facade.

"I wish I could have saved him." The Op cleared his throat and breathed heavily to regain his composure. He glanced up at Azha, asking for a moment to himself. His eyes were red, and he fought back the tears. As Azha walked away, the Op changed his mind and asked him to stay.

"That Ryquat was the bravest man I've ever known. He died saving us. I want to carry his body with us and give him the burial he deserves. That grieving woman over there is his wife and would rather die than leave him here to rot alone." Azha nodded yes and told him he was sorry.

Victis and Kigen crossed paths with the group at the iron trains near the entrance. Azha was in the middle of explaining why they had to move when Victis cut him off. Victis was in no mood. He told Azha to wait until he spoke with Rigdan, Steve, and Bibet, then yelled at them to get over here. When they didn't walk fast enough, he waved and insisted they hurry.

"I got through to Akio. But my frequency was intercepted somewhere on Zaurak. Not sure how much of the transmission they heard or if they got a lock on us. I asked for a few Trekachaws, Ops, and jets to meet us at Largo. Get everyone on their feet and ready to go. Akio is flying the shuttle down here. More like a *nosedive* down to the planet to minimize detection. The Crozin fleet is within sensor range, so we gotta go now. Soon as Akio lands, get these Ryquats ready to run. Anyone who can't keep up will be left behind. Akio will fly in low and fast between the buildings to get us out of the city. Steve and Rigdan, get your jets off this planet. We need them for what's coming. Bibet, you go with Steve until it's safe to dock on my battleship. Rigdan, tell Akio he is with you. Azha, Kigen, and I will fly to my battleship first and then Pify's.

"The shuttle Akio's flying has a limited defense system. But he does have lasers. There's enough food and medical supplies on the shuttle until we return. The Ryquats should be safe at Largo. As you know, we recently cleared it of Crozins again. Once we're out of this mess, I have important information, but it can wait." Victis told a few Ops to help him with the Ryquats. "When the shuttle gets here, move them fast! The Crozins will be right behind it."

Victis shouted for everyone to hurry up, over to the entrance, "When the shuttle gets here, run as fast as you can. Steve will explain everything on the flight. Go, go, go!"

The loud hum of a shuttle landing echoed into the subway. The Ops hoisted the injured over their shoulders and ran. The adults picked up the children and ran. The last of their precious memories were left behind lying on the ground. The hum grew louder, and the shuttle touched down with the ramp lowered. Victis shouted, "Run, don't stop. Move, move, move!"

A barrage of laser fire exploded near the entrance. A laser scorched the side of the shuttle with a jolt. The ramp bounced, and the Ryquats running on it fell.

Victis yelled, "Get up! Get up! Go! Go! Go! Don't stop!"

Some had to crawl on their hands and knees the rest of the way. Others stood up, grabbed the screaming children, and ran to the top. Bibet was the last up the ramp. She looked over her shoulder, searching for Azha. The hatch shut behind her, and she stared out of the small porthole. The shuttle surged and rolled, forcing her to hang on to a rail. Lasers blasted the subway entrance into rubble. She looked for Azha through the smoke and debris but could not find him.

The buildings they flew between exploded, creating a shock wave. The cockpit went dark, and Akio switched the autopilot to manual. This was not the first time Akio flew blind. He could feel the ship and what she could do. Akio banked hard, soaring and diving between the structures. He relied on pure instinct to navigate the shuttle. Another laser missed its mark. They were not coming from above; the Crozins were firing from the streets. A thought crossed his mind. He would not make it out alive. At this speed, one mistake and no one would survive.

Akio cleared his mind and concentrated on not clipping a wing or crashing into the next building. The Ryquats were screaming and hanging on to anything attached to the shuttle. Akio gambled on a long shot, and it paid off. He flew skyward, climbing as fast as the shuttle could without ripping her apart. His body pressed against the pilot's seat, and he watched the clouds disappear. Entering the black space gave him hope that they were beyond the reach of the lasers beneath them.

The screams had stopped, silenced by the sharp ascent. Akio was trying not to, but he could feel himself passing out.

Bibet made her way to the cockpit and sat down next to Akio. She did not seem affected by it at all. The bird stretched her neck and got in his face.

She told him that he needed to drop off Steve, Rigdan, and the Ryquats near Largo before docking on Victis's battleship.

It had slipped his mind in all the chaos, but he pretended to remember. Bibet smirked and rolled her eyes at him. She puckered her beak and said four more Ryquats died on the shuttle during the turbulent flight. Akio tuned her out, thinking how lucky it was anyone survived. But she kept chirping in his ear.

Akio raised his voice. "Bibet, do me a favor and stop talking. Go, get Steve and Rigdan. I need to talk to them."

Bibet glared at him and walked away.

Still feeling a bit disoriented, Akio stretched and rolled his neck. His hearing was off, and his voice sounded hollow inside his head. He wondered if the sharp ascent damaged his eardrums. He tried to clear them by yawning. When that didn't work, he stuck his finger inside to pop them. Sometime during his home ear remedies, Steve sat in the chair next to him. And to his right, Rigdan was leaning against the navigation console.

Steve sounded impatient. "Why aren't you taking us to our jets?"

Akio had had enough of everyone's attitude. "I risked my life to save all of you from a Crozin swarm. How about a thank you? And yes! I'm flying there now. Okay! Has anyone asked about my wife and two boys yet? I didn't see them get on the shuttle. Ask the Ryquats if anyone knows anything about them." Akio was very loud.

"Yeah, we forgot to ask. Not that we weren't trying to save Ryquats or anything. Don't get me wrong. I'd feel the same way if it were my family. There's been shuttles coming and going for days. I bet someone knows something. Hang tight, and I'll go ask."

Steve did not want to ask. What if someone told him bad news or she was dead? If that were the case, he'd lie and say no one knew. Once he got to his jet, he'd tell Akio the truth.

Just his luck. A Ryquat knew quite a bit about Mya and the boys—more than he wanted to know. But it could have been worse. He felt pretty good about sharing. So, what if she was with another man? That shouldn't be a problem considering their predicament. What mattered was that Mya and his boys were alive. Steve sat down next to Akio.

"I have good news. Remember I told you about Mark Keller? That's the Op who found your wife and boys hiding in your apartment after the first attack. He's kept your family safe. A few days before we found this group, Mark Keller, your wife, and the boys left the subway with a group of Ryquats. They were looking for a place to hide from the Crozins and planned on returning if they found one. He told me some other stuff, but it could be wrong. You might not want to hear it."

Akio frowned. "Just tell me, good or bad."

"Fair enough. If it were me, I'd want to know too. I'm not making excuses for her, but from what I heard, Mya thought you were dead. The Ryquat said he thought Mark Keller and Mya were married. She was surprised to hear that Mya was married to someone else. I guess the boys were calling Mark 'Dad.'"

Akio pounded his fists on the console. "What! Get ready to land. I'm staying here."

"No, you're not. Victis ordered you to go with Rigdan. Keep your head in the game, or you're no good to anyone," Steve was serious.

"And what if I refuse? Will you shoot me?" scowled Akio.

"Maybe! I should have lied to you. Victis needs you on his battleship. Acting like a jealous fool won't change a thing. You should be happy she survived. Think about it. If we lose this war, your wife and boys will be ripped apart by Crozins."

"Shut up! Can you just shut up and let me think? I hate this war. Get ready to land." Akio pulled his shirt up to wipe his eyes. Steve understood how this could screw with his head, but he couldn't let Akio go rogue.

THE SHUTTLE LANDED ON A grassy knoll under a canopy of palm trees. They could not see the ocean but were close enough to feel its breeze. For Steve and Rigdan, this was home. Eager to check on their jets, they were the first two off the shuttle.

The rescued Ryquats were busy helping each other unload. The group must have thanked them a hundred times for saving their lives as they exited the shuttle. Slowly but surely, the tattered group made their way down the knoll to the edge of town. They disappeared behind the buildings one after the other to a place Steve hoped would be their sanctuary.

Several Ops volunteered to stay behind with the group, while others wanted to board the jets. Steve welcomed the fighters but also warned of an imminent battle that had poor odds of survival. Six Ops were comfortable with those odds and adamant that flying a jet was where they wanted to be.

Steve took in a long, deep breath of Zaurak air. He loved this spot and hoped to return when this was over. This place reminded him of how it was before the war. Those blissful thoughts ended when he saw the last Ryquats leaving the shuttle carrying their dead down the ramp. That image, for whatever reason, bothered him. But then, there were plenty of memories he'd rather forget.

At the bottom of a ridge, Steve saw the jets. This was the life he knew and chose. It was a mistake when he retired. He walked, then ran down the hill to touch her. She was his jet.

It wasn't long until the others caught up and boarded. Steve sat in the pilot's chair, smiled, and secured his harness. Bibet sat next to him and blinked. He thought to himself, *what a strange little bird.* The Mic-12 jets shot into space toward Victis's battleship.

# fourteen

# AEON DEVOTIO TWO SOULS

**The Umdul Language:**
ЕOINY TOVOIBAI ЖIUMLIЖ


**THE** fight above Trinite had taken its toll. Vious was dead. And Deneb was left in command, dealing with dire reports on all frequencies. The battleship had sustained significant damage and was a sitting duck. Meanwhile, the war had shifted to Zaurak, giving Deneb a pardon from attacks. But she could not bring herself to care.

Without Vious, Deneb's resolve deteriorated. She refused to leave her quarters and ordered the bridge crew to go away. Out of options, a navigator requested assistance out of desperation.

Of course, it was Clyde who was told to respond to the unorthodox request. He was the last Trekachaw to see Deneb. At the time, she was upset but functioning. He would have stayed, but he was trying to save Vious. Since then, most of the fleet had been dispatched to Zaurak.

Clyde hid it well, but he was having issues himself. He was injured worse than he let on and was taking Vious's death hard. What if he had transferred his energy while on Vious's ship? Could that have made a difference? At the time, he thought he'd get help on Pify's battleship. That was not the case. Now, that option was long gone.

Meanwhile, he was ordered to advise Deneb of her husband's death. That wasn't going to be easy. There were no shuttles, and he was too weak to fly. Not being able to tell her in person was wrong. When he told her on a ship-to-ship frequency, all he could hear was crying. She never said a word and ended the call. Officially, Pify or Victis should have given her the bad news and responded to her navigator's request. But they were not in the sector. Yet again, everyone considered him the best Trekachaw to determine if Deneb was competent. Several hours later, he gained barely enough strength to fly over to Deneb's ship. If he had known, he would have waited to tell her in person. This was another crisis he wished for a redo.

Nervous about being in that position, Clyde first met with the reporting navigator. Come to find out; it wasn't just the navigator's concern. The bridge crew was worried about Deneb too. He was reluctant to take command of Deneb's battleship. She blamed him for not doing more to save Vious. Clyde told the crew he couldn't stay. He'd send another Trekachaw to assist them.

After hearing about Deneb's condition, Zeta volunteered to proxy command until a replacement captain arrived. Clyde was grateful. However, Zeta was not who he had in mind.

Clyde had grown attached to her since becoming a Trekachaw. Zeta's Human half reminded him of Earth's old school; they believed in the same God with the same values. But at times, the Human Beverly was not rational. Zeta kissed his cheek and said what he needed to hear—she'd be okay and that she loved him.

The transfer began immediately. All nonessential crew members boarded Clyde's battleship bound for Zaurak and the war. The remaining skeleton crew welcomed Zeta's presence.

The worst was over. Zeta figured now would be an excellent time to meet with Deneb. She knocked on her door, then waited. Zeta knocked louder and called out her name. She knocked again and asked if they could talk. Deneb screamed, *No! Go away!* Zeta called out to her that she'd be on the bridge and walked away. Little did Zeta know that Deneb desperately needed a friend in this life.

Aeon Devotio was tempting her, calling her by name. Past lives beckoned for her soul to rise. She listened for Vious on the other side but did not hear him. Her Quizan soul told her not to be afraid—that he was waiting. Thoughts of Kigen kept her from letting go of this life. Yet the urge to leave was intense. Beautiful memories of her life on Palatu made her rise into the air. She saw her body beneath her and felt betrayed. This violent world was intolerable without Vious. The songs of past souls grew louder, and she heard his voice call out to her. Deneb surrendered, and her grey-death energy rose above, touching the one she loved.

The war-torn battleship drifted into space while the engineers worked diligently to repair her. Trusting they would soon be on their way; Zeta had not considered complications. The truth is, she thought Deneb would join her once they talked about what was bothering her. Otherwise, she would not have been so eager to volunteer. That was all well and good. She wasn't going anywhere. The engineers informed her they found damage that required dry-docking for at least two weeks.

Zeta gave the order. They embarked with minimal life support, half speed, and no weapons systems. The crew was grateful the war was no longer a threat in that sector.

Opus was a desirable planet with state-of-the-art space stations. Spending time there was a pleasant turn of events. En route, the crew grew bored with too much idle time. The Ryquat engineers bet the bridge crew on who understood the Umduls better. The fact is, not one of them understood Umduls or their technology. But there was no doubt every Ryquat engineer wanted to learn. And the rest of the crew couldn't wait to spend time on the planet.

The trek was peaceful, and spirits were high. Twenty-two hours had passed since leaving Trinite, and all was well. Half asleep and leaning back with her boots on a navigation console, she stared at a monitor. Soon her eyes closed, listening to the hum of the ship. She jerked when she felt her head nod and sat up wide awake. Did she hear something? Pushing her chair away from the console, she waited and listened for the sound again. There it was—a Crozin battleship signature.

*No!* she thought to herself. *God help us. There are hundreds of them.*

Stumbling out of the chair, she ran to the captain's quarters and banged on the door. Zeta jumped out of bed, startled by the noise. The young navigator looked as if she'd seen a ghost. Gasping for air, she spoke in a panic.

"A fleet of Crozin battleships are headed our way. Captain, what are your orders?"

Zeta ran past her, shouting at her to keep up. "How far out are they? Have they detected us yet?"

"I don't think so, but they may have by now," yelled the navigator running behind her in a race to the bridge.

"Go dark! Now! What's their location? Get the rest of the crew up here!" Shouted Zeta.

Specks on a monitor showed over a hundred Crozin battleships headed straight for them. She searched the heavens for a place to hide in the cold, vast expanse. There it was in the dark, a rogue moon. A godsend in time of need. It was perfect for hiding behind. She asked herself if they would be lucky enough to elude the devil's wrath.

Zeta was distracted by her Human soul. Beverly was emotional and not suited for this life. Their merger was Human and Quizan. They were nothing like Ryquat Trekachaws, who grew up in this advanced world. During Beverly's Earth years, she was a successful realtor that lived a quiet, sane life. To even consider there were little green men was laughable. But the aluminum heads were right all along. Beverly recalled seeing Cole for the first time as an alien. Zeta snapped at Beverly to give it a rest.

The navigator at the helm was waiting for Zeta to give him instructions. Orion looked young, too young to be in that chair. He gave her a nod, and she returned the nod. Whatever Orion was nodding about, Zeta quickly caught on. He was asking permission to hide behind the crescent moon on the monitor. No telling how long it had been drifting in space, with its barren surface and deep craters. Orion flew to the opposite side and saw a wide fissure to hide the battleship. He traversed into the dark as far as the ship could go. Tensions were high, but for now, it was a waiting game.

Hours passed, and not a sound. Zeta figured the Crozins were out of range by now. Before checking, she wanted to learn more about the bridge crew. Or, at least, ask the navigator his name before something else goes wrong.

Zeta sat next to him. "You did quite well. What shall I call you?"

"Orion. I appreciate that, Captain. I'm an Ops jet pilot. This is my first time flying a battleship. Other than the size and a few more controls, it's all the same to me." Orion had an unusual accent. It sounded southern from Earth. She wondered how that was possible.

"Okay. Here's what we're going to do. I will leave the ship briefly to see if the Crozins are gone. Don't do anything until I get back, got it?"

"Yes, Captain, loud and clear," grinned Orion.

The crew looked worried but had good reasons to feel that way. They had already lost two captains. First Vious and then Deneb.

Zeta flew to the other side of the moon, expecting to find the Crozins long gone. But to her disbelief, she discovered a fleet of Gor battleships disturbingly close. She streaked to her battleship and morphed into body form on the bridge. Quietly, she tiptoed over to Orion and whispered, "The Crozins are gone. But now there's a Gor fleet passing by us on the other side of the moon. *Shh*, we need to stay silent. I don't know if these Gors are with the Crozins or friendlies from Trinite. My guess is the Crozins. Why would the Trinite Gors be out here?"

Zeta mimed with her arms and mouthed to the rest of the crew in silence, informing them about the Gors.

Terrified again, the crew froze, fearing the Gors' sensors might detect them. Several hours passed before Zeta whispered she'd check to see if it was safe to leave. In a flash, she disappeared to the other side of the moon. Not a ship in sight, she sparkled and streaked back.

"The coast is clear." She rejoiced by spinning and dancing in ancient Quizan lore.

Orion scratched his head. "Does the coast is clear mean the Gors are gone?"

"Yes, it does. That's a Human thing. Orion, I must leave now if I'm to beat the Crozins and Gors to Zaurak. But before I go, I need to select someone to take my place. I'm not sure how to do this officially. Guess it doesn't matter how. You're the new captain. I know you will do your best. But try to get this ship safely to Opus. Let the Umduls know what we saw out here as soon as you can. And get medical help for Deneb. If she's awake, I'll tell her I picked you to be captain until she's better. Sound good to you?"

"Sounds good. Straight to Opus."

The crew raised one hand in favor of Orion.

She would have rather not disturbed Deneb, but she needed to talk to her this time. Zeta knocked a couple of times and called out her name before entering. Deneb's quarters were dark, and she was sound asleep on the bed. Maybe Orion could check on her later. It seemed a shame to wake her up. On second thought, Orion had enough on his plate.

She spoke softly, not to startle her, "Deneb. We need to talk. I promise this won't take long."

Moving closer, she touched Deneb. Something felt wrong. Zeta leaned over. *Was she dead?*

She told the sensors to turn on the light and wanted to cry. Deneb's body was nothing more than a gray shell. Two souls and the gift of a mighty Trekachaw were gone.

If she'd had any idea Deneb would take her own life, she would never have left her alone. She must have ascended to Aeon Devotio. Beverly was screaming to let her speak. As Beverly surfaced, Zeta could hear her praying. She pulled the cover over Deneb's face and wished she could give her a fitting ceremony. These words gave her comfort when she was at death's door: *"Heavenly Father, bless my mind and body as I transform my life into something different. Carry me when I need you most, dry my tears, and guide me along this path. Amen."*

Zeta gave Beverly a moment to mourn, then resurfaced. She dimmed the lights and shut the door. On the way to the bridge, Zeta heard Ginger's voice praying inside her head. She must have heard Beverly's thoughts. How strange their customs are. This Earthly ritual seemed necessary for a Human soul to cope with the transition from death to Heaven. Yet her Quizan half welcomed her ascent to Aeon Devotio. The two didn't seem all that different. Except for Humans do not have grey-death energy, and they can't see the other side.

Then morbid memories flashed inside her head of Beverly's excruciating pain while waiting for her cancer-riddled body to die. Zeta winced. She did not care to share that pain. Beverly was questioning if Cole should have saved her. Was the sacrifice worth it? Her soul yearned for Earth's simplicity and innocence. Not every Trekachaw was suited to this violent, complex life. Zeta was appalled by Beverly's questions. From now on, this self-pity will not be allowed. Zeta was not going to let Beverly kill them.

Orion glanced over his shoulder when Zeta walked onto the bridge. He spun the pilot's chair around, questioning her with his eyes. He was an intuitive Ryquat. She chose well, selecting him to be captain. Zeta spoke softly to Orion so that no one else could hear. Deneb was dead. And to keep that to himself for now. Orion controlled his shock and confusion, then spun his chair as if nothing was wrong. Zeta hugged him and, in a flash, was gone.

# fifteen

# ALLY OLYPO, NO GO FOE NASTY BIRDS!

**The Umdul Language:**

ELILIYI ILIYIPAI NYI OGI

NYEЖBYI DAℨTЖ

**VICTIS**, Azha, Steve, and Rigdan arrived at Pify's bailiwick. For Victis, seeing Pify renewed his optimism as only the old salt could do. Even during the worst times, Pify was pleasant and five steps ahead of everyone else. And though he spoke in riddles and questions, what he had to say would inspire the worst defeatist.

Loud, jovial voices coming from the bailiwick were inviting. Victis recognized friendly faces he had not seen since the last meeting. For Azha, the room had quite the opposite effect. He hesitated in the doorway when he saw Zeta sitting at the far end of the table. Dreading another round with Cole's mother, he pretended not to notice her.

He took the long way around the room. That forced him to zigzag through chairs to avoid her. Which only made matters worse. From the corner of his eye, he noticed she was watching him. Her face didn't have that angry look. Had something changed? Maybe she'd forgiven him for Ginzal's death? Azha noticed Phera's stripes turning shades of purple, and she was tapping her fingers on the top of the table. No one knew a thing about the meeting. But Phera was impatient and cranky. Hopefully, this was not an indication of things to come.

Victis was still trying to get through the crowd. He growled at those standing in his way. Jostling, nudging, and squeezing, they stepped aside. Showing a bit of gratitude with the tilt of his head, he made his way over to Phera and sat down. Victis scowled, looking down at her tapping fingers. "Who are we waiting for?"

She stopped tapping and smugly replied, "Pify. He's with Gystfin Kogbor—the Gystfin Dux Ducis—Gystfin Survite, Gor Klop, Boo, and Atue. They're at the mezzanine monitoring Gor Olypo."

Victis shrugged. "Why are you irritated?"

"Pify asked me to stay here. I didn't want to. I wanted to watch the Gors ambushing the Crozins, who were going to ambush us. I can leave when everyone gets here."

"You know we hate to wait," grinned Victis.

"Yes, we do. But that's not what's irritating me. I'm worried about Pify's new heart. He's having problems, and like always, he's doing too much."

Victis struggled with Phera's dreadful news. He thought Pify was fine. "I thought he was okay?"

Phera made a fist. "No, he is not. Pify keeps pushing himself. He has this war won if nothing goes wrong. We need to find a Quizan willing to merge with Pify. Victis, he's running out of time. I'm scared. Belton's been trying too. One Quizan. That's not too much to ask." Phera looked down so no one could see her face. "I'm scared."

Victis leaned toward her. "I love Pify too. You tell me when, and we'll go together."

"Good, thank you. Maybe that will work. There's something else. Deneb's dead. I can't imagine what this is going to do to Kigen. Do you know where he is?"

"Yeah, he's on my ship. Or that's the last place I saw him."

Phera whispered, "Deneb took her own life and ascended. I heard secondhand that after Vious died, Deneb fell apart. She didn't care about her ship or anything else. Zeta agreed to proxy command until they reached Opus. But somewhere along the way, Zeta found Deneb dead in her quarters. I don't know how to tell Kigen."

"Don't worry, Phera. I'll tell him." He shook his head in disbelief.

Phera gasped and sat straight up in the chair. Kigen's blue eyes were staring at her.

"Victis, he's inside the table! He heard us. Kigen, don't go. I am so sorry you had to hear it this way. Please don't go. I can explain." Phera placed her palms on the table, wishing she could touch him. Kigen's blue eyes faded away.

An excited Umdul waddled in, yelling at everyone to follow him to the mezzanine. Victis and Phera stayed in the bailiwick, waiting to see if Kigen would reappear. They could hear the Umdul snorting as he led the group down the corridor.

Phera pushed her chair out to stand up. "We can't wait any longer. I'm translating for Pify at the mezzanine. He expects me to be there. No telling where Kigen is now." Phera grabbed Victis's hand and pulled him out of the chair.

The mezzanine's large monitor screens displayed Crozin battleships surrounded and outnumbered by the Gors. The Crozin Ukarus threatened to self-destruct and fire hyperbaric shock waves at the Gors, refusing to surrender. They were stalling for time, and everyone knew it. Crozins never self-destruct. They didn't know it yet, but retribution was unavoidable.

A few Gor V-Jak jet pilots were transmitting their surrender and requesting amnesty to dock on a Gor battleship. A barrage of lasers cut across space. The Crozin battleships destroyed the V-Jak jets before the Gors could answer.

An ally Gor battleship transmitted: "Crozins surrender, or we will fire! Ukarus, I am Gor Olypo, Jarb of battleship with the Fidus Achates Coalition. Resist, and you will die. Captain Pify of Opus awaits your answer."

Multiple overlapping transmissions from the Crozin battleships were requesting reinforcement. No response.

Olypo transmitted, "Gor death is not honored by a Crozin, only the victory from our death. Crozin tyranny is not a threat. We are free to choose our fate, and now yours. Surrender or die." End of transmission.

Two Crozin Ukarus appeared on screen. "Captain Pify of Opus, heed my fleet with Ukaru Jaddug of Tajat Rakta battleship. I am Ukaru Redaxtar, son of Narthex, destroyer of worlds. Surrender not way for superior Crozins."

Captain Pify leaned forward in his chair. "Weak is nasty birds spread wings torn apart. Forbidden War Zone draw line—Son of Narthex, Redaxtar savvy. Prig Jaddug belch empty threats. Thunder boosts foolishness."

Jaddug heckled, "Do not understand the riddles of frail, Umdul squat."

Phera helped Pify belly roll out of his chair and waddle out of monitor view.

"Umdul hide!" roared Redaxtar.

Phera sat down and adjusted the monitor to speak. "I am Trekachaw Phera. Captain Pify has delegated me to translate for him. We do this so that you understand who's ignorant. Ukaru Redaxtar, being the son of Narthex, will not save you. He is our prisoner on Pify's battleship. How great is he now? If it were my decision, you would all die. Jaddug, your fleet is in the Forbidden Zone and awaiting your surrender to negotiate with Captain Pify."

The Ukarus cut the live vicast, and the battleships in space returned on the screen. Jaddug opened a ship-to-ship frequency with Redaxtar.

Pify snorted and motioned for Victis to come closer. "Jarb Gors primed tip-bell Crozin words *Car-duc Gen* Crozin no relent. Scramble to quash."

Victis agreed. "If Jaddug orders the strike, the Gors must distance themselves to clear the hyperbaric shock wave. If not, their ships will disintegrate along with the Crozins. I know you disapprove of eradication, but we can't afford to lose this battle. What we do right now will determine if we win or lose the war. I can hikari speed to Jaddug and eradicate his battleship. Seeing what we are capable of may convince Redaxtar to surrender. The Gors shouldn't have to sacrifice themselves."

Pify's eyes were tired, and he had to catch his breath before talking. "Faith, versus, paradox. Dream peace, war crux of will. Crozins hate reflects verdict tenable, empowers Victis. Eradication final trumpet save worlds." Pify grinned at Phera, and she smiled back at him. Words were not necessary to comfort one another. She respected his will and adored his humble elegance. And most of all, his allegiance for as long as his failing body permitted.

The monitor cut to live vicast with Redaxtar on the screen. His nose split, and he glared at Phera before speaking, "Negotiate with Captain Pify, not you!"

Phera adjusted the monitor screen to include Captain Pify. "I will translate for him. There can be no misunderstanding of terms. Agreed?"

Redaxtar twisted in his chair, exposing his contempt. "Agreed, Trekachaw."

Pify nodded his head in approval.

Phera continued by reading the terms from a tab pad.

"The Fidus Achates concurs with Captain Pify's terms of the nonnegotiable Concordat. The terms and conditions of said agreement are as follows: the Crozin species shall not enter the Galaxy Uncharted X-Region's expanse, nor the Forbidden War Zone charted in space. In addition: consecutive planets and the interspace-defined perimeters of said planets are forbidden and prohibited. Gardux of the Gystfins. Storsa of Gors. Palatu of Quizans. Opus of Umduls. Trinite of Mejou Flowers. Earth of Humans. Zaurak of Ryquats. Crozins shall notify the Fidus Achates before negotiating trade, services, and contact, including communications with planet inhabitants. Failure to comply will be considered a breach and an act of war.

"A cargo ship is on standby to secure the Crozin jets and battleships for docking and transfer. The Ukaru captains, Ruks, Crozins, pilots, and crew will immediately board the cargo ship for departure to Galak. Trekachaws will inspect battleships and jets pre-departure to confirm a complete transfer. Noncompliance to evacuate or sabotage ships will result in eradication. Our goal is to complete a transition with no fatalities. The Concordat will be in effect for five Crozin generations, equal to seven hundred and fifty Ryquat years. Upon the completion date of the Concordat, the Umdul regents will reinstate negotiations in good faith. Captain Pify awaits your response."

Redaxtar glared at Phera and spoke not a word. The transmission ended, and the screen went dark.

Captain Pify scooted forward in his chair. "Olypo anchor-jawed foresee posthaste. Forthwith Gor Klop plus Trekachaw Boo in trench on abaft witless Jaddug?"

Olypo confirmed transmission. "Affirmative, Captain Pify. Klop is in range to engage Jaddug. Crozins one to two. Trekachaw Boo and Gystfin Kogbor Survite await command."

"Tally sums engage, *zoe, pu, opi, toof, ula*." Pify authorized strike.

Phera transmitted, "Countdown in, five, four, three, two, one."

"Halt! Negotiations not discussed," shrieked Redaxtar on the monitor screen.

Captain Pify raised his fist. "Drop chicanery! Option expires, tout de suite."

"What? I hear Umdul gibberish!" Redaxtar hissed, and his nose twisted.

"Captain Pify said, take it or leave it. You started this war. You enslaved and murdered the Gors. You slaughtered Gystfins, Ryquats, Kikis, and any species who disagreed. You raped and tortured Ryquat women. No more! The Umduls developed a vaccine to free the Gors of your tyranny. You boast we are inferior and expendable. You are the inferior ones. Crozins are a plague of filth and evil. No excuses. None! Board the cargo ship, or we will kill you. It's that simple," raged Phera.

Redaxtar screeched, rolling his head as far as the bulge in his sagging skull permitted, *"YES!"*

Phera refused to react to his anger. "Order your Jager-Ki jets to return to your battleships. Dock and transfer all on board to the cargo ship."

"Captain Pify, as one Ukaru to another, I Redaxtar request my Tajat Rakta. I implore you."

Phera's eyes narrowed to slits, and she shook her head. *No.*

"Old, hardened war inflicts. Years imbibe obvious certainty conflict. Regret perhaps? Ukaru Redaxtar recalls tolerance beget rapport," advised the old Umdul, relying on kindness to atone for the risk.

"I do not understand?" Redaxtar waited for a translation.

Phera looked at Pify, confused. "Are you sure about this?"

"*Uketotta.* Raison d' être. Lineage not genocide, decide whom?" Pify explained, trying to put it into words that Phera could understand or accept.

Phera reached over to Pify and touched his hand. "I trust you have a reason for everything you do. Redaxtar, Captain Pify will allow you to keep your battleship. Have the other battleships dock immediately to complete the transfer. Before the bridge crew disembarks, have them send remote capability to Captain Victis's ship."

Redaxtar bowed his head and gave the order. Jaddug's fleet flew past Captain Pify's battleship, escorted by the Gors. The Ukaru underestimated the courage and determination of the Gors they had once enslaved. In doing so, their failure to ambush Captain Pify was pivotal in the war. Punishment for this negligence would be swift and painful. Therefore, Ukaru Jaddug concerted his death with the other Ukarus in his fleet by ingesting poison. As a final act of solidarity, they honored each other on the bridge moni-tors before switching the screens to gaze upon vast space with its infinite stars. Sitting at their helms, the Ukarus paused to look at their Tajat Rakta bridge for the last time. To be given such an honor to command a mighty battleship was a divine prophecy held by bloodlines. Proudly, they sacrificed themselves for the dynasty. They activated the self-destruct sequence and waited to die honorably. The Ukarus' last thoughts were most likely that of anger. Their battleships did not self-destruct. The Trekachaws had already changed the sequence.

The disgraced Jaddug crew was the last to board the cargo ship, and their punishment was to become the new enslaved.

The loaded cargo ship engaged and rolled onto its side to begin the trek. As if a snake was shedding its skin, the empty Crozin Tajat Rakta battleships and Jager-Ki jets remained in space behind her wake.

Until now, dreaming of this victory was foolish, considering the overwhelming odds. Where the Crozins failed was underestimating the influence and respect of one Umdul.

If not for Captain Pify's masterminding a plan to liberate the Gors from tyranny, the Crozins' evil reign would have spread across the galaxy. Still, watching the massive ship fade away did not satisfy the suffering or thirst for revenge of those who sacrificed the most. Cruelty, death, and destruction prevented forgiveness. Their fight to win the war had been paramount so long that life beyond it was a fantasy.

Be that as it may, a new dawn had risen. Of course, that depended on the Crozins truly being defeated and not just another Crozin deception.

# sixteen

# HOLD ON TO THE GIFT OF PROMISE

**The Umdul Language:**

HIEILIT INY BI BHIEO

OGAFAB IFA PAℨIMAЖO

**THE** Fidus Achates remained on high alert, even though they had not detected a Crozin ship for some time. For good reasons, everyone had a hard time believing the war was over. Could it be the Crozins accepted defeat or grew weary of war? Still, that had nothing to do with forgetting or forgiving the Crozins' wrath. Perhaps worse than the Crozins were the traitor Ryquats. How and when did the Crozins infiltrate? And why was it so easy to corrupt them with cheap bribes of fortune and power?

The war had taken its toll and altered the future, but it also exposed evil and freed the suppressed. The bloody war was their testimony. Never again allow the Crozin plague to spread.

Slowly but surely, loved ones scattered across the galaxy reunited. And, in goodwill, they shared a common goal with diverse species to populate and rebuild battle-scarred worlds. The gift of promise began to heal old wounds and intolerance. Regardless of lineage, all agreed on one thing. How quiet and beautiful the galaxy is when seen through the eyes of peace.

Not so for some. Not all were free to do as they pleased. The brave Ops remained diligent. The Crozins left behind on Zaurak were still a problem. Hidden in the shadows, they were the ghouls that haunted the living.


## *BHIEO OGIЗЖ*
### The Gors

KLOP AND THE GORS RETURNED to planet Trinite. The Mejou flowers celebrated and welcomed the Gors home. However, Gor Olypo chose a different path. He volunteered to follow and spy on the Crozin cargo ship and Redaxtar's battleship to Galak. If the Crozins deviated from their destination, Olypo would notify Pify. He knew this was risky, but it justified checking on his home world.

Olypo heard horror stories about Crozins retaliating on Storsa. What puzzled him was why the migration to Trinite had stopped. There were secret transports to defect still in place. He suspected the Gors on Storsa were unaware of the Ectype vaccine. Could it be the Crozins took away all communications and ordered the planet on lockdown? Or were they being punished for the acts of others? If that were the case, how grievous and how many?

Most species in the galaxy were blind to the atrocities forced upon the Gors before Captain Pify's intervention. One reason was the location of their planet. Storsa is the farthest planet from other civilizations in the galaxy. Yet it neighbors Galak, the Crozins' world.

This quandary still begs the question. Why would millions of Gors choose to remain on Storsa suppressed by tyranny?

Olypo remembered the first time he met Captain Pify. And being in awe of his generous offer. In the beginning, only a few Gors believed him. Most refused to listen and distanced themselves, fearing Crozin punishment. It didn't take long before Olypo's story was leaked to the Crozins. From then on, Olypo, his family, and close friends were forced to hide. The Umduls had arranged to help them escape Storsa in case this happened. While en route to Trinite, they were given a new lease on life, the Ectype inoculation. Captain Pify introduced them to the Trinite Mejou flowers and their first taste of freedom.

Within a short time, Olypo convinced many Gors to join the revolution. He proved freedom was possible, and they could live beyond thirty years. As an example, the Crozins made capturing Olypo a priority. Hunt and kill, no matter the cost. Little did they know Olypo was not on Storsa. For months, the Crozins hunted in vain. Enraged, they vowed brutal torture and death to any Gor who sympathized with Olypo.

Despite the risk, Olypo still wanted to see Storsa for himself. Besides, he could not rest until he knew the truth.

He kept his distance from Redaxtar's battleship and out of sensor range. Once they entered the Forbidden Zone, Olypo changed course to Storsa. By now, the Crozins would have deviated if that was their intention. He hadn't given it much thought about what he'd do if he got this far.

The sensors confirmed a worst-case scenario. The Crozins had infested Storsa, and the sky swarmed with Jager-Ki jets. They were locked down to prevent Gors from escaping. Pify assumed the Crozin fleet was depleted. Not true. The sensors showed thousands of Crozin ships coming and going from another location in that sector. From what he saw, the Crozins were just getting started. Pify should have let us kill every Crozin when we had the chance.

Olypo felt horrible about leaving the Gors. He knew they were suffering. But he had no choice. Captain Pify had gifted him one of the few friction-energy battleships. Above all, he could not let it fall into the Crozins' hands. Olypo set course hikari speed to intercept Captain Pify's battleship.

## OE3BHIE
### Earth

EARTH. THAT IS WHERE AZHA wanted to go, and Victis agreed. Both had unfinished business on the planet. For Victis, Ryquat Captain Doug Smyth still had Choan imprisoned there.

Smyth consorted with the Crozins on Palatu, which played a significant role in empowering the enemy. But cowards like Smyth always seem to know when to save themselves. And that is what he did. Smyth fled to Earth, where he watched the fallout unscathed. Victis had not forgotten nor forgiven Smyth. Penance for his sins was due, and Victis was coming for his old friend, Trekachaw Choan.

Like it or not, when Zeta's Human half, Beverly, heard about the trip to Earth, she insisted on going. And since she was going, Clyde came along to keep her company. Granted, he had his own reasons that he kept to himself.

Bibet was raring to go. She didn't need to ask because Azha wasn't ever leaving her behind again. But life got even better. Azha gave her a shuttle to navigate. Unbeknownst to the little bird, Azha promised his Human soul they'd find Frank and Cole Jr. A shuttle was necessary to transport the Humans. But Azha liked making Bibet feel special.

The trip to Earth spread like wildfire. Before Azha could throw water on it, dozens of Human Trekachaws were asking to tag along. Victis was, let's say, not pleased.

"How did this get out of control? A short trip, that's all I asked! C'est la vie. Tell the Human Trekachaws to meet me on the lower port docking bay. I already told Akio he could furlough to search for his family on Zaurak. Who's capable of commanding my ship while I'm gone?" Victis was red and sounded irritated.

"What about Roon?" suggested Azha.

"That's it? That's all you've got. He's a science officer."

"Cheap shot, Victis. He's more than that, and you know it. If you don't want the Trekachaws to go, tell them no. I can't think of anyone else unless maybe Umdul Captain Yagi. The Umdul captains always have four or five proxy commanders qualified on their bridge."

"Nah. Roon will do. Have him respond to the docking bay. We won't be gone long."

Victis watched the Human Trekachaws walking and flying into the docking bay. Who were they? He remembered the veterans he'd met while on Earth at the hospital. But as Trekachaws, he did not recognize any of them. Victis knew etiquette was not his strong point. He poked Azha in the chest and asked, "From right to left, tell me their names."

"What? Why would you think I remember their names? You ask them if you want to know."

"Right, Azha. Duh. That's why I asked you to do it. They won't care if you don't remember."

Roon's energy morphed into body form next to Victis. "What's going on?"

"I want you to proxy my battleship for a few days while we visit Earth."

Roon looked surprised. "Sure. Thank you. Are all these Trekachaws going with you?"

"I suppose. Roon, move. Give me some space and stand next to Azha."

Roon took a few steps sideways and made a face at Azha. "What's going on?"

Azha returned the face. "Let's listen. This oughta be good." And then mouthed, "Wow."

Victis relaxed a little after he recognized a few of the Human Trekachaws. Perfect, he would direct his questions to them.

"Ta-da, Cooty, Nikki, A-jar, Dur . . . Dur?"

"Duroc, Captain, sir."

"Yes, you. Okay. You five, I'm putting you in charge of supervising the rest. Let's call it a temporary promotion. If you do well, I'll make it permanent," commanded Victis in an authoritative voice while rocking back on his heels.

Takeda raised his hand, "Ah, Captain, I'm Takeda. This is Cody, Nikki, Ajax, and Duroc."

"Right, I knew that. Azha, you got their names wrong. I expect you five to enforce my rules on Earth. Number one: never turn into body form in front of a Human. *Ever! Any Human.* Two: do not cluster or draw attention while in energy. Three: do not contact Humans by those phone things, devices, or your mouth. No contact! Observing them is permitted. Four: if a beastly dog attacks you, control your stripes and get out of there. Rule five: you have two Earth days to complete your visit. Six: don't make me regret this, or Earth will be off-limits permanently. Those are my rules. I will share with you an Earthling quote. It may serve you well: *check your risks for crooks in crannies.*

With that out of the way, Takeda, Cody, Nikki, Ajax, and Durod, uh, Durick, take turns rotating to Europa. That's where Bibet will be waiting in a shuttle. Don't frighten her unless you want Azha to go bonkers. Any questions?" Victis stood up tall, looking back and forth at the Trekachaws.

Nikki raised her hand. Victis remembered her as the vicious female veteran who threw the IV pole that hit his foot. *She was a mean Human.*

"Yes, Nikki," replied Victis, wishing he could ignore her.

"Ah. Don't you mean, *check your six?*" Nikki asked, puzzled.

Azha stepped forward. "We all know what Captain Victis meant."

Victis's eyes narrowed. "We'll revisit this conversation, Nikki. Any other questions?"

Cody pulled on her arm. "Not smart, Nikki."

Victis's voice deepened. "Two days. That's it. Rendezvous on Europa, and we'll return to Zaurak together. Azha and I will check on Bibet tomorrow. If there's trouble, go to Europa and wait for us there."

The Human Trekachaws flashed into a spectacular burst of colors and spiraled in all directions. Victis hoped letting them visit Earth was not a mistake.

Victis did not question why Azha always chose the old winery. For whatever reason, that deserted dusty dungeon was his sanctuary on Earth.

For Azha, it was evident. The old winery was his beginning. His journey from Palatu to Earth was much worse than he had imagined. Finding the old winery kept him safe from Humans. As a Quizan, he could not breathe oxygen. To morph into body form would have meant a painful death. Call it fate, intervention, or a miracle. The Human police officer called Cole saved Quizan Azha from death's door that night. They were the first Trekachaw.

To everyone's surprise, Clyde asked Azha to speak with Cole. Being in the winery stirred the old veteran's soul, turning his stripes green. And rarely seen—a smile.

I know this place. I used to come here with my wife when we were young. She liked wine sampling. Never much liked wine myself; more of a hard liquor man. That's not why I wanna talk to Cole. My son is a police officer in this town. His name is Clyde Swartwood, Jr. You may know him as Charley. I was wondering if Cole might know him?"

Azha couldn't believe his ears. Cole rose to answer. "Yes. He was my sergeant. He's your son?"

Clyde leaned against the cold rock wall and looked sad. Zeta didn't understand why this would cause him grief. Not knowing what else to do, she hugged him.

It was like he had a moment to think about it. And then, whatever it was, he came to terms with it. Clyde rubbed his eyes and clapped his hands, shouting, "By god, I get to see my son! My baby boy. Never thought I'd see Charley again."

Victis interrupted, asking who was speaking—Cole or Azha.

Cole had had enough. He was tired of being silent. "Victis, I've been Azha's equal since the day I left this winery. I admit at times, my anger prevented me from being cooperative. Didn't you ever wonder how a Quizan would know so much about Earth? Who do you think corrected you when you botched Earth sayings or when we talked about old movies? Or TV. Or anything else? It sure wasn't Azha. I used my experience as a police officer to train the Quizans. Azha is brave, but he doesn't know how to fight. I was angry until I spoke with Phera. When I thought Ginzal was Myosis, I wanted to blame Azha for her death. How could I kill my wife? It was Phera who explained why all this craziness happened to me.

"Between us, coming here that night was not a coincidence. Think of the odds—the sequence of events. My sergeant told me I could take that night off. But no, I didn't. Poor Ginger, the pain I must have put her through. I had no idea she was pregnant at the time. If she had told me, would I have taken the night off?

"Let's face it; what-ifs can drive you insane. Could have, should have, would have are excuses for bad decisions. But that entire night was not normal. Sergeant Swartwood rarely reassigned beats. He switched mine with another officer thinking he was doing me a favor. It was slow that night, and I was bored stiff. I came so close to asking if I could take off early. Instead of using more comp or vacation time, I decided to check out this old winery. What made me think of doing that? I hadn't been down here since I was fourteen. Unless you believe we were preordained, it makes no sense. If I had left early or not come down here, the Quizans would be extinct, and the Crozin would rule the galaxy. I accept my calling; I was meant to be a Trekachaw.

"Victis, Azha is your brother. But I am the reason we have so much in common. Enough about me. Clyde, I'll go with you to see Charley. Then we'll find my son and Frank. I'm guessing you may know who Frank is. He probably worked with Charley. Frank is Cole Jr.'s surrogate father. As far as I know, Frank is the only Human that knows about us. We can ask him the who, what, and where."

Victis was speechless for once in his life. Clyde seemed better but was now comforting Zeta, who was speaking gibberish. To be specific, Beverly was the one speaking gibberish, and Zeta was disgusted by the Human drama.

Choosing his words carefully, Victis spoke in Azha's defense. "Azha flew to Earth and saved us all. He risked his life on an old fable thousands of years old. My Quizan half, Zygo, told me what Azha did, and we should respect his bravery."

Clyde agreed. What Azha did as a Quizan was incredible.

Azha smiled at Victis and silently told Cole he was sorry for stealing his soul.

Beverly's blank stare at Azha was not encouraging. And she probably did not appreciate Clyde agreeing with Victis if pushing his hand away was any indication. But above all, Clyde was a gentleman. He asked Beverly if she wanted to see her grandson and Frank before he visited his son.

Victis spoke before Beverly could comment. "Clyde, we'll talk to Frank first. He may know when your son is working and where he lives. How long has it been since you last saw him?"

"Might as well be a lifetime ago. I was MIA in Nam for twelve years. Was comin' back till I lost my hand and legs. Like that, I'd be a burden. Besides, my wife died when I was in Nam. The military told my kids, make your peace. Your dad's probably dead being MIA that long. I kept track of them. Not that it did any good. My oldest son drank too much. Wound up dying in a car crash, but the whiskey is what killed him. Charley's my youngest. Had a new wife and in the police academy. Real proud of him. Filed papers, making sure he got my money and medals. No telling what the military told

Charley after I disappeared from the vet hospital. I thought about calling if I ever had the chance. But what would I say? Best to leave it alone. When you guys found me, my organs were failing. I was in a lot of pain. Thought you ought to know that."

"You're welcome," smiled Victis, looking over at Azha. "All right, let's go to Zeta's house; that's the last place we saw Frank." Victis flashed into energy first, and the other Trekachaws followed.

The house was dark. Frank had dozed off, watching some old movie, and Cole Jr. was asleep, curled up on the couch next to him.

Frank opened one eye and squinted several times at their light orbs. Victis flashed red and Frank jumped to his feet. "Is that you, Cole?" he whispered, trying not to wake Cole Jr.

"Daddy?" The little boy was sitting up and pointing at the lights.

"It's nothing. Time to go to bed." Frank picked up Cole Jr. off the couch and then set him down. Before Cole Jr. could turn around, Frank gave him a little nudge toward his room.

Cole Jr. sat on the floor and mumbled, "Spaceman, Daddy."

Frank squinted, wondering if it were a dream. "Hey, if it's you, give me a sign?"

The lights morphed into Trekachaws across the living room.

"Wow, that will do it." Frank sounded nervous. He picked up Cole Jr., who had toppled over and fallen asleep on the floor.

Azha laughed and introduced the others. "I told you I'd come back. That's Victis; over there is Clyde, and she's Beverly. We call her Zeta now."

"Beverly? Cole's mom? Ah, um, where do I start? Thank you for naming me in your will. Leaving me this house, the money, and Cole Jr.'s college fund. How's Ginger?" Frank sounded a bit overwhelmed but still handled it better than their first encounter.

Zeta was gone, and Beverly had returned. Azha thought it strange how he was beginning to recognize who was whom, by their expressions.

Beverly wanted to touch her grandson but kept her distance. "I'm grateful that you're such a good dad to Cole Jr. There's no amount of money that can repay that. You should know, Ginger ascended to Aeon Devotio and is no longer with us." Beverly squatted down and reached out to Cole Jr.

The young boy leaned into Frank shaking his head no. She lowered her arms. "Maybe next time. How do you explain it if Cole Jr. talks about us?" Beverly was making small talk, trying to avoid questions about Ginger.

"I tell people he has a vivid imagination. Probably will do the same thing this time. He's still young enough for me to get away with it. Wherever Ginger's at, I hope she's happy. Can you let her know I miss her? I think she'd like to see her son." He couldn't hide his disappointment.

Azha felt Cole's soul rise. "Frank, are you still interested in leaving Earth?"

"Maybe someday, not now. After your last visit, I thought about it a lot, and I don't think it's a good idea until Cole Jr. is older. He's a happy boy, and I have a lot of support here. I was exonerated of any crimes, and the PD reinstated me." Frank was getting nervous. The more they talked, the tighter he held on to Cole Jr. It was time to go.

"Frank, you will always have a choice. If it's okay, Beverly and I would like to visit now and then. We promise not to reveal ourselves to Cole Jr. without your permission. If you know where Sergeant Swartwood lives, or if he is on duty, it would sure help us out."

Azha's soul gained control, but he could feel Cole's anguish. He wished he could do something, but that burden was Cole's alone.

"Why do you want Sergeant Swartwood's information?"

"Long story short, over there is Clyde Sr."

"A Trekachaw? No way. I thought his father died in Vietnam. Why not? Why should I be surprised? Sergeant Swartwood is swing shift today. Did you know they have a new baby girl? Last sign-up, he went to swings to help out with her in the morning. His shift started about two hours ago. Briefing should be over by now. You should know that everyone likes Swartwood—the cops and the community. He's on the fast track to becoming a lieutenant."

"Thank you, that means a lot to me." You could see the pride on Clyde's face.

Victis clapped his hands. "Azha, lead the way to PP. The night is short."

Azha and Frank smiled. "PD, not PP."

Victis grinned. "HA! Gotcha. You have no sense of humor."

Azha wondered if Victis had punked him all along.

The Trekachaws flashed into energy. They circled the ceiling to bid farewell and then disappeared.

Frank was not going to get much sleep that night. He carried Cole Jr. down the hallway and gave him a big hug before tucking him into his spaceship bed.

Charley was sitting alone in the sergeant's office reviewing reports. Clyde was beside himself. A man with age lines and a wrinkled brow had replaced his Charley. He stopped reading and listened to dispatch describing a suspect on a vehicle stop. Like tonight and every night, his shift would be dangerous and unpredictable. Watching from above, Clyde desperately wished he could explain what happened in Nam and why he disappeared. Seeing his son made him question his decisions. What could he possibly say to justify not being in his life? Someday, he'd return and talk with Charley about the future, not the past.

Victis grew restless and was flickering. He circled Azha, asking if he wanted to check on Bibet. Whatever his reasons, Clyde wanted to go with them. Zeta was surprised, but she kept quiet. Maybe seeing his son was too much. Victis did not care to judge. *We all have our demons,* he thought. It made sense that Victis would see it that way. He danced with the devil more than most.

A couple of Human Trekachaws were entertaining Bibet on the shuttle. Victis recognized them but not their names. They thought she looked like an Earth bird called an egret. Bibet liked the Human Trekachaws. They said she was beautiful. She fluffed her feathers and blinked her eyes. Watching them dote over her, Azha got jealous. He'd never admit that to anyone.

Bibet sashayed over to Victis to report important news.

"Phera sent you a message. The cities on planet Zaurak remain infested with Crozins. When the Ukarus were ordered to leave, the nests on Zaurak were left stranded. They're angry, hungry, and killing the locals. She asked for assistance ASAP."

"How long ago did Phera contact you?" growled Victis.

"An Earth hour." Bibet's eyes got big.

"Bibet, stay with the Human Trekachaws."

"You two clowns. What are your names?" barked Victis.

"I'm Mike, and he's Tony."

"Mike, you two are responsible for getting the Trekachaws to Zaurak. Round them up quickly. No one stays on Earth, got it?" Victis, glaring back and forth at them.

"Yes, sir," nodding their heads in concert.

"Bibet, you stay in charge of this shuttle. Follow the Trekachaws to Zaurak. I'll pre-set the coordinates. Mike and Tony, get going."

Victis was disappointed that time ran out for him to look for Choan. He'd find a way to come back for his friend.


*UTEUMЗЕЖ*

### *Zaurak*

STEVE, RIGDAN, AND A HANDFUL of Special Ops waited outside the capital city limits to rendezvous with the Gystfins and Trekachaws. Tired, dirty, and on edge, they searched the skies for a sign. They had nothing to talk about. It had all been hashed out before. To talk about what went wrong meant blaming those who were no longer alive. Their soundest tactics had failed. Boasting of victory or defeat had become a curse in itself.

A young Op was the first to notice the dark shadow forming on the horizon. The cavalry had come and was indeed a sight for sore eyes. Though grateful for the help, many had died needlessly. This was their second attempt to clear the capital of Crozins. They assumed most of the Crozins departed when their ships left for Trinite. From then on, it was downhill. They were stuck at ground zero and in survival mode.

Most of the Ryquats living in the cities had fled to rural areas. And for whatever reasons, the stranded Crozins made their nests in the cities. For a while, the Ops were not risking their lives to save the city Ryquats. That is, until shuttles dropped off civilians smack dab in the middle of the Crozins' nests.

Clearing the Capital again was just as important as the first time. The problem was how many Crozins were there, how long it would take, and at what cost.

Mic-10 and 12 jets landed alongside Gystfin Krof and an array of hijacked Crozin Jager-Ki and Gor V-Jak jets. Steve raised his arms and whooped a battle cry, *"Hoorah! Take that, ya cold-blooded Crozins!"*

Rigdan and the other Ops joined Steve in shouting, *"Hoorah!"* This was the break they needed. A few days earlier, the team had made a pact to stay and fight to the death. They were convinced Zaurak had been defeated. But then, rumors began circulating about an old Umdul captain who united the Gystfins and the Gors. The Gors? That was difficult to believe. Still, if it was true, they'd like to shake the hand of the Umdul who accomplished the impossible. Without the Gors, the Crozins might lose the war.

Two battle-scarred Kogbor captains walked toward them with an older Gystfin Steve did not recognize. Walking behind them were Trekachaws Boo and Atue. The rivalry and mistrust between the Trekachaws and the Gystfins had evolved into a worthy alliance. Of course, Boo was instrumental in bridging that gap as a mediator. But with or without Boo, history dictates, wars have and will create unlikely partners. The Gystfins are a good example to make that claim. They were forced to flee their home planet and rely on the Umduls for survival. Their loss was great, but their will and pride never wavered. They were known as fierce adversaries with the strength of three Ryquats. And a reputation for not being afraid of hard labor that most species could not endure. Because of their strength, when merged, they inherit physical advantages as a Trekachaw. Yet, there are only two Gystfin Trekachaws, Boo and Myosis. But other than strength, they are opposites.

Boo's merge created a kind and incredibly handsome creature. His thick fur glistens in the sun, and his muscular body towers over the other Trekachaws.

Myosis is that of a troll. He mirrors a malformed frogtite with patches of fur. The beast's broad head resembled a jackal with hollow yellow eyes and dingy fangs. Some say that Myosis's ugliness and cruelty came from a corrupt Gystfin. But the blame goes both ways. Myosis stole the Gystfin's soul, knowing he was addicted to grey-death energy. Indeed, Myosis was the spawn of evil.

Kogbor Gystfin Tysug proudly introduced the older Gystfin Serlof as one of the few surviving Dux Ducis dignitaries. Serlof looked old and tired. Being forced to leave the planet he called home had taken the fight out of him. He raised his head and gazed at the blue sky toward Gardux. For the longest time, he paused before discussing his plan to rid Zaurak of the Crozins. Serlof began by warning Steve and Rigdan about a Crozin assassin they call Zloy. Whether you knew him as Myosis or Zloy, his reign of terror was the same.

Serlof struggled to continue. "When the Crozins attacked our planet, Zloy butchered the Dux Ducis dignitaries." Serlof covered his ears, saying he could still hear them being slaughtered.

Serlof raised his head to look at Boo. "Someday, we sit by the Temple of Jaaju and speak of this war. If not together, promise me, Boo, to carry me home," implored Serlof.

On bended knee, Boo vowed. "Together, we share Temple of Jaaju. Boo find a way."

Steve and Rigdan listened to Serlof's testimony. How could a Ryquat fight such a beast? A Trekachaw that powerful, intent on destroying without remorse. Steve wondered if Boo was good and Myosis was evil, who would prevail in mortal combat? It was best Steve didn't know that Boo almost died fighting Myosis to save Atue. The Trekachaws learned the hard way never to confront Myosis alone.

Akio ran down the ramp and across a lot to catch up with the group. "I have information about where swarms of Crozins were recently seen in the subways and buildings with basements."

Steve and Rigdan knew that area and were confident the information was correct. Steve whistled and waved for everyone to gather closer.

"We've been here fighting Crozins since the beginning of the war. If you all agree, I'd like to take the lead?" Steve felt like a kid inside the circle of giant beings. They were twice his height and built like tanks. The thought crossed his mind. *Damn, he wouldn't want to piss one off. It's a good thing they're on his side.*

Holding the tab maps as high as he could, Steve pointed to the best spot to start clearing the Crozin infestation.

"Right here, and this is why. The subway runs east and west. We push the Crozins to the east cuz there's less exits at that end to cover. Exterminate them as you go and flush the rest out onto the streets. I'll station Ops at the exits to get 'em coming out. The Crozins had laser traps. If they're still down there, those are probably your biggest threat. After the subways are cleared, we can fortify the tunnels and use them as shelters for the Ryquats we rescue in the city. Another thing before you go. The Crozins know we won't eradicate the tunnels if civilians are down there. And they've used Ryquats as shields. Any questions about what I've covered?" Steve put away his tab map and waited.

Azha raised his hand. "Hey, back here! Is eradicating the same as sterilizing?"

Victis rolled his eyes at Azha. "Yes. And you knew that."

"It's good to be right," grinned Azha.

Steve stretched his neck to see them. "Glad to see you two. I was hoping you could join us. When did ya get here?"

Victis stepped forward. "Wouldn't want to miss this. I have Human Trekachaws on the way too. And by the way, tomato, potato, eradicate, sterilized. The results are the same, Azha. Vaporized!"

Steve agreed, "I've heard it called both ways."

Victis sneered at Azha. "There you have it!"

Azha bickered, "There you go!"

Steve laughed, shaking his head. "You two act like you're married. Is this a Trekachaw thing or what?"

Boo and Atue spoke at the same time. "No! It's these two."

"Okay, well, that's good to know. Any questions?" grinned Steve.

Akio pushed past Azha. "I have a favor to ask. My wife and two boys are out there somewhere. After we clear the subways, can I get help finding them?"

Victis did not hesitate. "Azha and I will help you."

Akio let out a sigh of relief and thanked his captain.


OUTSIDE THE EAST SUBWAY ENTRANCE, a nest of Crozins were feasting on freshly killed Ryquats. The crunching and chewing sound they made was repulsive. And watching their noses split to shove bloody meat into the hole they call their mouth could make anyone gag. That was bad enough, but the wind shifted, and the stench could knock you over.

The Gystfins did not seem affected by the smell. They roared and stomped their feet. Before Victis could react, the Gystfins charged the Crozins, firing lasers. Several Crozins stiffened their long noses and trumpeted to warn the others of danger. The nest of Crozins froze. Another laser flashed, triggering the swarm to stampede toward the narrow subway entrance.

Fighting to be first, they shrieked and viciously clawed each other as they disappeared inside the dark tunnels. The Ukarus at the bottom of the stairs fired lasers, not at the Gystfins but at the Crozins. *Fight or die*, they screeched. Either way, the Ukarus didn't care. It would create chaos and allow them time to escape. Besides, according to the Ukarus, a Crozin with no rank was not much better than a Gor. Especially ever since there were fewer Gors to use as cannon fodder.

When the chaos ended, and the Crozins lay wounded or dead, the Gystfins urinated on them. This vile act is what the Trekachaw's Quizan half remembered about Gystfins. And that was a terrifying memory. True to nature, the Gystfins were brutal. If a wounded Crozin moved or groaned, the Gystfins tried to bite the Crozin's head off. But no matter how much they tried, they could not shove the Crozin's elongated skulls inside their mouth. Instead, the Gystfins bit the back of the Crozin's skull to pop the membrane. Azha's Human half remembered popping bubble wrap sounding the same way. From now on, that good Earth memory was permanently noxious.

The Trekachaws and Ops did not intervene. The Crozins decimated the Gystfins' planet and almost succeeded in their genocide. As bad as it was for the Ryquats and Gors, the Gystfins suffered worse.

When it was finally over, and there was a bloody pool of Crozins, the Gystfins sang their ancient battle cry and stomped their feet. Boo's Gystfin soul surfaced and joined in claiming his ancestral rights. He threw his head back and roared thunder to the heavens. The Gystfins' god, Jaaju, led them to victory.

Gystfin Kogbors bowed and offered to enter the subway first. Boo respectfully declined. "Crozins blind to energy. Here wait. Soon hunt together."

The Trekachaws flashed into energy and flew into the dark subway. Victis and Azha knew the tunnels well from their recent rescue of stranded Ryquats.

Not so for Boo and Atue. They lagged behind, distracted by everything. Boo caught a glimpse of a shadow on a wall and spiraled above to see what it was. Atue rode the rails as a Ryquat but seeing them from this perspective was entirely different. Conveyors connected stacked platforms to elevated hubs. In the dark, it gave the illusion that the rails disappeared into an abyss.

Atue heard the scraping of claws and hooves. The Crozins were everywhere. They had strategically positioned themselves to ambush any poor soul who traveled on the ground below. Boo and Atue dimmed their orbs and flew to the highest terminal. They saw hundreds of them swarming and crawling in and out of iron trains. The clicking noises they made could not be heard in the tunnels below. Boo flickered; it was time to go. They followed the rails until there were no more Crozins.

Atue and Boo met Azha and Victis, who had already doubled back to look for them. Boo morphed into body form behind a train and motioned for them to do the same.

He spoke softly, "Up, Crozin nest. Hundreds see. More hiding, not seeing. Eradicate smart. Many terminals. More Crozins."

Victis wasn't about to risk any more lives. "We're using the eradicators. If Pify were here, he'd do the same. Whether they're stranded or were strategically left here doesn't matter anymore. There's no food down here. I've seen the Crozins eat their young when hungry. That's probably why they were at the subway entrance eating Ryquats. They were in the city sniffing for Ryquats."

All agreed to use whatever means to rid the Crozins—the sooner, the better.

There were six eradicators on the jets. Dignitary Serlof was escorted to a Gystfin jet. He was too old to fight a Crozin, and his wisdom was crucial for the future. Steve, Rigdan, and a group of Ops positioned themselves outside the terminal exits to ambush the Crozins coming out. Meanwhile, the Trekachaws and Gystfins mobilized at the subway entrance. Today could be the last battle for some, but they all agreed there was no worthier way to die.

Victis handed an eradicator to Boo, Atue, Survite, and Tysug. Before they continued, Victis liked to give a speech he called the down-and-dirty, nitty-gritty logistics. Whether or not it helped, he never asked. Azha told Boo and Atue his speech started out being called Logistics by Captain Victis. Then he called it The Nitty-Gritty Logistics by Captain Victis. Now this. Boo and Atue had no comment.

The Gystfins had never held an eradicator before. Tysug and Survite sniffed it, rolled it, flipped it back and forth in their enormous paws. And then they smiled, exposing their long, yellow-stained fangs. This caused Victis and the other Trekachaws to wince again. Memories of how the Gystfins massacred Quizans for their grey-death energy wasn't something they'd soon forget. Victis told himself to get over it. Bygones were necessary to conquer the common enemy. Just the same, the Quizan souls of the Trekachaws disagreed.

And so, the eradication began. The Trekachaws and Gystfins entered the subway using a utility staircase between terminals. Of course, being in energy would have been easier for the Trekachaws, but then Tysug and Survite would be on their own. At any turn, a horde of Crozins could overpower two Gystfins.

Hugging the subway walls, the team moved toward the nest. The Gystfins fell behind, waiting for their eyes to adjust to the dark. Not far into the tunnel, they heard faint echoes of Crozins clicking. Following the sound, they were headed in the right direction.

Victis threw his hand up, signaling them to stop. He thought he heard a woman's voice. There, he heard it again. A female Ryquat was screaming and cursing. It sounded like someone was slapped hard, then dragged. Then he heard clothes ripping and the Crozins shrieking in ecstasy.

He handed his weapon to Tysug and flashed into red energy. Trekachaws Boo, Atue, and Azha flashed, leaving their eradicators on the ground next to the Gystfins. Victis streaked toward a horde of crazed Crozins. Was he too late?

A Ukaru had thrown her to the ground and was getting on top of her. He lowered his body and straddled her to begin the rape. She screamed and fought. Twisting sideways, she closed her legs. The Ukaru shrieked. She had stopped him from raping her. The fight aroused the horde of Crozins, creating a frenzy, waiting to be next. Enraged by her defiance, the Ukaru's eyes bulged, and he sliced her leg with his claws. When she screamed in pain, the Ukaru slapped her face with his nose. She begged him to stop, but that made him want her even more. He lowered his body and forced her legs open with his claws. She twisted and kneed the part that hung stiff between her legs.

Victis flashed inside the Ukaru's brain. "Stop, or I'll kill you!" screamed Victis, drowning out the Ukaru's thoughts of stabbing her chest and raping her until she was dead.

The Ukaru hesitated to question the voice in his head. He'd heard that a Trekachaw could control thoughts.

Victis answered, "That's true."

The Ukaru screeched, "A Trekachaw's in my head!"

Victis surged his energy to kill the Ukaru and then streaked inside the female's head. She watched the Ukaru's eyes flickering and roll back, revealing greyish-white orbs. His body stiffened and spasmed, then collapsed, flopping to her side.

"Get up! I'm a Trekachaw inside your brain. Do as I say, and I'll try to save you. If a Crozin touches you, keep running. I will kill that one the same way I killed this one. Run to the terminal staircase. Don't stop until you're on the lowest floor. You'll see two Gystfins there. Stay with them. Do you understand?"

"Yes!" she screamed out loud.

A Crozin swiped her shoulder with his long claws. Victis streaked to the demon's head and surged into a bright light. The Crozin's eyes ignited into flames.

Shrieking and turning in circles, it swiped at the air until it fell, smoldering to the ground. Victis streaked back to the female, yelling, "Don't stop. Don't look back. Run!"

Seeing through one of her eyes, he saw the staircase. She ran down the first flight, then stumbled on the platform leading to the second staircase. A laser from above hit the platform with a jolt. The metal creaked and twisted, slamming against the subway wall. She stumbled and grabbed onto a rail to avoid falling to her death.

Victis yelled, "Get up! Run!"

The female looked up, and Victis saw a Crozin with a laser aimed at them.

Victis streaked inside its brain and surged. The Crozin's head exploded as Victis flew out of its eye. A barrage of laser blasts vaporized the Crozin into thin air. Victis felt dizzy, and for a brief moment, lost track of the woman.

He heard claws scraping and hooves pounding the ground behind him as they ran on all fours.

"Trekachaws rapacious! Trekachaws rapacious!" the Crozins screeched.

Boo, Atue, and Azha were jumping from one head to the next. The frantic Crozins were killing each other with lasers before the Trekachaws could surge. A swarm ran into the dark subway tunnels, fleeing for their lives.

Azha leaned over a rail to shout at Victis, "There's fifty or more Ryquats up here inside these iron trains. What do you want to do with them?"

"Stay up there. I'll be right back." Victis flew to the Gystfins and found the female he saved sitting on the ground.

"Tysug, you and Survite stop the Crozins from coming through the tunnel at this end. There are Ryquats up there. We need to move down here before we eradicate this section."

Victis yelled up at Azha, "Get them out of the trains and down the stairs. Tell them to stay with the Gystfins on the ground floor!"

Dozens of starving Ryquats exited the trains and ran toward the staircase. Victis waved at them, running down the stairs, "All of you, this way!"

Boo and Atue morphed into body form and carried the injured Ryquats across the platform to the edge. They stepped off and slowly descended to the ground below. Victis was surprised they had learned how to fly with the weight of a Ryquat. To their credit, it made getting the injured to the ground floor faster.

The last few Ryquats to leave the train were elderly. Shuffling and limping as fast as old bones permitted, they were still incredibly slow. The Trekachaws scooped them up and flew them to the Gystfins. They were delighted and laughing on the way down. One kissed Boo's cheek, telling him he was the most handsome creature she had ever seen.

Pure adrenaline got the Ryquats this far. They were dirty, tired, and in desperate need of food and water. Victis told Azha to leave the subway and meet Akio at the jets. They were to bring back rations with a couple of Ops to help. As Azha flashed into energy, he heard Victis yell, "Bring a lot of rations."

In the meantime, that section of the subway was ready to eradicate.

Worthy of notice, the Gystfins followed Victis's orders to the letter. Relinquishing command to another species was humiliating for a Gystfin. But they never complained. Be that as it may, the Gystfins were disappointed they did not get to participate in the killing of the vile Crozins. If Victis was ever going to trust them, now would be as good a time as ever. Victis motioned for them to bring their eradicators and walk with him. Away from the Ryquats, he told the Gystfins they were going to use their eradicators.

"A word of caution before you shoot those. Aim into the center of the tunnel. Not the sides or up or down. Set one, one hundred RDS. Push the top slide to engage, wait until the blue beam stops, and count to five before moving. Are my instructions clear?"

Survite smiled, displaying his yellow-stained fangs. Victis caught himself making a disgusted face but then made several weird faces hoping they didn't notice. Survite and Tysug tilted their heads sideways and looked puzzled as to why Victis made such strange faces. In turn, they mimicked weird faces back at Victis. The two Gystfins raised their weapons and aimed down the tunnel. "Understood."

Victis ordered, "Ready. Fire!" Survite and Tysug pushed the slides forward, and two brilliant blue beams lit the tunnel displaying a spectacular aurora of light. How could something be so soothing and beautiful yet so deadly?

Watching it mesmerized the Gystfins, followed by a state of calm. The blue beam vanished, and the tunnel became dark as night.

Tysug counted to five, *"Nag, ak, vite, jar, tajok!"*

Survite and Tysug lowered their weapons.

"Captain Victis, tunnel sterilized?" Tysug asked, looking down at the eradicator in his hand.

Boo had walked up behind them to watch. He looked at Victis, then answered the question. "Blue light metazoan disintegrates. Sterile evil begets evil. Immense power comes great responsibility," explained Boo, who rarely spoke more than a few words.

Victis listened to Boo's words and reflected on the role Trekachaws play in the balance of nature. Victis's Quizan half stirred, awakening Zygo. He reminded Victis about the story of Earth's beginning long before Humans fled Mars. This era was blissful. But Earth was changing, and they would be forced to leave in search of another world. The short time spent with Humans created a bond the Quizans would never forget. And though time and space separated them for eons, their journey to meet again was destiny. Victis and Zygo proudly accepted the role as a superior species faced with a galaxy raging war. The Trekachaws came to be when the universe was in need. Selfless warriors born without a planet. So, who's the judge of evil begets evil? Zygo predicts a reckoning will come with judgment day. But for now, good versus evil was at bay, and they were shepherds of the flock.

Steve and Rigdan told the Ops to ready arms. They heard the screeching Crozins getting louder inside the subway. The nest emerged from the exits and poured out onto the streets. A steady fire of lasers did not come close to killing all of them. Hundreds ran past them, disappearing between the buildings.

The Crozins that ran out of the subway had infested the city again. That put a stop to eradicating the buildings. One block at a time. One structure at a time. Now one floor at a time had to be searched. Fighting hand-to-hand combat and short-range lasers would be unavoidable. Purging Zaurak of Crozins would take much longer than before.

Akio and several Ops arrived at the subway carrying food and supplies. A group of stranded families walked out of a building from across the street. They were hungry enough to risk exposing themselves to ask for food and water. Akio split the rations and stayed with the families. Steve and Rigdan took the other half and headed down the subway stairs.

Akio thought it odd that some Ryquats left the city while others stayed. It seemed reasonable not to stay where Crozins were. But that could change at any moment. Look what happened in the city. The Ryquats on the battleships were transported back to the city they escaped from. Whoever said it was safe was a blithering fool.

The group huddled together, terrified to be in the open. Though starving and weak, they talked among themselves before taking one bite of food. Several stronger individuals gave their food and water to the children, the elderly, and the injured. They carried the remaining rations to Akio and set them on the ground. Akio did not understand until one of them explained why they would do such a thing. His explanation reminded him of how extraordinary Ryquats can be.

"Please, do not think we are ungrateful. But many others in hiding have gone without food longer than we have."

The Ryquat reached out and shook Akio's hand. There were no words to express how much that meant to him. This Ryquat's kind act restored his faith that good would prevail. Akio told him not to worry. The rations were for them. As Akio walked away, he saw the same Ryquat helping a child open her water pack.

Seeing the devastation was depressing. There were few buildings fit to live in, and they had no resources. The streets were littered with rotting debris, and transportation was nonexistent. Akio wondered how anyone survived this long under these conditions. He kept his mind busy by handing out rations to hungry families.

Akio had hoped his family would be there. His only screenshot of the boys was when they were much younger. Why he kept this screenshot all this time, and not a recent one, was shortsighted. He'd show it around anyway. Maybe he'd get lucky.

Victis was tired of being in the dark subway tunnels and morphed into body form next to Akio. Screams, grabbing children, and running amuck ensued. It took a moment for the families to realize he was a Trekachaw. They apologized profusely and went back to eating. Victis was tapping his foot and asked Akio if he needed anything.

"Have you heard anything about my family?"

Victis felt terrible that Akio could not be a priority. "No. Have you asked this group?"

Akio held up the screenshot and walked back and forth. "Does anyone recognize or know anything about this woman or the two boys? Anything would help. I've been looking since the invasion."

A woman spoke up. "I know Mya and the boys."

Akio's heart raced. "Where? Where did you see them? When? Are they okay?"

The woman nodded her head yes and smiled. "They were fine the last time I saw them—Mya's with her husband and the boys. It was a week ago. But I'm guessing they'd still be there. They're at the building across the street from the next subway entrance. It's a high-rise with only a few glass windows. You can't miss it. I think it's called the Train Station Estates."

He was elated, relieved, and angry. Akio wasn't sure which emotion he felt the most. What would he do if Mya was still with Mark Keller? That would destroy him. He told himself it didn't matter as long as the boys and Mya were alive. That was a lie. It mattered.

PHERA RECEIVED A TRANSMISSION FROM across the galaxy. The news could not have come at a better time. Pify was free to leave Zaurak. He had done his best to give them a fighting chance.

A hundred years ago, when Pify was spry, he saw virtue in the Ryquat/ Human species. He vowed to keep them safe, even if it meant sacrificing himself. Little did he know that someday he'd find a protégé that meant the world to him—a young wild Ryquat in need of a father.

The old salt seldom asked for anything. But he wanted Victis and his Umdul sons to be by his side. Phera had sent several urgent transmissions for Victis to contact her immediately. For one reason or another, Victis did not receive her messages until Pify's battleship was well underway.

If only it were that simple. Since there were only two battleships in orbit, Victis felt it necessary to leave his behind. The other ship was Boo and Atue's. Their battleship could not leave orbit. Boo's position of liaison was pivotal. He was waiting for the arriving Gystfin Trinite refugees and in contact with the Gystfins on Zaurak fighting the Crozins. For all its worth, Boo and Atue had more problems and obstacles than they could handle. All the other battleships were in dry-dock or at Opus for refitting. It would be days before another ship could arrive. Seeing no other way, Victis made a difficult decision. Take a shuttle and leave his battleship at Zaurak, knowing Pify might not be able to wait for him. It was a lousy situation, but he'd try to get there before the merger. But in the end, none of that mattered. Today was the best day ever. Belton found a Quizan willing to merge with Pify.

Victis informed the Trekachaws and Steve that he was leaving on a shuttle with Azha and Bibet to meet Phera and Pify orbiting Palatu. Bibet sat in the pilot seat and set course. She looked over at Azha and blinked. Victis was gazing out the bridge porthole as the stars sped past in a race to the Quizan's world. If all went well, he could say goodbye to his father.


## *PAELYEBUM*
### *Palatu*


PHERA REFUSED TO LEAVE PIFY'S bedside during the trek to Palatu. She didn't want Pify to know, but she was terrified he would die before they got there.

Pify's artificial heart was not the only problem this time. His arteries and veins were thin and compromised, restricting his blood flow. He didn't want his life to end this way. He should have died in battle. But all that changed when he met Phera. He didn't care if he was ill. Every day he was alive was another day with her. He wanted to merge but was afraid to believe it would happen in case it didn't. His pain was becoming unbearable. Life itself was becoming unbearable. He lost track of how many days he lay in bed, hoping for that miracle. Now it was real. He just needed to stay alive long enough to get there.

Phera was angry that it took forever to find a Quizan, but it finally happened. And not a moment too soon. She could focus on getting him there and getting it done. Belton assured Phera they were ready as soon as she arrived. The Quizan was healthy and eager. Belton was encouraging, but Pify's Toogus Oiba was fretting and frazzled. That was not a good sign.

Now she was overthinking everything, and her mind was all over the place. Since Pify was the first Umdul to merge, she tried to imagine different versions of that mix. The Human and Ryquats were a natural fit. Of course, there were those few Gystfin misfits. But one could argue not all mergers were successful. A couple of Humans were failures, and Myosis was the spawn of evil.

Whatever Pify was after his merger, she would love him the same. Besides, no matter what, they would share five hundred years of adventure. They were a new species with unseen abilities limited only to their willing restrictions. With such power, the vast universe held endless wonders to explore. She would find the perfect planet to call home with Pify. He had to make it. Phera could not fathom a future without him. She leaned over in the chair to look at him. They needed to hurry.

Phera received confirmation that Pify's Umdul sons, Jifney and Pubney, were orbiting Palatu. The Umduls and Ryquats would remain on their ships due to Palatu's toxic atmosphere. Besides, there was no need to scare the shy Quizans with strangers in scary space suits. On the other hand, the Quizans cannot breathe oxygen while in body form. The little Quizan would remain in energy while on the ship until he merged with Pify.

Trekachaw Belton and Quizan Pogo eagerly awaited Phera's arrival at Cavern Village. She would escort them in energy directly to Captain Pify's battleship, where the long-awaited merger would create a new Trekachaw.

It hurt when Pify spoke or lifted his head, but he insisted on seeing his two Umdul sons and Victis before becoming a Trekachaw. Phera had hoped Victis could get there in time, but they could not wait any longer. Pify could not hide his disappointment when he was told. She whispered in his ear not to worry, that Victis would meet them on Palatu.

He whispered in a raspy voice, "A new me my son shall see."

Phera contacted the battleships and urged Jifney and Pubney to board immediately and keep the conversation to a minimum.

The robust father they knew was gone. How could the jovial, pudgy Umdul lose so much weight? It hadn't been that long since they last saw him. But thinking back, his uniform did seem too big. His body had withered to skin and bones, and his face was gaunt with deep lines and hollow eyes that could no longer mask the pain. Their father was dying.

Jifney and Pubney sat beside Pify's bed, consumed with grief, and fighting not to moan as Umduls will do. The old salt's voice cracked, and his words were forced. "Care for Fizz Noggin-Stomp. Eyes, for me, never fail. Not die if I die. Life on Trekachaw is quixotic. Famous Noggin-Stomp chose best share crown dome."

No one considered Pify and Fizz parting, but then no one ever thought that would happen. If agreeing to adopt Fizz Noggin-Stomp would provide even the slightest comfort for their father, making it happen was a privilege. Fizz Noggin-Stomp parted Pify's hair to look out at them. He had not been eating and was sick from mourning.

Pubney reached his hand out. "Fizz Noggin-Stomp, my tit, Kaufnphartz. Passive he is. Benefit nervous young tit—Indeedy, brave warrior reputation Fizz famous. Notable impulse defines title, *Kaufnphartz*. Forgive his quirk, son of Pify. Kaufnphartz young tit."

Fizz Noggin-Stomp frowned and held tight to a clump of Pify's hair. Jifney stepped forward and lowered his head so Fizz Noggin-Stomp could see his tit. She was beautiful with big eyes. Fizz stretched his neck to get a better look. Jifney was talking, but Fizz did not hear a word. She was perfect.

"I, proud if chosen. Prefer sublime tit. Embrace equals fabulous. *Ta-dah*, Razzle-Dazzle! Renowned marquises of tits." Jifney smiled.

Pify was relieved that Fizz took a liking to Razzle-Dazzle. "Noggin defend, Fizz years my eyes. My son regrets not. Trekachaw anew, as you too," cooed Pify to his faithful friend.

Jifney extended his hand to Fizz and waited for him to let go of Pify's hair. Fizz sat down and shook his head no.

Jifney waited. "Not last to share Pify. Often visit, you see," promised Jifney.

Fizz stood, gazing up at Jifney. He hugged Pify's clump of hair before slowly crawling onto Jifney's hand. As Jifney's hand moved away, Fizz looked down at the old Umdul, feeling lost. Pify was his world, his life, and his cohort. Who would warn Pify when danger appeared?

Grudgingly, he stepped onto Jifney's head, overwhelmed with dread and guilt. He questioned abandoning Pify in his most time of need. He'd fly back and die with him or stay until he became a Trekachaw. But something distracted him. He felt Razzle-Dazzle take his hand. Fizz turned to look at her; she must have understood his sorrow. She squeezed his hand, shook her head no, and then asked him to join her. Fizz knew why he had to leave, but accepting the harsh reality of losing Pify was yet another matter. Fizz held on to Razzle-Dazzle's hand and bowed his head to cry.

Phera's heart broke watching the separation of Fizz and Pify. After the merger, Fizz could jump on Pify's head to visit. Then he'd be okay living with Razzle-Dazzle on Jifney's head.

It was time. Phera kissed Pify's cheek, assuring him she would return soon with Quizan Pogo and Belton. Pify's shaky hand reached out and touched her, and he smiled that enchanting big smile she'd fallen in love with from the moment she met him. She kissed him one more time on the forehead and flashed into energy. Pify watched her light disappear.

Palatu brought back memories—some good and some bad, but mostly good. Looking down at the sparkling silver ocean reminded her of when she was a Quizan. That is, until the invasion of Gystfins, Ryquats, and Crozins. Before their onslaught, her planet was one of peace and tranquility. So simple, yet so divine. Would she go back in time if it were possible? No. You are never the same when your eyes are open to the unimaginable. Like that of a caged bird set free to spread its wings and fly high into the sky, she had soared to worlds beyond that life.

Phera circled Cavern Village. Her instincts told her there was something wrong, but it could be nothing more than raw nerves. That was it. All was well. Belton was standing in front of Cavern Hall entrance with a group of curious Quizans. Perhaps they were the village soldiers. And to think, sticks and stones were all they had to defend themselves. Even those simple weapons took away their innocence. The Trekachaws promised to cherish and protect them, though that promise came at a cost.

She landed next to Belton and morphed into body form. Her old friend was the perfect Trekachaw for Palatu. From the beginning, Belton volunteered to stay with the Quizans. Not that she understood it, but he had no desire to explore the cosmos.

Phera was eager to meet the Quizan called Pogo. There he was, a tiny little Quizan peeking out from behind Belton's leg. At best, he was knee-high. So young and happy with a great big smile. He was an excellent match for Pify. Phera squatted down and motioned for him to come to her.

"I'm Phera. I was told your name is Pogo. You are my hero. I am forever grateful for your bravery and willingness to merge with the great Umdul Captain Pify."

Pogo giggled and disappeared behind Belton's leg.

"How old is Pogo?"

Belton walked toward Phera with Pogo hanging on to his leg. "Pogo is young but old enough. He's just shy. The Gystfins killed his manany and papay.

I've taken care of him since. Pogo wants to be like me. He knows Pify is not a Ryquat, and he's fine with that."

Belton patted the little Quizan on the head. "Pogo, this is the Trekachaw that we talked about. She is owaried with Captain Pify."

Pogo made a curious face and jumped off Belton's leg to show off his green stripes.

A massive figure, shadowed by the dark cavern walls, stood behind Pogo. Phera strained her eyes to see what it was.

*NO!* She knew those yellow eyes. She panicked. It couldn't be. *Myosis?*

Phera screamed, "Pogo, run! NO, this way. Run to me!"

Pogo ran inside the cavern, believing he would be safe there. The little Quizan ran straight into Myosis's arms.

Belton and Phera ran after him but froze when they saw Myosis holding Pogo by his neck with his feet dangling in the air.

Belton spoke calmly, not to provoke the Trekachaw beast. "Myosis, I beg you, let him go. Please spare him. Tell me what you want. I'll do anything you ask."

Myosis squeezed Pogo's neck and guffawed. Phera gasped, and Belton fell to his knees. From the depths of hell, pure evil had risen. The young Quizan and Pify's fate was the beast's sword to wield.

Phera saw the purebred's blue eyes behind the beast in the dark—Kigen. Not all was lost.

# THE END

# prologue

**THE** trilogy intensifies with Trekachaw Planet Muskelon.

The Crozin War is no longer a galactic threat. Freedom reigns as the battle-scarred worlds share an influx of diverse aliens to rebuild. The weary masses must find a way to cohabit and make peace with those they mistrust. Compromise will be imperative for their survival.

Transformed, the Trekachaws find themselves questioning who they are and their future. Were they created to counter evil in the cosmos? Perhaps as divine warriors or archangels that worlds have known by many names. The Gystfins call them Jaaju. Whereas Ryquats envision angels with golden wings as guardians. But that is not what burdens Victis. A surreal awareness of the staggering loss weighs heavily upon him now that Pify is no longer his mentor. The birth of a prophecy falls to the unforeseeable and cannot be rekindled. So with a heavy heart, Victis accepts his role in leading the Trekachaws with Phera. As nomads, they search the heavens for a planet to call home. That is, until their souls remind them of their calling. Sooner or later, a day of reckoning will come, for evil never dies. It hides in the shadows to gain strength and waits for complicity. Earth is vulnerable, and Humans are unaware of the infiltration of those in hiding. Moral depravity walks among their primitive ancestors while bracing for the Trekachaw's return.

# Trekachaw Glossary

Earth, our home. Not long ago, astronomers believed she was flat and that the stars circled around us. We are far from those dark ages. But understanding and exploring vast space with all its wonders and secrets is a journey yet to unfold. Now is the apex of an evolution. The next generation of seekers who dare to take chances. Those who dream of what could be and are willing to explore the impossible. This is the story of a man who sacrificed his soul to another willing to risk everything. New worlds and those who have been protecting us will be revealed. This is a journey into our past and future. We are not alone.

## QUIZAN SPECIES

Quizans are one of the original 243 species to occupy the fifty-eight documented universes within the Vastuscaelus. They explored the universes millions of years before Ryquats or Humans were capable of building fires. Originally, Quizans were indigenous to a planet called Pala located within another universe. Billions of years ago, Quizans were not as physically evolved. Like Humans, they required food, water, and shelter. They were an advanced, compassionate species who engineered spaceships to rescue endangered life on compromised planets.

| | |
|---|---|
| *Planet*. | Palatu |
| *Sun:* | Targus |
| *Life span:* | 300 years |
| *King/Leader:* | Rulers of Palatu |

| | |
|---|---|
| ***Fathers/Mothers:*** | Papay/manany |
| ***Marriage:*** | Owari bond |
| ***Quiey:*** | Quizan babies or children |
| ***Ayak:*** | Palatu bird |
| ***Grut:*** | Rat-like creature |
| ***House:*** | Caverns at Cavern Village |
| | Cupola pod/odeum pod at Kismet Ebb |
| ***Bodo:*** | Gas bubbles released from the bottom of Quizans' feet when they absorb too much energy |
| ***Vox Populi:*** | Unanimous vote |
| ***Ola:*** | Three feet |
| ***Pavo:*** | One hundred |
| ***Aeon Devotio:*** | Life after death/grey-death energy (Latin) |
| ***Atmosphere:*** | Combination of carbon dioxide/sulfur dioxide/ carbon monoxide/helium/$H_2O$ |
| ***Phosphorus-Urodela:*** | Extinct Earth lizard DNA used for creation of Quizan hybrid |
| ***Sopa tree:*** | Palatu tree |
| ***Jacko tree:*** | Palatu tree |
| ***Villages:*** | Cavern Village, Kismet Ebb Village, Silwat Village |

## QUIZANS

| | |
|---|---|
| ***Zith:*** | Palatu prince, son of Myosis |
| ***Rodia:*** | Azha's Quizan wife, from Cavern Village |
| ***Pogo:*** | Quizan/Captain Pify |

Quizan/Ryquat Merges
| | |
|---|---|
| ***Life span:*** | 500+ years |

| | |
|---|---|
| ***Zygo***/Victis: | Zygo from Cavern Village/Ryquat battleship captain |
| ***Phera***/Tara | Azha's first love, from Kismet Ebb/Special Ops Tara |
| ***Roon***/Simon: | Friend of Azha, from Kismet Ebb/Science Ofc. Simon |
| ***Atue***/Einstein: | Friend of Azha, From Kismet Ebb/Engineering Ofc. Einstein |
| ***Pax***/Jacet: | From Kismet Ebb/battleships' MD Jacet |
| ***Choan***/Bruce: | From Silwat Village/Sgt. of Special Ops Bruce |
| ***Vopar***/Eric: | From Cavern Village, brother to Vious/Special Ops Eric |
| ***Vious***/Dillon: | From Cavern Village, brother to Vopar/Special Ops Dillon |
| ***Duroc***/Washington: | From Silwat Village/Special Ops Washington |
| ***Belton***/Larry: | From Cavern Village/Special Ops Larry |
| ***Deneb***/Darcy: | From Cavern Village/Special Ops Darcy |
| ***Kigen:*** | First purebred male Trekachaw, parents Vious and Deneb |

## Quizan/Human Merges

***Life span:*** 500+ years

| | |
|---|---|
| ***Azha***/Cole: | Azha traveled to Earth; first Trekachaw hybrid with Human Cole |
| ***Ginger***/Quetzal: | Cole's Human wife Ginger/Quetzal, renamed themselves Ginzal |
| ***Beverly***/Zeta: | Cole's Human mother (Beverly)/Zeta |
| ***Human Duroc:*** | Veteran from Earth/Quizan merge, Human parents were pig farmers |

| | |
|---|---|
| ***Human Ajax:*** | Veteran from Earth/Quizan merge, Human parents are computer tech(s) from California |
| ***Human Clyde:*** | Veteran from Earth/Quizan merge |
| ***Human Nikki:*** | Veteran from Earth/Quizan merge |
| ***Human Cody:*** | Veteran from Earth/Quizan merge |
| ***Human Takeda:*** | Veteran from Earth/Quizan merge |
| ***Human Joshua:*** | Veteran from Earth/Quizan merge |
| ***Human Nick:*** | Veteran from Earth/Quizan merge |
| ***Human Mike:*** | Veteran from Earth/Quizan merge |
| ***Human Tony:*** | Veteran from Earth/Quizan merge |

## HUMANS

| | |
|---|---|
| ***Cole:*** | The first Human-Quizan merge with Azha |
| ***Frank:*** | Cole's childhood friend/married Ginger after Cole's disappearance |
| ***Cole Jr.:*** | Cole's Human son with Ginger |
| ***Judy:*** | Frank's ex-wife/adopted parent Cole Jr. |
| ***Andrew:*** | Ginger's blind date after Cole disappeared/ bioengineering |
| ***Ella:*** | Young female prisoner on Crozin jet |

## RYQUAT SPECIES

Ryquats were once inhabitants of Mars. During that era, Mars was a warm planet with oceans of water and rich in oxygen. The Ryquats had evolved into a thriving industrial species that made their presence known across the Milky Way galaxy. But tragically, Ryquats became stranded on Earth. Those beings were to become Humans.

| | |
|---|---|
| ***Planet:*** | Zaurak |
| ***Sun:*** | Hoshi |
| ***Life span:*** | 150 years/Human ancestors |

## RYQUATS

| | |
|---|---|
| ***Akio:*** | Battleship navigator |
| ***Anna:*** | Nurse assigned to Trekachaw book 1 battleship |
| ***Connie:*** | Captain Victis's first wife |
| ***Heidi:*** | Captain Victis's first child with Connie, murdered via Crozin Ukaru Narthex |
| ***Marilyn:*** | Ryquat who cared for Connie's/Victis's second child while captive via the Crozins |
| ***Tilly:*** | Connie's/Victis's second child, born during Crozin captivity |
| ***Vexy:*** | Captain Victis's second wife/Viceroy on Ryquat Council |
| ***Doug Smyth:*** | Evil Ryquat battleship captain/Choan's uncle |
| ***Steve:*** | Special Ops |
| ***Rigdan:*** | Special Ops |
| ***Orion:*** | Special Ops |
| ***Mark Keller:*** | Ops who saved Akio's wife Mya and two sons |
| ***Mya:*** | Akio's wife |
| ***Benji:*** | Akio's youngest son |
| ***Wren:*** | Akio's middle child |
| ***Kim:*** | Akio's eldest child |
| ***Skylon:*** | Young female prisoner on Crozin jet |
| ***Fidus Achates:*** | The coalition of species within the Orion Belt to protect planets threatened by hostile aliens |

**Decree:**                 Fidus Achates laws
**Decretum code 5-1**   Prison or death sentence
**Viceroy:**               Government officials
**Council:**               Titles of Viceroy officials
**Neco weapon:**        Laser handgun capable of lifting, moving,
                        and holding items up to 45 kg;
                        multi-levels of lasers, fits hand
**Vita brevis:**           Ryquat custom space suit; means
                        "Life is short" in Latin
**Hikari speed:**          Maximum battleship speed
**Jets:**                  Mic-10 and Mic-12
**Linguistic chip:**       Microchip embedded under skin,
                        provides translations of alien languages
**Chovo:**                 Ryquat bird species; hybrid ostrich/chicken/vulture
**Vastuscaelus:**          Fifty-eight charted universes
**Caltaboone:**            Ryquat whiskey
**Mito drink:**            Liquid nourishment

## Japanese Words

**Endo dens:**             End transmission
**Anzen'na tabi:**         Safe journey
**Keijo:**                 Breach/battleship lockdown
**Baka yarou:**            Stupid asshole
**Damare:**                Shut up
**Unko:**                  Shit
**Nanda:**                 Hell

## UMDUL SPECIES

The Umduls are prominent members of the Fidus Achates Territory and close Ryquat allies. Throughout the galaxy, they have a reputation for being formidable warriors and respected spacecraft engineers.

They are sort of cute but ugly, and everything they say seems to be a riddle. Umduls are approximately four feet tall with squatty bodies and colorful, bushy, baby-fine hair standing straight up on their heads. Their hair is long to their waist at the back of the head. Either it grows in a straight line like a ponytail or is attached to their spine. Either way, it is by far the most attractive feature of an Umdul. For thousands of years, the Ryquats provided avian-nautical blueprints and raw materials to the Umduls. In return, the Umduls provided the Ryquats with reliable high-tech battleships, cargo ships, transports, and shuttles. Umduls are brilliant engineers, shrewd in combat, brave, and loyal. They are by far the quirkiest species in the Orion Belt.

| | |
|---|---|
| *Planet:* | Opus |
| *Sun:* | Uta |
| *Life span:* | 200 years |
| *Government:* | Regents |
| *Advisers:* | Chancellors |
| *Physicians:* | Toogus |
| *Oiba:* | Cpt. Pify'sToogus |
| *Pify:* | Battleship captain and old friend of Victis |
| *Cpt. Jifney:* | Battleship captain/Pify's son |
| *Cpt. Pubney:* | Battleship captain/Pify's son |
| *Yagi:* | Battleship captain |
| *Teltoo:* | Battleship captain |
| *Oyee:* | Battleship captain |
| *Poipu:* | Battleship captain |
| *Teepug:* | Umdul soldier |

| | |
|---|---|
| ***Marriage:*** | Pali-otos |
| ***Tabula rash:*** | Clean slate/fresh start |
| ***Inter nos:*** | Just between us |
| ***Umdul sex:*** | Ou-dim-fa |
| ***Bailiwick:*** | Umdul captain's office |
| ***Jets:*** | Mic-10 and Mic-12 |
| ***Bogtu-urp:*** | Battleship on high alert |
| ***Raison d' être:*** | Reason or justification/being or existence |
| ***Uketotta:*** | Affirmative |
| ***Tit:*** | Pets that live in hair on Umdul heads |
| ***Fizz Noggin-Stomp:*** | Pify's tit |
| ***Razzle-Dazzle:*** | Jifney's tit |
| ***Kaufnphartz:*** | Pubney's tit |

## KIKI SPECIES

They come from a galaxy called Coma Berenices, about thirty million light-years from Zaurak. Their planet, Kowok, has a third of Earth's gravity. The Kikis are highly sophisticated, courageous, and beautiful creatures. They walk upright gracefully on two legs with colorful, iridescent, short feathers except for long, brilliant tail feathers. They are fast and have very slender, sleek bodies. An adult Kiki stands approximately five to six feet tall. Though they resemble Earth's egret, the Kikis have arms instead of wings and cannot fly. Kiki battleships are unique and iridescent, like the feathers of the species. For millions of years, the Kikis and Umduls have been allies.

| | |
|---|---|
| ***Planet:*** | Kowok |
| ***Sun:*** | Jiju |
| ***Galaxy:*** | Berenices |
| ***Life span:*** | 175 years |

| | |
|---|---|
| ***Hai:*** | One hour |
| ***Pasha:*** | A battleship |
| ***Bevy:*** | A fleet of battleships |
| ***Covey:*** | Kiki crew |
| ***Cifron:*** | Physician |
| ***Jagnar:*** | Name of Kiki government officials |
| ***Mikado:*** | Title of battleship captain |
| ***Thude:*** | Battleship captain/Captain Pify's comrade |
| ***Watoto:*** | Thude's adjutant |
| ***Bibet:*** | Assigned to the Trekachaws as a liaison |

## GYSTFIN SPECIES

The Gystfins have the reputation of being mercenaries and not to be trusted. They are known for dangerous manual labor contracts within the galaxy. Gystfins resemble Earth's hyenas, except they're much more significant. They have broad shoulders, long muscular arms, and short legs. Their hands look more like paws with three fingers and a stubby thumb. When squeezed, the fingers extend, revealing six-inch claws like that of a cat. A Gystfin's face is broad and ugly, with a wide muzzle baring long, baboon-like yellow fangs. Merged with a Quizan, a Gystfin is more powerful and faster than a Trekachaw.

| | |
|---|---|
| ***Planet:*** | Gardux |
| ***Sun:*** | Mushfig |
| ***Life span:*** | 100 years |
| ***Dux Ducis:*** | Dignitary |
| ***Kogbor:*** | Battleship captain |
| ***Jaaju:*** | Gystfin god |
| ***Cargo ship:*** | Used for large interspace transports |
| ***Jets:*** | Krof |

### Quizan/Gystfin Merges

| | |
|---|---|
| ***Myosis***: | Quizan king, later deposed, who becomes fixated on destroying his former species |
| ***Zloy:*** | The Gystfins call Myosis "Zloy"/ stole a Gystfin's body and soul for revenge |
| ***Noyac:*** | Myosis's chosen heir |
| ***Leaders:*** | Noble Quizans of Myosis's cadre/stole Gystfin souls |
| ***Boo:*** | The Gystfin who reported the genocide of Quizans to the Ryquat Council/a Quizan-requested merge |

### Gystfins

| | |
|---|---|
| ***Serlof:*** | Dux Ducis dignitary |
| ***Tysug:*** | Kogbor |
| ***Survite***: | Kogbor |

## CROZIN SPECIES

Ryquats despise Crozins, and they consider them a vile, ugly species. Likewise, and for good reasons, that same sentiment is felt by most galaxy inhabitants. Crozins walk upright on three-toed hooves but often run slumped, using their forearms to gain speed. Their faces are long and narrow, with a split nose that can separate. Even from a distance, it is easy to recognize Crozins by their oversized skull hanging freakishly between their shoulder blades. But despite their terrifying appearance, the Crozins are intelligent and ruthless warriors.

| | |
|---|---|
| ***Planet:*** | Galak |
| ***Sun:*** | Akuma |
| ***Life span:*** | 150 years |
| ***Ukaru:*** | Battleship captain |

| | |
|---|---|
| ***Ruk:*** | Officer |
| ***Tajat Rakta:*** | Crozin battleship |
| ***Jets:*** | Jager-Ki |
| ***Car-duc Gen:*** | Battleship on alert |
| ***Narthex:*** | Crozin Ukaru who imprisoned Connie (Victis's first wife) |
| ***Redaxtar:*** | Son of Narthex |
| ***Jaddug:*** | Ukaru |
| ***Flurg:*** | Ruk |

## GOR SPECIES

The Gors are descendants of the Crozins. They evolved into smaller, thick-skinned beings with armored scales covering most of their backside. When threatened, the Gors curl into an impenetrable ball. They are difficult to kill and multiply quickly. The Gors hunt the Gystfins for food and consider them a delicacy, until they discover the Cerbalus spider on Trinite.

| | |
|---|---|
| ***Planet:*** | Storsa |
| ***Sun:*** | Zon |
| ***Life span:*** | 30 years without Ectype vaccine/unknown years with vaccine |
| ***Jarb:*** | Battleship captain |
| ***Jets:*** | V-Jak |
| ***Olypo:*** | Captain Pify's trusted ally |
| ***Klop:*** | A Gor and Kogbor Survite's trusted ally |
| ***Ectype:*** | A vaccine created by the Umduls to counter the effects of a virus |

## MEJOU SPECIES

The Mejou flower is an indigenous species on planet Trinite. Unlike Earth or Zaurak, these flowers are ambulatory and prefer a plant-based appetite but can be carnivorous. The one enemy of the Mejou is an indigenous predator called the Cerbalus spider. These arachnids are large creatures that will inject venom to paralyze their adversaries. The toxin is potent and provides the spider ample time to spin its web to prevent resistance or escape.

| | |
|---|---|
| *Planet:* | Trinite |
| *Life span:* | Unknown |
| *Mejou flower:* | Ambulatory flower with large white petals and large teeth |
| *Cerbalus spider:* | Large spider, enemy of the Mejou flower |
| *Ikiniku:* | A Mejou flower and ally of Gor Klop |

# Acknowledgments

My world changed the day I attended the La Jolla Writers Conference. Jared Kuritz along with a cast of expert speakers lectured on specific topics that gave me a new perspective on the publishing industry. Everything I thought I knew or was guessing became evident and transparent. How can anyone thank another for the gift of a lifetime? My special thanks to Antoinette Kuritz, my mentor, my guiding light. Without her knowledge my first book would never have been published.

Thank you.

# About the Author

**POLICE SGT. BRENDA FLORES** was a pioneer. One of the first women in law enforcement assigned to patrol, she also created the canine police program for U.C. Davis, training canines in police work and bomb detection. A gifted artist, she served as a composite artist for her department. And she was at the forefront of handling domestic violence and abuse issues while on the force. Brenda is currently writing her third book in the Trekachaw series, Trekachaw Planet Muskelon. As a writer, she can create worlds and dream of venturing out into space. Though far from walking on Mars, she never tires of watching the rocket launches blast into space from her backyard in Florida.

Learn more about Brenda at www.brflores.com